THEIR LAST DAYS OF SUMMER

WELCOME TO PARADISE. NOW TRY TO SURVIVE IT.

MARIA FRANKLAND

AUTONOMY PRESS

First published by Autonomy Press 2025

Copyright © 2025 by Maria Frankland

All rights reserved. No part of this publication may be reproduced, stored or transmitted in any form or by any means, electronic, mechanical, photocopying, recording, scanning, or otherwise without written permission from the publisher. It is illegal to copy this book, post it to a website, or distribute it by any other means without permission.

This novel is entirely a work of fiction. The names, characters and incidents portrayed in it are the work of the author's imagination. Any resemblance to actual persons, living or dead, events or localities is entirely coincidental.

Maria Frankland asserts the moral right to be identified as the author of this work.

First edition

Cover Design by David Grogan www.headdesign.co.uk

JOIN MY 'KEEP IN TOUCH' LIST

To be kept in the loop about new books and special offers, join my 'keep in touch list' here or by visiting www.mariafrankland.co.uk

THE BROTHER IN LAW

KEEP YOUR ENEMIES CLOSE...

Maria Frankland

We were together. I forget the rest.

— WALT WHITMAN

PROLOGUE

BY THE END *of the week, one of us will be dead. And one of us will be a killer.*

I scroll through the photos from our first day – all sun-flushed skin, matching cocktails and smiles frozen in time. Borrowed time.

We thought we were escaping real life, but we were racing straight toward the worst of it.

I yearn to go back – to be able to warn those grinning versions of ourselves that someone among us isn't who they seem. And another member of our group is going to take things too far.

When I close my eyes, I can still see the water, bright and glinting like broken glass. But the water was never a threat.

We were.

I keep replaying the same questions in my mind, *what if I'd told the truth about the past when the holiday was still merely an idea?* And, *what if I'd stopped the stupid game we were playing before it turned so toxic?*

But it's too late for *what ifs* now.

1

TINA

'Anyone would think you were getting ready for a funeral.' Andy zips his case. 'You could at least *try* to be enthusiastic.'

I tear my gaze away from the row of neatly hung skirts and tops to look at my husband, his face softly illuminated by the glow of his bedside lamp. There's something different about him – he looks younger, lighter, as though life has loosened its grip on him these past few months. The boys have teased him about having a midlife crisis. He's taken up running, updated his wardrobe, and has even started wearing aftershave again. I joked not long ago, *You're not thinking of trading me in for a younger model, are you?* He laughed and told me he couldn't imagine life without me, but the way he said it made me wonder. It sounded more like habit than passion, like comfort rather than love.

'Come on, Tina – we need some sleep. If we get to bed in the next hour, we'll at least have a chance of a few hours of shut-eye before the taxi arrives at four.'

'I never wanted to go on this holiday in the first place.' I sigh as I wedge my sandals into the corner of the case.

'You're the only person I know who wouldn't be looking

forward to a holiday like this.' He shakes his head. 'Most people would give their right arm to be getting on a plane to Aruba in the morning.'

'I'm not most people.' I yank the drawer open and start rummaging. Truth be told, I'd rather Andy left the room. Sorting through my underwear in front of him feels oddly intimate for two people who've barely touched in weeks. He never sees it on me anymore, so I doubt he'd care to see it off me either. Just another subtle reminder of how far apart we've drifted.

'No shit.' He reaches for his phone from the bedside table, and his face lights up in its glow. A ghost of a smile plays on his lips as he reads something on his screen, but he quickly straightens his face. Is it because he's realised I'm watching?

'Who's texting at this time of night?'

'Just Rick from the club – telling me to go easy on the Balashi beer while we're out there. It's apparently very moreish.'

'I don't see why we couldn't have just done what we do every year.' I throw a couple of tops into the case, wishing my clothes were a size or two smaller. I meant to slim down, to match my effortlessly toned friends, but life's too short to say no to cake, especially now I'm fifty. Besides, I've got to take my pleasures where I can in life. But even when I try to undo the damage in the only way I know, the weight still clings and it's become far worse since the menopause.

It's Andy's turn to sigh. 'If it weren't for Siobhan organising this holiday, we'd once again,' – his voice takes on a dreary tone, – 'be heading to Tenerife. Same old, same old.' He drags his fingers through his newly-cut grey-flecked hair. 'Don't you want to do something *different*, Tina? Aren't you happy to be going away without the boys for a change?'

Now that *is* an encouraging question. 'Aruba *is* a honeymoon destination.' I smile for what feels like the first time this evening. Perhaps I *can* look forward to this holiday after all.

'We're way past all that, aren't we?' He chuckles as he looks back at his phone, blowing my last thought out of the water. 'It's a looong time since *our* honeymoon.'

'Thanks for the reminder.'

Andy doesn't reply. He's too busy tapping a message into his phone, presumably to 'Rick from the golf club.' I drag a couple more items from coat hangers and fold them into the case. The echo of grungy music from one bedroom and the incessant beat from the other has ceased, and the house is silent. Our sons must be asleep.

'The boys are the other problem, now you mention them.' I wish Andy would give me his attention, instead of his phone for a change, but he never does. 'They'll probably burn the house down while we're away – or have a wild party.'

'Stop bloody worrying, Tina. A bit of responsibility will be the making of the pair of them. Besides, you've batch-cooked and labelled meals for the entire week – all they've got to do is chuck them in the microwave.'

'Are you still texting Rick?' I try to keep my voice nonchalant, but it's hard. 'You normally only say four words to me, like *pick up some milk,* or *I'll be late home.*'

'No one now – I'm all done.' He rests his phone on the bedside table. 'You need to get some more clothes in there.' He points at my suitcase. 'That isn't going to keep you going all week. Anyway, what's got into you? It's not like you to leave all this until the last minute.'

He's right. If this were our usual holiday, I would have had a list written out for what I wanted to take and had my case packed three days ago. I wrench more things from the hangers.

'You've been at home all week too.' He's still going on, but at least he's got his attention on me now instead of his phone. 'We're not all so lucky to only work in the term time.'

I chuck two pairs of shorts on top of the growing pile. 'I'll be done in ten minutes.'

'We need to get some sleep.' He reaches for his phone again. It's as if he gets twitchy if it isn't in his hand. 'Oh look,' – he enlarges a photograph with his fingers and holds it in front of my face, 'Mr Flash is already crowing on Facebook about our holiday.'

Andy's had a grudge against Jo's husband, Cameron, since she met him online ten years ago, no matter how hard Cameron has tried to get along with him. I think it's down to how much he earns. There's a ceiling on what Andy can make as a partner in a legal firm, and restrictions on what he can and can't do, but as the owner of a kitchen manufacturing company, Cameron's got full control and the sky's the limit for him, as he repeatedly proves.

'Spending a week with *any* of them isn't exactly filling me with the warm and fuzzies.' I hold my pashmina to my nose. It's soft against my skin and still smells of the perfume I bought for Tenerife last summer. 'We might have been close friends when we were young, but we've all changed hugely over the years.'

'So why still see them every year if being with them feels like a chore?' Andy throws his newly sculpted, muscular arms in the air. 'Especially as you're always so pushed for time.'

'Once a year for a few hours is hardly onerous.' My case is half full now. Usually, I'm asking Andy if I can squeeze items inside his case. But I feel so rotten about myself at the moment, that my mindset isn't focused on looking 'nice.' Not like Jo. She's probably planned outfits for each day and night, plus a new bikini for every day. 'An entire week in Aruba with them is another matter – like I said, I'd much prefer to be going away as a family.'

'You're such a stick in the mud, Tina. We stay in the same hotel, year in-year out, doing exactly the same activities and eating exactly the same food.' He counts the items on his fingers as he always does when he's making a point. 'You've got to admit that Aruba looks amazing.'

'Stuck with *that* lot, I'm not so sure.' I begin packing items from my dresser. Aruba's supposed to be a windy island, so I don't know why I'm bothering with my hairdryer and diffuser, but my hair is the one thing I've got going for me. Even Jo, who barely has a kind word to throw in anybody's direction usually, said recently, in her capacity as a hairdresser, that people would pay good money for curls like mine.

'Other than Cameron being there, everyone else is alright. In fact, I'm really looking forward to spending some time with Caleb.' Andy unbuckles his belt and slides it from the waistband of his trousers. He's still wearing what he's worn for work all day, but at least he's taken his tie off.

'So you and Caleb will be talking shop all week?' Like Andy, Siobhan's husband is a solicitor. 'Great.' Another reason I don't really want to go away as a group. My husband and I won't get *any* time alone.

'You'll be spending time with your friends.' He begins unbuttoning his shirt.

'But I want to spend time with *you*.' I might sound petulant, but I don't care.

'You'll be too busy in spas and going shopping.' He smiles.

'Do you have to be so patronising?' I stare at him. Since his mid-life transformation, I can once again see echoes of the handsome teenager I pursued all those years ago.

'Why are you being like this, Tina? Why are you trying to spoil our holiday before we've even left the house?'

2

TINA

Andy slides his trousers over his feet as he waits for my reply.

'Because you've changed.' I drag more clothes from hangers without paying proper attention to what I'm choosing. 'You don't even notice me these days. You're far too wrapped up in yourself.' I rake my fingers through my unruly dark curls. It's too late to wash it now – I've been too busy cleaning and organising the house to a standard I'm happy for the boys to maintain. My friends will be preened and glorious when we meet them at the airport, whereas I, as always, will look like I've been dragged through a hedge backwards. 'And you come home later and later every night. Even tonight, it was eight o'clock before you showed your face.'

'You're talking rubbish.' He shakes his head as he plugs his phone in to charge at the side of the bed. 'I wanted to get one last gym session in before the holiday.'

'I just don't want us *all* to be stuck together for an entire week.' I lower myself onto the edge of the bed beside him and rest my hand on his leg. It's barely perceptible, but his muscle tightens, as if he's flinching at my touch. 'Like you said, we've got this time without the boys.'

Their Last Days of Summer

'I'm sure we'll get some time together, love.' His voice has an edge of resignation as if he's just saying it to shut me up. Now that he's undressed, he picks up his phone again. I might just end up throwing it overboard during one of the boating trips Siobhan's planned.

'Right, I've packed enough clothes.' With one final toss of a cardigan on top of everything else, I roll the zips around and clip them into the suitcase lock.

Once upon a time, my husband would have helped me close the suitcase *and* carried it down the stairs. These days, he doesn't offer to do either.

'Are you getting some sleep before this flight, or what?' He jerks his head at the pillows on my side of the bed. 'Come on, Tina – at least *try* to look forward to your fiftieth celebrations.'

If it was only *my* birthday, I'd have celebrated in my own way, with Mum, with fellow teachers from the school, then with Andy and my boys. But because Jo, Siobhan, Becky *and* me are all turning fifty in quick succession, I got dragged along in the wave of enthusiasm that's become this holiday. On the face of it, it sounds like it should be wonderful, but we haven't been together for an extended period of time since – well, I don't even want to think about the last time we all went away.

I'm all over the place lately. A part of me wishes Andy wasn't coming at all – and that the other husbands would stay away too. Their presence will only stoke the slow-burning fire that's been smouldering beneath the surface of our so-called friendship. There are too many secrets after what came out of our youth club days. There's too much at stake.

'Look, I'm sorry, love.' I drop my head into my hands as I sit at my dressing table to carry out my nightly face cream ritual. 'I'll snap out of it, really I will. I'm just knackered.'

'*You're* knackered. You should try waiting around in court all day.'

'You should have taken the day off, like I said all along.'

'It's alright for you, with your long holidays from school. You don't have clients that could get sent to prison if you don't turn up for work.'

This is one of Andy's regular lines. 'Forget work now, eh? And that goes for when you and Caleb get together as well.'

'Have you finished all your packing?' The way he changes the subject suggests he's got no intention of forgetting about work.

'Yeah, I just need to grab the sun cream and the insect repellent from downstairs before we set off – and my toiletries from the bathroom.' I glance around our cosy bedroom, not really wanting to leave it for a week. As Andy has pointed out several times, the wallpaper is chintzy and outdated, and the patterned carpet needs replacing, but it's home. It's where I feel safer and less vulnerable.

Andy taps at his watch. 'We're going to be ruined if we don't get some sleep soon, especially with the long flight we've got in front of us.'

∼

Andy, as usual, is asleep within five seconds flat. I lie, ruminating over whether I've remembered everything. Passports, travel money, and medication. I wish I could feel excited. I didn't even feel excited when I was shopping for new clothes. I generally take extra care with my appearance when I'm meeting with the old-school crew, especially Jo, who always looks impeccable. I guess with having her own hair and beauty salon, she has to, but she still puts me to shame. Still, it was kind of her to invite us all in for a manicure and pedicure last weekend. I stretch my hands out to admire my Shellac nails in the light coming in from the streetlamp – painted in 'bluebell kiss.' At least my hands and feet will be in keeping with the others.

Let the snoring begin. Great. I reach for my earplugs and glance at the curve of my husband's back as he lies facing in the other direction. There was a time when we fell asleep in each other's arms, but those days seem to be well and truly over. Or I would tuck in behind him and would fall asleep nestled into his body heat instantly, but I no longer feel welcome enough to encroach on his side of the bed as he once made me.

Even with earplugs in, I can still hear him snore. Wonderful. I badly need some sleep. As he said, we'll be *ruined* if we don't get some before that flight. The taste of minty toothpaste lingers on my tongue as I stare around the familiar dark corners of my room, as I have so many times. I *hate* not being able to get to sleep. Especially when I have to. It's when my mind works overtime the most, when I've nothing to distract me from my intrusive thoughts.

I can't shake the memory of Andy smiling at something on his phone. I need to know that it *was* Rick from the golf club, and I need to know *before* we go away. I've always managed to shake away the temptation to read his messages, but I've never had a feeling as strong as this one in the pit of my belly.

Sliding myself from beneath the duvet, I creep around the bottom of the bed to his bedside table. Gently lifting the phone, I'm horrified to see the message, *face not recognised*. I try the passcode – no, that's not working either.

We've always had passcodes, thumbprints and now, facial recognition set up for each other's phones, but that's all changed. For the first time since we got together, he's locked me out of his phone.

With tears stinging my eyes, I crawl back into bed. Really, I'd like to wake him and demand to know what he's got to hide. But I'd only make things worse if he thought I'd been trying to snoop in his phone, and I don't want to arrive at the airport with a horrible atmosphere between us.

I can't bear the thought of Andy leaving me – I don't want to start again in my fifties. The prospect of navigating the online dating scene, which I've heard about from some of my younger colleagues and Jo, from when she met Cameron, makes me want to break out in a cold sweat. Not that anyone would want me anyway. I've been with my husband since our university days, when he was studying law and I was training to be a teacher. I was drawn to his geekiness and introverted nature, but nowadays, it feels like he's come into his own and has completely outgrown me.

Andy's more than happy to spend his free time golfing with his legal cronies and seems to get far more pleasure from his endless business trips than anything we might do together. He claims I live vicariously through our sons, clinging to their milestones as if they're mine. Maybe he's right. Sometimes I catch myself envying them – the way their futures stretch ahead like a sun-drenched nineties summer, wide open and full of promise. Now that I've hit fifty, I'm painfully aware that more of my life is behind me than ahead. If I dwell on that for too long, it usually ends with me having an eating binge.

My husband and I have become like an old pair of slippers that have seen better days. I can feel they're falling apart, but they're so comfy and familiar, I'm petrified at the prospect of them being thrown away.

That this holiday will either make or break us is a feeling I can't shake. And I'm heavily leaning towards the latter.

3

JO

'OH MY GOD, I can't believe we're all together.' The holidaymakers behind us tut as Siobhan squeezes past them, oblivious to her claims that the rest of us have been holding her a place. I let go of my Gucci suitcase as she reaches us in the queue at the check-in desk.

'Group hug.' Siobhan pulls us all together, and I get a whiff of her expensive perfume. She's made a *lot* of effort to say it's so early in the morning, even more than me. 'I can't wait for us to get there. Come on, Tina – get in.'

'All that plotting and planning has finally paid off.' Becky pulls an excited face as Tina steps forward. Tina's face looks more like she's heading off for a rainy weekend in Scarbados than a week in Aruba. I won't ask her what's wrong, though I reckon I could hazard a guess. She confided in us the last time we met about Andy's mid-life crisis, as she called it, as well as how distant he's become. I didn't really know how to reassure her.

'You just wait until you see what I've got lined up for us this week.' Siobhan steps in closer.

'Did you manage to sort the jet skis?' Zane squints under the fluorescent lights. They're very bright for *this* early in the morning.

Siobhan taps the side of her nose as if she's keeping a very important secret. 'You'll have to wait until we arrive.'

Andy winks at me as I smile at him over Tina's shoulder. She smells of shampoo and jadedness, but he, as always, looks cheery and ready for action. She's right – he really *is* enjoying a new lease of life now he's officially middle-aged.

After a few seconds, the four of us let each other go.

'How long has it been since we all met up?' I ask. 'I know you came in for your nails separately, but it must be nearly a year since the four of us were together.'

'It's longer than that.' Becky looks thoughtful as if she's trying to recall.

I don't mean to be judgmental, and like the rest of us, she's got up in the middle of the night, but Becky doesn't even look like she's brushed her hair. She's been with Zane since we were at school, so she probably feels like she no longer has to impress him. It's the same with Tina and Andy.

'Well, you'll all have plenty of time to catch up this week, won't you?' Zane grins around at us all, his final gaze lingering on me, which never feels comfortable.

'It's good to see you, Andy.' Cameron, my always suave and confident husband, thrusts his hand towards Tina's husband like they're about to do a business deal. But it's nice to see Cameron dressed casually in his combat shorts and t-shirt for a change, even though it's not exactly warm out there. In contrast, Andy still looks like he's set to do a day's work in his sensible chino shorts and short-sleeved checked shirt. We all laugh at his straight-laced ways, but he's always been the same, and I guess it's part of what makes him who he is.

I wasn't brave enough to wear my holiday clothes for the

journey and was shivering even in my jeans and cashmere jumper when the taxi dropped us at the entrance to the airport. It can also be chilly on the plane, so I'd rather keep myself cosy.

'You can take the men out of the office.' Zane laughs as he turns around in the queue. 'Don't worry, Andy – Cameron shook my hand when I arrived as well.'

I cast my gaze over the shine of the concourse, expecting to see Siobhan's husband, Caleb, rushing around the bustling queues towards us, having visited the loo or something. We haven't seen him for a while, so it will be nice to catch up. Like Becky and Zane, he and Siobhan have also been together since they were teenagers.

'So where is he then?'

'Who?' Siobhan follows my gaze before averting it to glance at a dark-haired man loitering on the fringes of our gathering, seeming to be watching our group. He's familiar – too familiar. I glance at Becky and realise I'm not the only one with colour draining from her face. It's *him*. I try to catch Tina's attention, but she's not looking my way. It's *really* him. I hope he doesn't try to talk to any of us.

'Caleb, of course. Who did you *think* I meant?'

'Oh– er,' Siobhan looks apologetic. 'We actually split up a couple of months ago.' Her voice is casual as if she's telling us she changed jobs or something.

'So he's not coming?' Andy looks crestfallen. We all used to laugh at how well he and Caleb got along, calling it *the bromance*. I can't believe they've *split up*.

'Nope.'

'You're joking?' Suddenly, every eye in our group is on Siobhan. Even *my* husband appears to be interested. Normally, Cameron's only interested in his own affairs, but whatever explanation our friend's about to divulge about her marriage split has definitely caught his attention.

'Well, I didn't see that one coming, Siobhan.' Becky's eyes are wide as we all await further information. But judging by Siobhan's face, we'll be waiting a while.

'It's a long story, and I'll bore you with the details some other time, but for now... well, I've met someone new.' She flushes, looking coy for a moment.

'What?' Tina's voice is a squeak. 'No way.'

She beckons to the man dressed in jeans and a Ted Baker t-shirt, the one I noticed a moment ago. I hold my breath. Looking at Tina and Becky, I'd say they're doing the same.

'*This* is my new boyfriend.' Pride beams from Siobhan. 'Everyone, meet Marty.'

He steps forward, his Converse pumps squeaking against the polished floor as he joins our group. He's flushed in the face as his gaze wavers from me to Becky. As he smiles around at the men, a stunned silence hangs between us women. Suddenly the echoes of conversations carrying on around us in the queue seem louder than ever.

'Oh my God.' Becky seems to freeze as she stares at him.

'I'm sorry.' He blinks and gives her a scrutinising stare as if he's trying to place her.

'It's *you*.' She sounds like she could choke on the word *you*.

'Do we know each other?' He looks puzzled, but I can tell he's acting.

Becky flicks her gaze towards me and Tina, who looks equally horrified, and then back to Marty.

'You know full well we *know each other*.'

'I'm really sorry – I—'

'Otley Youth Club. Thirty-five years ago.'

'I don't think so.' But he shuffles from foot to foot as if he's really uncomfortable. As well he should be. 'In any case, how many years have passed since then?' He laughs.

'I was Becky Harding.' She points at herself and then at Tina. 'She was Tina Maidley and *she* was Jo Seddon.'

Their Last Days of Summer

He shrugs. 'Means nothing to me.'

I harden my face in her direction, hoping to convey my wish to be left out of the conversation. Cameron's looking quizzically at *me* now and will no doubt be grilling me later on to find out what I know about this man who's infiltrating our holiday. My husband prides himself on knowing *everything* about me. But even when you're married to someone, *some* secrets should be locked away. Some things are best left in the past. And for all our sakes, especially *his*, the secret concerning *Marty* must always stay locked away. This might be easier, since he's pretending not to know us.

Siobhan looks confused, but her smile doesn't fade. 'You all used to *know* Marty? But I was *always* with you, so surely *I'd* remember him as well.'

'You might have been away.' Becky frowns and her voice wobbles, as if she's uncertain. 'You were *always* on holiday.'

'*I* remember you like it was yesterday.' Tina's eyes narrow further. 'You were about three years above us.'

'I knew *lots* of people.' Marty appears to relax as if he's now on more solid ground with us. 'Some are more memorable than others.' His gaze flickers towards me.

'So the two of you...' Siobhan nudges Becky as she keeps her eyes fixed on Marty. 'Were you...'

'No, she bloody wasn't.' Zane's tone is snappy as he joins in our conversation. 'She was seeing me by then.'

'Anyway, however you think you knew me, it's all ancient history.' Marty's steely blue eyes remain crinkled with a false smile as he reaches for Tina's hand, which she tugs away sharply. 'I don't remember you so it's good to meet you.'

Everything feels like it's in slow motion as he reaches for my hand next. And before I can stop him, it's brushing against his lips. 'It's good to meet *you* as well.'

Siobhan doesn't look at all happy as I wrench my hand away. 'You lot have got some explaining to do,' she hisses.

'And so have *you*,' I snap back at her as Marty turns his attention to Andy and Cameron.

Andy offers his hand. 'It's good to meet you, Marty.' I didn't think *Andy* would be the first one to make him welcome. He and Caleb have always been as thick as thieves.

'Don't you think you should have told us *he* was coming instead of Caleb?' I jerk my head in our 'intruder's' direction as I face Siobhan. The men seem pretty shocked by Marty's presence, but are mostly gentlemanly enough to make polite conversation with him. 'We had a right to know who we'd be forced to spend a week with. And poor Caleb – I hope you haven't just kicked your husband to the kerb to make way for *him*.'

'Jo.' Siobhan widens her eyes at me as if to say, *don't be so bloody rude.* I look away.

'I still don't know how you all think you've known Marty before.' Siobhan continues. 'Who's going to enlighten me?'

'We didn't know him for long.' I can't be the only one from our group who feels like their throat is closing up. We all need to leave that little period of our teenage years well behind us. It's become one of the unmentionables, yet here we are, with a stark reminder of it standing loudly and proudly before us.

'But *how* long?' There's an accusatory edge to her voice as she glares at me. 'And more importantly, how *well*?'

'What do you mean, how *well*?' Really I know exactly what she's getting at.

'None of this matters – as Marty just said, it's all ancient history.' Tina slings her arm around Siobhan's shoulders and shoots me a look. 'We just want to know what's happened between you and Caleb. We didn't even know you were having prob—'

'You never said a word when you came in to have your nails done?' I glance at the nails spread out in her Birkenstock sandals. Rose blush. I could tell there was something amiss with Siobhan when she came into the salon, but I never imagined that her marriage had broken down. Siobhan's always bright and breezy, but that day she was almost manic, and she kept checking out of our conversation.

'I wanted your first meeting to be a surprise.' She lowers her voice.

'Oh, it's that alright.' Becky's tone couldn't be any more sarcastic.

'Ah, come on, you must surely agree that he's absolutely gorgeous?' Siobhan looks coy as she courts our approval. 'I bet that's the problem – jealousy.' She's smiling, but still she flashes me a look that I take as a warning.

'Beauty is only skin deep.' Becky still isn't taking her eyes from the new member of our group. 'How did you meet him anyway?'

'He was right under my nose at the gym.' Siobhan wraps either arm around her shoulders as though hugging herself as she sways from side to side. 'Can you believe it?'

'I can't believe he's *here*,' Tina mutters in my ear. 'Not after what happened.'

'Anyway, whether you all knew him over thirty years ago or not, and whatever you might have thought at the time, that's all in the past.' Siobhan bustles us forward as the check-in queue moves before smiling back at him. 'He's here now and we're all going to have a great time.' Her voice bears the edge of a warning just as much as the look she flashes at me.

'Right then.' Siobhan rubs her hand against Marty's bulging bicep. 'At least the introductions have been taken care of. See.' She shakes her long auburn hair behind one shoulder. 'There was nothing to be nervous about.'

Oh, but there is.

Marty smiles around at us all. 'Cheers for inviting me.'

I bite my lip to stop myself from blurting that he *wasn't* invited – not by the rest of us anyway. He's probably only here as the place was already paid for. The place which should have belonged to Siobhan's ex. Poor Caleb – I wonder if he knows anything about this man.

Whatever it is, it won't be what *we* know.

4

JO

'Next, please.'

We surge toward the check-in desk, wheelie cases rattling behind us across the polished floor. As we move, I catch sight of a young couple by the entrance – he's clutching a suitcase, she isn't, and the tears on her cheeks say everything. She's staying. He's going. Airports always make the hairs on the back of my neck stand up. There's something about them – soaked in both anticipation and sorrow. By their very nature, they're places of passage, stitched together with nothing but hellos and goodbyes.

'Let the partaaay begin,' yells a voice from the back of our group.

Everyone grins back at Zane, except me. I don't feel like grinning at anyone. Zane revels in his self-appointed role as the group's fun guy, even though he and Becky have the least money, and she's aged more than the rest of us. Not from time alone, but from years spent lamenting her life instead of taking charge. She's settled – for a lacklustre career as an administrator, for a version of herself that no longer tries, and for drab clothes that seem more like surrender than style. Zane's easy on the eye, sure, but she's never looked truly happy with him. She doesn't talk about it, but it's obvious there's more going on between them than she'll ever admit.

I've offered to give her a confidence boost by doing something awesome with her hair and to donate her a few bits from my wardrobe but she always gets uppity and accuses me of treating her like a charity case.

If only she'd see that she could do so much more with her life, she might begin to live a little like the rest of us do. Given the choice between marrying a mediocre gardener like Zane, no matter how good-looking he is, or a CEO of a furniture manufacturer like Cameron, I know I've made the correct decision.

'Are we all excited?' Siobhan beams around at us all. 'I can't believe we're finally on our way.'

'I'll be more excited when we've got this flight over and done with,' Becky replies with the usual edge of despair in her voice. 'The longest I've ever flown for is three hours, and that was years ago.'

Cameron steps forward so he's first at the desk.

'Maybe you should ask about an upgrade after all?' I murmur, ignoring Becky's latest round of complaints as I nudge my husband. When I booked the flights, I couldn't exactly ask Siobhan to bump Cameron and me up and leave the others behind – it would've drawn a line between us before we'd even boarded. But after a sleepless night, the thought of stretching out on a recliner sounds infinitely better than being wedged into economy like sardines, wearing garish pressure socks and jostling for a sliver of armrest. And at least the coffee up there will be real – not watery instant rubbish. I run my tongue along the roof of my mouth. The bitter aftertaste of the flask of coffee from the car ride still clings there, dry and stale.

'I can't believe you didn't ask Siobhan to book business class for us in the first place.' Cameron shakes his head. 'What were you thinking?'

'Like I told you, not everyone can afford it,' I reply through gritted teeth, not wanting any of the others to hear, namely Becky.

'I'd have covered the difference.' My husband flashes his perfect teeth as he smiles at me, and I don't doubt that he would. There's no one more generous than Cameron. There's a school of thought that suggests the wealthy hang onto what they've got by being frugal and tight-fisted, but Cameron has certainly proven otherwise. The main problem is that when he gives, he nearly always expects something in return. Not in a monetary way, but *everything* has a price.

'Good morning, Sir.' From the look on the travel assistant's face as she stares into my husband's eyes, she appreciates my husband's chiselled good looks as much as most of the women he encounters. 'How can I help you?'

'Good morning, Michelle.' He checks out her name badge, and she flushes. 'You could help me even more if you have any upgrades available.'

Zane nudges him. 'I'm not being funny mate, but—'

Dismissing Zane by turning his body away, Cameron continues addressing *Michelle*. 'And you look like the sort of lady who'd do us a wonderful deal.'

I don't know how Becky and Zane live like they do, so hand to mouth and paycheck to paycheck. It'll be a wonder if it doesn't put them into an early grave.

'I'll see what I can do.' Michelle presses buttons on her keyboard, a smile dancing on her perfect lips. Cameron can charm the birds from the trees, so if there are any upgrades to be had, he's sure to secure them. 'How many of you are there?'

'Eight.' He gestures around at everyone. 'And it's a very special occasion. You see, if I'd have been in charge of booking the flights, we'd have all flown business class to begin with.'

Siobhan frowns. She'll possibly take this as a personal criticism.

'What's the occasion?' Michelle looks at Cameron intently.

'My wife, – he gestures to me, – and her three childhood friends are all celebrating half a century on this beautiful planet.'

I wish he wouldn't say *half a century*. It makes me sound haggard. I'm having injections, fillers, lasers, facials, you name it, but it's getting increasingly difficult to hold back the march of time. It certainly isn't a problem Cameron has to worry about. The appreciative glances he gets from his younger employees when he saunters into his work events with me on his arm make me feel increasingly invisible. And judging by my friends' reactions to him when we first encountered one another this morning, there are at least two of them who wouldn't think twice if the opportunity arose.

'I have three upgrades available this morning.' Michelle raises her clear blue eyes to look at my husband. I've never seen eyes as attractive as hers, and from the way he's holding her gaze, I'm pretty sure my husband hasn't either.

'How much?' I ask. Not that I'm bothered. Whatever they cost, it's pocket change to my husband. I don't splash the cash on everyone else like he does, but I don't mind splashing it on myself – besides, I see it as an investment. I've come up the hard way, so giving copious amounts of money away isn't in my psyche.

Michelle spins the screen around to show us. They must be extremely pricey seats for her to be showing us, as opposed to telling us the cost.

'They're very reasonable.' Cameron reaches for his wallet, his wedding ring glinting in the overhead lighting. 'We'll take them.'

'I'll just need the names and passports of those looking to upgrade their tickets.' Michelle seems to be back to business as she stares back at her screen instead of at my husband, the tips of her eyelashes brushing the top of her cheek. I used to have natural eyelashes like that. Nowadays, I have to apply fake ones.

'So we're not going to be all sitting together on the flight now?' Siobhan's voice is laced with irritation. 'I thought that was the whole point of this trip?' One thing I know about my old schoolfriend is that as a redhead, her temper can flare from nought to a hundred in five seconds flat, and it appears we just might be igniting it.

'We can't turn an offer like this down.' Cameron points at the computer.

'Great.' Andy shakes his head. 'What did I say to you?' He looks pointedly at Tina.

'What are you talking about?'

Tina's expression is one of discomfort as she looks away. The two of them have clearly had words. Andy makes little secret of not enjoying being around Cameron, who I know he calls, *Mr Flash*.

'We need to decide who's having these tickets.' Cameron steps away from the desk. 'I vote that Becky and Zane get them.'

'*What?*' I stare at him. 'But there are only *three* upgrades.' I wouldn't mind Becky coming in with us – but only Becky.

'We fly business class all the time.' Cameron looks from me to Becky to Zane. 'We should let one of the others enjoy it. It's my treat,' he continues, 'give this lovely lady your details and the tickets are yours.' He gestures at Michelle behind the desk.

Becky starts to protest, but Zane nudges her sharply. 'It'll be ace,' I hear him say. 'Who are we to look a gift horse in the mouth?' His voice is loud, clearly as an attempt to drown out his wife's misgivings, probably that she's being treated as a *charity case*. This sort of attitude is one of the things which has held her back so much in life.

'Have *you* ever flown business class?' Marty stands back so that Siobhan is directly in Cameron's line of sight.

'Well, no, but—'

'Well, I vote for *you* getting the third seat,' Marty says. 'After all, you've organised everything.'

Bloody hell. I could almost taste the champagne and the sumptuous meals I'd have been offered throughout the flight. I'd only resigned myself to cattle class because I thought we'd all be sitting together, albeit in adjacent rows. And who the hell does *Marty* think he is, offering *our* seats out like they're his?

'But you've only just met everyone.' Siobhan frowns at Marty, looking to be stopping herself from adding the word, *again*.

'It'll be even easier for me to get to know them *better* then, won't it?' He grins, and his face takes on a more sinister edge, showing more of a side we once experienced.

Siobhan looks uncomfortable. 'No, honestly – it's too long a flight to be sitting on my own.'

'You won't be sitting on your own.' Zane smiles. 'You'll be sitting with *us*.' He gestures from himself to Becky. I'd expect her to smile, considering where she's going to be sitting, but she narrows her eyes. As we get older, she seems to be growing more possessive of her husband.

'Believe me...' Cameron rakes his fingers through his still-ample fringe. 'You won't care who you're sitting with when you're on the other side of those curtains.'

Siobhan looks thoughtful. 'I can't say I'm not tempted.'

'Well, that's settled then.' Cameron gestures to them and turns to the counter. 'If you could put these three lovely people in the upgraded seats, please.'

I try to smile, but it's probably never looked more false. Cameron should have booked two of those seats for *us*. I hope he's not going to carry on like this for the rest of the holiday. Making decisions without consulting me first.

As well as putting others before *me*. It's because of him doing that so often that we've got to where we are.

5

BECKY

'Thanks so much,' Siobhan gushes to the air hostess who's been serving us for the last ten hours. 'This has been my first time upgraded, and you've made it really special.'

'It was my pleasure,' she replies.

Siobhan's driven me mad throughout the flight with her p's and q's. She's used the posh telephone voice we always used to laugh at when we were kids, and if I had a tenner for every time she's said *thank you*, I'd be as loaded as Jo and Cameron. I'm all for being polite, but you don't have to thank someone when they put your cutlery down, then ten seconds later when they give you your starter and then again ten seconds later when they pour your drink.

That said, I've enjoyed it too – I'm just not as vocal as Siobhan. I slept for at least half the journey, the taste of champagne lingering on my tongue as I drifted off. With the window blind down and the face mask they provided, I could almost pretend it was nighttime. Unlike the normal cabin, the temperature was just right too.

'Well, that was awesome.' Zane rises from his seat and stretches his long limbs beneath his jeans and t-shirt. 'I can't believe how different it was. The delicious food, the comfy recliner seats, the tablecloths. I even slept for three hours.'

I'd like to comment on how his attention has been more on Siobhan than on me throughout the journey, but I'll keep quiet. Whoever's going to cause the first fall-out between the four of us isn't going to be me. Judging by Tina's pouty face since we arrived at the airport, it will more than likely be her.

'Did you see the little tubes of face cream and lip balm? They smelt gorgeous.' Anyone would think Siobhan had never encountered such items. 'I don't want to travel in economy ever again after *that* experience.' She offers a parting glance of sadness at her seat as we begin to walk away from where we've spent the journey, our soft blankets and pillows strewn over our seats.

'I do think we stood out like a sore thumb.' I wait between my friend and my husband as we queue to disembark. 'Did you notice how posh some of those people were?' I point towards the line of people waiting in front of us. 'They probably go away several times a year and fly like that every time.'

'They're only *people*, like us.' Siobhan turns back to me. 'Just because they've got more money doesn't make them any more special.' If Jo were here, she'd probably mention Siobhan's former gambling habit, which fuelled her credit card addiction. There's no one more inclined to try keeping up with the Joneses than Siobhan used to be. But I'm not as cutting as Jo.

Plus it's alright for Siobhan to have confidence alongside *anyone* with her luscious auburn hair, deep blue eyes and milky skin. If she were as skinny, mousy and covered in freckles as I am, she'd have the same inferiority complex I've always struggled with. Not to mention the life I have back at home.

'I couldn't put it any better.' Zane says from behind me, taking yet another opportunity to agree with my friend as we queue at the door of the plane, looking out at the cacti and the clear blue sky. 'Wow, will you feel that?' The thick wall of heat and smell of aviation fuel hits us as we reach the steps. 'And here's me in jeans and trainers. I need to get changed, sharpish, and work some more on my tan.'

I half expect Siobhan to make some comment in reply, but thankfully, she holds back. Zane's been bordering on flirtatious towards her throughout the flight, and I don't like it – I don't like it one bit. I can't imagine she'd ever reciprocate; but it shows the level of respect he has left for me. 'Aren't we waiting for the others before we head through security?' I look back up at the door to the plane.

'Like the captain said—'

I grit my teeth. Because he came around to meet us all at the start of the flight, Siobhan's acting like she knows the captain personally. 'Business class disembark first,' she tells me like I'm an imbecile. 'The rest of them will still be waiting until everyone in front gets off before they can even move from their seats. 'We'll just wait down on the tarmac.' She looks wistfully back towards the front of the plane. 'Wait until I tell Marty about how well looked after we were. He'll be soooo jealous.'

I got the feeling that Marty won't be all that bothered. He seemed more interested in reacquainting himself with the others – namely Jo, judging by the appreciative looks I've noticed him giving her.

∾

'How was it?' Cameron grins as the rest of our party lands one by one at the bottom of the steps.

'Incredible.' Siobhan hugs him as if he's just bestowed a life-saving gift. A dark expression enters Marty's eyes.

He must sense me staring, for his expression darkens even further as our eyes meet. Sooner or later, Siobhan's going to grill me about how and when we became acquainted. *How would I even begin to answer?* Looking away from me, he quickly rearranges his features into a smile as he turns his attention to Andy.

Meanwhile, Cameron moves from Siobhan to my husband. 'Thank you, man.' Zane holds out his hand. 'I won't forget that journey in a hurry. You guys are so lucky to do it all the time. What an awesome start to our holiday.' Zane's so cheerful it's sickening, especially since we're probably going to run out of spends by day three. I get so sick of this way of living. We shouldn't even be here and we wouldn't be without Siobhan's help.

'You're welcome.' Cameron accepts his handshake before turning to me.

I want to hug him too, but I daren't, so like Zane, I offer my hand. 'Thanks so much,' I mumble. There's something about Cameron that always ties my tongue up in knots. I wish I had Siobhan's confidence.

'It's a shame we've landed just as the sun's beginning to set.' Siobhan sounds almost manic, clearly still buzzing from her experience in business class. I follow her gaze to the glint of the sun behind the whitewashed airport buildings.

'Well, I for one won't be up too late tonight.' Jo smooths strands of her bobbed hair behind one ear, and I'm almost certain from the way Andy's watching her that he longs to smooth it for her. Tina's watching him too. I'll have to keep my eye on them – something is definitely amiss. 'I didn't get a wink of sleep on the journey. That *bloody* baby. I mean, who takes a child that small on a long-haul flight?'

'It wasn't the *baby's* fault, love.' Cameron glances in my direction and rolls his eyes. I don't know why he's being so attentive towards me all of a sudden. Usually, he barely acknowledges me, which I've always put down to being worlds apart from him.

Jo catches up with Siobhan as I lag at the back of the group. Zane would rather walk and talk with Marty, who he's only just met, instead of with me. I get the feeling he's bored of being in my company after spending the flight at my side, lap of luxury or not. After so long together, it's like we've run out of things to say to each other, which is why I was irked that he had so much to say to Siobhan.

'What's first on the agenda?' Zane calls out as we follow the signs along the baking hot corridor.

'We'll get a couple of cabs to the villa.' Siobhan turns back, her voice authoritative. 'We'll dump our bags and then head out for drinks and some food.'

'But it'll take forever to get ready.' Jo's voice is whiny. 'It'll be midnight before I've showered and got myself anywhere near presentable.' She tugs at the skin beneath her eyes as if to demonstrate how haggard she believes she looks. Her skin springs straight back into position. She shares her hair salon with a beauty therapist and couldn't look any less haggard. Sure, she's got a few laughter lines around her eyes, but it's better than the deep grooves that have etched themselves in and around *my* face over the years. If I had her job and money, I'd probably look like her as well.

'Can we make a pact to all go out just as we are tonight?' Tina pauses and spins around to face the rest of us. 'We're *all* dishevelled after the early start and the long journey.'

'You couldn't look dishevelled if you tried.' Siobhan reaches for Tina's hair, brushing the tips of her fingers against her curls.

I smooth my hand against my shoulder-length hair. I've worn it in the same style since I was eleven years old - around the time I first encountered Tina, Jo and Siobhan at high school. I can't imagine my hairstyle will ever change or that I'll ever be able to afford regular highlights to brighten my mousy mop. I'll probably be a dowdy administrator until the day dawns when I retire on a state pension, and then I'll die in my front room while watching Loose Women.

'What's up, Bex?' Jo throws me a look. 'Flash us that fifty-year-old smile.'

Only me and Jo have turned fifty so far. Tina's birthday is in a couple of weeks, and Siobhan's is on the last day of August. She only just made it into our school year, but despite being the youngest, she was probably the cleverest out of our group. It certainly wasn't me.

'Nothing,' I reply. 'I'm just tired.'

'Come on, Bex – spill it. We're in *Aruba* – you're supposed to be giddy with excitement.' Jo smiles as we pass a giggling gang of younger tourists in resort wear.

'Perhaps I would have been if I were fifteen instead of fifty.'

She gives me a knowing look. We both know this isn't true – for any of us. There wasn't much giddiness *or* excitement when we were fifteen.

'I just hate being so old,' I continue. 'You lot might all think fifty is something to celebrate, but I don't.'

'Why don't you try to reframe how you're feeling?' Siobhan hangs back to join in with our conversation as we finally reach the queue for border control. 'Have you ever considered age to be a privilege? After all, not everyone makes it to the ripe old age of fabulous fifty, do they?'

'Hark at her wisdom.' Marty looks around, presumably checking if his words have amused the others. Andy, Cameron and Zane laugh along. The rest of us don't. I'm surprised how deftly Marty's slipped into the shoes of Siobhan's ex-husband as far as the other men seem to be concerned. It's as if he's been around for far longer. For some of us, he has.

'Let's change the subject, shall we?' Now Cameron's joined in with the chat, I don't want him knowing anything of how I feel about myself. It's embarrassing.

'Well, I, for one,' Siobhan says, 'am more comfortable in my own skin now I'm fifty than I've ever been, whether it's saggy or not.'

6

BECKY

GETTING through security is painless enough. We wait for five minutes surrounded by the hum of fans and the shouts of customs officers, then we're in. I'm not well-travelled in the slightest, but the four of us, usually renowned for our poor sense of direction, seem to be leading the men the right way around this tiny airport without too much trouble.

'It's going to be fab-u-lous,' Siobhan gushes as she heads us up in the direction of the baggage hall. 'I've booked us yoga on the beach, a Caribbean cooking class, a sunrise hike—'

'A sunrise *hike*,' Zane echoes. 'Aren't we supposed to be on *holiday*?'

We stand at the baggage conveyor as if we're contestants on The Generation Game, waiting for our cases like our lives depend on it.

'Imagine if they lost one of our bags.' Jo clutches her chest, proving my point. 'I can't imagine anything worse. All my clothes, shoes and makeup.'

'It wouldn't be the end of the world.' Siobhan taps her on the back. 'We'd all lend you our stuff.'

'Hmmm, yeah.' She looks Siobhan up and down as she replies, evidently thinking *I wouldn't wear the bohemian crap you do.* Jo wouldn't be seen dead in my clobber, and as for Tina's clothes, well, they'd hang off her. Tina used to say Andy loved her just as she was, describing her as 'voluptuous,' but the way he keeps looking at Jo suggests otherwise. Bloody Jo – she always got the boys when we were younger as well. She exudes so much confidence that men have always flocked to her like crows surrounding a dead rat. Meanwhile, other women just watch on, wanting to *be* her.

Mine and Zane's luggage is the easiest to spot - ours are the shabbiest suitcases. It's difficult not to compare the ancient case I borrowed from our next-door neighbour with the gleaming designer thing Zane passes to Jo as it arrives. Life's fallen into her lap over the last decade. Even Tina and Siobhan are ten times happier than I am.

But I can't let myself dwell for too long on this unfairness. If I do, it risks making me act too resentfully. Or worse, it might force me to divulge the event from our teens - the one the four of us swore each other to secrecy over. We were all equals then, and we should be now.

'Since you're being the hero, Zane.' Siobhan points at her case as it approaches.

'I'll get it.' Marty swoops in, and I roll my eyes. He's trying too hard.

'Cheer up, for God's sake, Becky.' Siobhan nudges me. 'We're here to celebrate.' Great, *she's* on at me as well now. 'Especially since I've been telling Marty how amazing you all are.'

'It'll be good to get to know you all better.' Marty spins around, this time avoiding my eye and feasting his gaze on Jo.

Their Last Days of Summer

Even after her crammed-up flight, she still looks impeccable. But she seems uncomfortable under his sudden scrutiny.

'There's nothing like a holiday...' Zane begins, looking at Siobhan. I'm going to kill him when I get him on his own. I know he's had more than a few drinks on the plane, but I can't believe he's still flirting with her so blatantly. 'To be *really* able to get to know people.'

The four of us women exchange glances, our unspoken words conveying knowledge of what the others are thinking. We already know way too much about each other. Maybe, as I was telling someone at work, that's what's kept us in touch for so many years.

'Let's hope we're all still speaking in seven days.' Siobhan laughs.

'Yeah,' Andy adds. 'Things will come out whether we want them to, or not. All our bad habits, everybody's irritating little ways.'

'You haven't got any of those, surely?' Jo touches his arm, and I steal a glance at Tina to see if she's noticed this gesture.

'You'd know all about irritating little ways.' Tina nudges her husband as she falls into step with him, and it's difficult to tell if she's joking. By the look on her face, I'd say probably not. She's been so quiet since we all met at the airport. At some point, I'll have to check in with her and make sure she's alright.

'So if anyone's got any dark secrets,' – Cameron concludes the conversation with a sweep of his hand, – 'you should come clean before we leave the airport. As this is the week where everything will worm its way out.'

7

SIOBHAN

Jo scrambles into the taxi with Cameron, Tina and Andy without asking who wants to ride with who. It was always the same at school. Jo claims that I try to push our group around, but really, it's *her*.

'I'll sit in the front.' Becky gives Marty a look I can't work out as she grabs the passenger side door handle before anyone else can. I'll be able to collar her on her own soon and find out what she's got against my new boyfriend. She got on well with Caleb, my ex, so hopefully, it isn't much more than that. Jo, however, could be another matter – I'm getting a definite sense that something's happened between them. Clearly from many years ago, but still... When the drinks flow and everyone's dressed scantily on the beach and in the hot tub, I hope that he doesn't notice her more than he does me.

'A rose between two thorns.' As I rest my bag at my feet in the dark interior, Zane nudges me. Becky twists in her seat and shoots me a scathing look. Never mind *me* feeling jealous over Jo, Becky seems to have it in for *me* all of a sudden. Every time Zane speaks to me, she looks like she could cheerfully wrap her hands around my throat. I've never known her to be as insecure as she seems to have grown with her husband. I move my knees so they're not touching Zane's anymore, but pointing towards Marty.

'Speak for yourself, Zane.' Marty laughs from my other side. 'You might feel like you're wilting, but I'm still in full bloom.'

I glance at him. I wasn't sure about inviting my new boyfriend along, but there's no denying how easily he's fitting in with my friends' husbands, even if there's an atmosphere from Becky, Jo and Tina towards him, which I really think is more to do with their loyalty towards Caleb.

Perhaps they're just jealous. Becky, in particular, was always punching above her weight with Zane and never seems to have grasped how lucky she is that he's stuck around, even after she denied him the chance of parenthood. We once tried to broach it with her, but she closed us down, saying it was none of our business. Which is obviously right.

Even with the air conditioning in here, I'm still struggling for breath as I sit pressed in the middle of the back seat between the two men.

'Isn't it great to be around palm trees?' I point from the window, trying to distract myself.

'It's impossible to be rid of those.' Marty laughs as we pass a row of fast food chains I wouldn't eat at if you paid me. I'm looking forward to eating well this week, and my research included identifying some of the finest restaurants for us to visit.

Zane and Becky remain silent as if we've touched a nerve. Judging from my friend's pasty, dull complexion, the fast food chains our taxi is speeding by probably serve up the crap she's most accustomed to. Hopefully, this week, we can introduce her to a better way of being – and not just in the food department.

'How are you for spends?' I lean forward in my seat and whisper into her ear. 'Let me know if you start to run low.'

She stiffens as if I've just offered her an insult instead of a helping hand. She's really defensive, but then I guess an entire childhood of being bullied made her that way. If it wasn't for the three of us, she wouldn't have had *any* friends at school. She doesn't reply. I didn't want to embarrass her – I only wanted to help.

She's not the only one who's known poverty, but she wears it with more dignity than I was able to. Not many people know how badly I coped with being broke, nor how it nearly landed me in prison. I hope my friends will stay quiet about it as I'd hate for Marty to find out.

We spend the rest of the journey listening to the small talk made between Marty and the driver. Places to eat, sights to see, where to go. I don't know why he's bothering, as I've got it all sussed.

The others have unloaded their cases by the time our taxi pulls up outside number 7a, a pure white villa which will be our home for the next week. I can't wait to see inside the accommodation I so carefully chose with my oldest friends in mind. Excitement dances in my belly as I climb from the back of the taxi, relieved to be free of the stench of the awful air freshener swinging from the rear view mirror. Marty pays, refusing a donation towards the cost from Zane.

'You can cover the journey back to the airport,' he says. I follow him from the taxi, the sound of cicadas filling my ears. It's their buzz that I associate with being on holiday.

As I take in the outside of the villa, a weird, prickling sensation crawls over me. A sense that when the day of our return journey arrives, everything will have changed – and not for the better.

8

SIOBHAN

MARTY HOISTS all four cases from the boot and passes them to each of us, his muscles taut beneath his t-shirt. I'm lucky I met him, I know I am. Most men in our age bracket are rejects or defects, yet as far as I can see, Marty is neither. He doesn't even have any children from former relationships, which is unusual but welcome. From listening to Jo's experience with Cameron's two daughters, I know what a problematic experience stepfamilies can be.

As if sensing my eyes on him, Marty turns and winks, a gesture he seems to reserve just for my benefit. He says he can't help but wink at me and calls it a reflex action – one which he's never experienced before. He always says all the right things, but I often get the sense that he's well practiced in his one-liners. I just hope I'm not one in a long line of women he'll eventually grow tired of.

I hope Tina and Jo have saved us the best room, the master bedroom with the ensuite, which overlooks the pool. I'm certain they will have done – after all, it's me who arranged *everything* and disseminated all that everyone needed to know ahead of the holiday. The need for a tetanus, the disembarkation form, and the fact that certain sun creams and insect repellents aren't allowed in the ocean because of the damage they will do to the coral reefs.

But then, the others don't care about stuff like that as much as I do. Jo and Cameron are frequent long-haul flyers, not giving two hoots about their effect on the environment. I've noticed when we've visited Tina that she doesn't bother recycling, and Becky's too focused on her own survival to be bothered about the survival of the planet.

All anyone else did for the planning of this was transfer their money to me and organise their own insurance. Apart from Becky, who still owes me for nearly half of the holiday. However, I'm getting the sense I'll end up having to write that money off. I wonder if Zane knows that I've been forced to finance their trip. Perhaps his demeanour wouldn't be so relaxed and assured if he knew he was only here because of me.

If I were to add up all I've loaned Becky since I got back on my feet financially after what I did in my thirties, I'd have no problem affording business class whenever I wanted. She always promises to pay me back, and I'm sure the intention's there, but she never seems to manage it. I shouldn't continue to help her really, but our group of four wouldn't be the same without her. *How could it be?*

'Don't you think it got dark quickly?' She says as we head through the courtyard towards the lit-up villa, which is the most inviting building I've ever seen. 'One minute the sun was setting, but then it only felt like a few minutes later that it was completely dark.'

I follow her gaze to the sky, marvelling at the constellations. It still isn't a dark sky, more a beautiful shade of midnight blue. 'This place is gorgeous enough at night, don't you think? I can't wait to see it in all its glory during the day.'

'You're such a hippie.' Marty tugs at one of my plaits, the

style I always adopt for travelling. 'But that's one of the many things that caught my eye.'

Becky scowls, making me wonder if that's because Zane never says anything sweet like that to her anymore. Zane glances at me and then looks away. I wish he'd pack it in with whatever he's harbouring. All he's doing is causing trouble between himself and his wife – as well as making *me* uncomfortable.

I'd better lighten the mood. 'Oooh, just look at that pool. I'll be jumping in there as soon as possible.' Lights gleam beneath the water's surface, and I don't think I've ever seen anything look more alluring. I'd be in there right now, but my need to go out for a glass of something is far greater. I smack my lips together. I'm parched, having not drunk anything since we left the plane.

'It's the jacuzzi I spotted on the link you sent us that I've got my sights set on.' Marty winks at me again. 'Hopefully, we can all fit in there at the same time.'

'No thanks.' Becky looks like she'd rather sit in an ant's nest than the jacuzzi with the rest of us. I'm sure there will be plenty of those around as well.

'You two go on into the villa.' I tug on Becky's arm to hold her back. 'The two of us need a quick word.'

'We do?' Becky swings around to face me as Zane calls, *hi honeys, we're home* into the entrance at the main set of patio doors, his voice echoing around the marble kitchen.

I wait until they've disappeared inside before I swing around to face my friend. 'Right, out with it, Bex – what *exactly* is your problem with Marty?'

'I don't know what you mean.' She's avoiding my eye, a sure sign she's lying and instead, she's fixing her gaze on the shimmering pool which is lapping gently against its edges in the warm breeze.

'You're being *really* off with him.' I move myself so I'm

standing in her line of vision. 'You said you knew him from the youth club?'

'We only went there a couple of times.' She's still avoiding my eye. 'Like I said, I think you were on holiday.'

'How *well* did you all know him? Did he and Jo—' My voice trails off. It shouldn't matter what might have happened between him and Jo all those years ago, yet somehow, it does. Especially now that we're all here together.

Becky opens her mouth and for a moment, it looks like she might impart whatever's on her mind. I'm unsure what reason she could have to dislike Marty, especially since thirty-five years have elapsed since we were at school. He's been friendly enough and couldn't have tried any harder with my friends.

'It really doesn't matter, Siobhan.' She turns towards the lights emitting from our villa.

'Of course it *matters* – you're one of my best friends.' I reach out and touch her arm, hoping this will reassure her that I mean well, even though I've collared her on her own like this. 'If Marty's inadvertently said or done something that could have upset you, or the others – or if *I've* said or done something, let me know so we can get it put right.' Zane's laughter roars from inside. It may just be because of her husband's over-friendliness towards me that she's being off. It's probably nothing to do with Marty.

'Just leave it, will you?' She tugs her arm from my grasp. Her face suggests she's arrived for a wet caravan weekend at a soggy seaside resort instead of a week at a paradise island.

'You're not jealous, are you, Bex?' I hate to accuse her of this, but I can't imagine what else could be eating her. 'Because if you are—'

'Jealous? Of *what*?' She spits the word out like it's something nasty in her mouth. 'No – I am not *jealous*. Come on, let's just get in there, shall we?'

I get a feeling that what she'd really like to say is, *let's just get this holiday over with, shall we?*

Becky *and* Tina have been out of sorts since we all met at the check-in desk back in the UK. And I'll find out what's up with them if it's the last thing I do.

9

THIRTY-FOUR YEARS AGO

'Nobody would dare try to get into the dorm with the four of you.' Miss Smith, the teacher leading our Year Ten residential laughs, though I can tell it's forced. At school, she tries to keep us all separate in class, as, instead of concentrating on our work, our greatest talent lies in distracting each other.

'I should have had a plaque made for your door telling everyone else to keep out,' she continues.

None of us reply. Really, we just want Miss Smith to clear off so we can discuss more important matters.

'I trust I can count on you all to behave yourselves if I don't try to split you up.' She'll know as well as we do that separating us would be pointless. We'd all sneak back together during the night. Especially with, unbeknown to her, what's currently going on between us.

'Of course.' I arrange my face so it's at its most angelic, and the others laugh.

'You need to sleep and not be messing about all night, girls.' She wags a commanding finger. 'Especially with a schedule as packed as ours is over the next couple of days. There's a lot of walking, so you'll need to be well rested.'

Finally, she leaves us to it, and the four of us look at each other.

'I thought she'd never leave.' Noticing the two top bunks have already been bagged by two of the others who've rolled out their sleeping bags onto them, I throw my duffle bag on one of the bottom bunks.

Snooze, you lose has always been the philosophy among the four of us. But next time, I'll win – I get sick of losing all the time.

Of course, one of us has no choice other than to sleep at the bottom. Climbing ladders to a top bunk at eight-and-a-half months pregnant wouldn't be the most sensible thing. Besides, she's getting up for the loo several times during the night. All she has to do is forget she's up a ladder, and things could get disastrous.

I stare across at the other bottom bunk. While it's just the four of us, she can let everything hang out. And I mean *literally*. Now Miss Smith has been and gone, she unzips her baggy cardy and shrugs it off with a grunt of *thank goodness for that*. The only people in the world who know about her being knocked up are us in this room. No one else has a clue.

Her mum and stepdad would kick her out for sure. All her mum cares about is the shame her fifteen-year-old daughter might bring on their family, especially since she claims not to know who the father is. We've quizzed her until we're blue in the face, but she won't divulge it. I've found myself constantly observing her when we're in assembly or the dining hall, looking to see if she's watching anyone, or just as importantly, if anyone's watching her. But so far, I've seen nothing out of the ordinary.

We've supported her through the sickness, then through the food cravings and over the last few months, between us, we've sourced her increasingly big and baggy clothes to hide her growing midriff. But her due date is marching ever closer and beginning to loom over the four of us like a nuclear cloud. Not one of us has anything resembling a plan for when labour starts or what might happen after that. Least of all, her. She must be terrified – I know I would be.

'You OK?' I rise from the edge of my creaky bunk bed and head over to hers, resting my hand on her arm. 'You look wiped out.'

'It was the journey.' She lifts her head from her pillow. 'I don't do coaches at the best of times. But I'll be fine after a lie down.'

'I can't imagine Smithy letting us rest in here for long.' I glance at the door. If she or any of the other girls charged in now, they'd immediately lay eyes on the enormous belly beside me and instantly gain knowledge of our predicament. 'You heard what she said about lots of walking. How long's the Dracula trail – does anyone know?'

'You'll be a mother in a fortnight,' comes an all-knowing voice from the bunk above me, ignoring my question. The Dracula trail is planned for after dinner, and I'm hoping it won't be too far – not when she's in this state. She looks like she could barely walk to the door at the moment. 'I take it you *still* haven't seen a doctor?'

'You really should.' I squeeze her arm as she shakes her head. 'You don't even know if the baby's healthy. Women can die in childbirth.'

'I'm not a woman,' comes the reply. 'Besides, they'll only tell my mum. If I were older, things might be different. People might call me less names too. I wouldn't be at school anymore, for starters. It's awful – I just want it all to be over.'

'That's what we're all here for,' I reply. 'Do you think we'll let anyone get away with calling you *anything*? Plus, like I've told you, my mum might let you stay with us if yours kicks you out.'

Even as I say this, I don't hold out much hope – Mum would

be horrified at us keeping this pregnancy a secret, especially for this long, and I don't think I could prevent her from telling someone.

With all this going on, I asked Mum a few weeks ago how she'd react if I came home when I'm not even sixteen, saying, *Mum, you're going to be a grandma.* Once I'd peeled her off the ceiling and convinced her that I was only *asking*, she replied that she'd be disappointed but that she'd stand by whatever I wanted. This is what made me think she might help my friend. I've wanted to tell Mum so many times, but the three of us have all been sworn to secrecy. If I break that, I risk losing the friendship we've built over five years with the girls I know better than my own family. I'm certain they suspect my secret too, but their silence suggests it's safe for now.

'Another kick?'

She nods and gestures for me to rest my hand on her belly. Her stomach's as tight as my brother with a bag of sweets, and is rippled with strange wavy marks. Within a couple of seconds, the baby kicks.

'It must be like being possessed.' I tug my hand back, not wanting to feel it kick – it's all too weird and makes it all the more real.

We're here in Whitby, a town that smells of salt, seaweed and fish, for the next three nights. It's a two-hour drive from home, and I know from all the research I've done that the baby could come at any time.

Perhaps I should be researching whether there's a maternity hospital nearby.

10

TINA

I RUB my eyes as I stare through the open window at the movement of the palm leaves against the night sky. Andy's snoring yet again. It wouldn't matter whether we were at home or in Timbuktu, he will *always* snore. He's wearing a mouth guard, but he might as well not bother. The menopause has played enough havoc with my sleep, but add in a snorer, and it's no wonder I look a hundred years old.

I need to pee, but am scared of who I might encounter on my way to the loo. At least it won't be Cameron. I'd die of embarrassment if I encountered him in his boxers. Much to Siobhan's dismay, Cameron and Jo took the best room – the only one of the four with an ensuite, which I could tell she was coveting. But Jo clearly believed that she had more of a right to it, and what Jo wants, Jo usually gets. Becky and I wouldn't have even been contenders for the room. Jo also opened the fizz that had been left by the owners of the Airbnb, and as Siobhan remarked on, put the complimentary flowers inside her room. She's out of order, but really can't see it.

My head's fuzzy after the cocktails we were guzzling at the bar on the seafront after we dumped our cases. With the

Aruban breeze in our hair and the backdrop of steel drums, everything felt perfect - for an hour anyway. I was so caught up in the moment that I asked Zane to take a first-night photo of the four of us with our matching cocktails and excited smiles. It will probably end up pinned to my fridge with the others. At least, I hope it will.

I defy anyone not to feel uplifted when in a place like this. Life seems so chilled out here, on what's described as *one happy island*. The favourite word used by the locals seems to be *awesome*, and the heat is enough to penetrate the chilliest of demeanours, even Becky's, who also had a smile on her face by her third cocktail.

My enjoyment stopped when I noticed Andy being all cosy with Jo, placing his hand in the small of her back at the bar. Cameron sat between them when they returned to the table. I'd love to ask him if he's sensed what I have.

The stress I was feeling swiftly gave way to exhaustion, and I realised well before our food arrived that I was beyond eating, probably not a bad thing after all the junk I ate on the plane. I never even got the chance to purge myself of it all – I haven't had a minute on my own. I'd planned to go to the loo when we landed, but Siobhan followed me. She seems to suspect that I'm still dealing with my problem weight in the same way I always have. Like I've repeatedly told her, if I wanted advice, I'd ask for it. And if I *wanted* treatment, I'd see a doctor. There's nothing wrong with me. Being sick is as natural as breathing. Or childbirth.

I managed to nod and laugh along for another endless hour before admitting defeat and saying I'd get a taxi back to the villa on my own if the rest of them wanted to stay out until later. Thankfully, the others mostly felt the same, all apart from Zane, Jo and Marty, who looked as if they could have gone on all night. Marty looked almost angry when Siobhan insisted we get a taxi back to the villa.

Jo won't admit to it, but I know she cheats to find that energy. Most mere mortals rely on caffeine as a pick-me-up, but Jo instead relies on the finest white powder money can buy. She has no idea we know about her coke habit, and I'll keep it that way – unless she dredges up something I'd rather leave buried. Wherever it comes from, I'd love to still have that level of energy, instead of constantly feeling as if my get-up-and-go has got up and gone.

The boys are old enough not to need me, I've been on a break from school for the last week, and I've no major stresses in life apart from my marriage hanging by a thread. Andy keeps quizzing me on why I'm always so wrung out. He helped me so much when we were at university together that if he suspected I was still up to my old bulimic tricks, well, I don't know how he'd react. He'd either be furious or perhaps he wouldn't even care anymore.

I don't know how many more nights I can lie like this, staring at shadows pooling in the corners of the room. I long for sleep to rescue me, but I am also dreading what tomorrow may bring.

11

TINA

'I'VE BEEN awake since four o'clock this morning.' Becky arrives in the kitchen behind me, stretching her arms above her head so high that her nightie rises up her thighs. 'That bed of ours is too soft.' Seeing her in her nightie reminds me of being in our dorm in Whitby. It's so many years ago, it feels like another lifetime.

'Me too.' I yawn. 'By the time we get used to the time difference, it will probably be time to go home. What are we - five hours behind the UK?' The faint smell of bleach in here isn't doing much for my stomach. The kitchen must have been cleaned not long before we arrived.

'Something like that. But I can't carry on like this all week.' Becky rakes her fingers through her hair. I'm pleased to see she took Jo up on her offer to do her nails, as it's rare for Becky to be able to afford any pampering for herself. It's been her way of life for as long as I've been her friend. With her constantly overgrown hair and hand-me-downs when we were at school, we had to constantly protect her from the bullies. Sadly, this poverty has remained her norm. 'But aside from that, isn't it wonderful to wake up to that sunshine?' She points at the patio doors. The first thing I did was to draw the curtains back when I came in here just as the sun was rising. I follow her gaze to the doors, the brightness out there making my eyes ache.

'What do you make of *him* being here?' She jerks her head in the direction of the room next to ours, the one Siobhan and Marty have taken. I might have to buy myself some earplugs – they've only just met, so are bound to have an active sex life, which is something I can do without being forced to listen to. Thankfully, Siobhan looked knackered, as was I when we got back last night, so I can't imagine sex was on the cards.

'Who, Siobhan's *new* bloke?' I draw air quotes around the word *new* as I lower my voice. With its high ceilings and marble tops, the kitchen amplifies our voices. 'Yeah, what a shocker.'

'Poor Caleb.'

'He was really looking forward to this holiday, according to Andy.' I plug the coffee machine into the wall. Now I need to work out how to use it. At least the coffee aroma will mask the smell of bleach.

'I know. It's not the same without him.' Becky leans against the back of the chair. 'Has Siobhan tried grilling *you* yet?'

'About *Marty*?' I point towards their room.

'Yes, who else?'

'She tried cornering me last night, but Andy walked in, so she left it alone.' She'd stopped talking so abruptly that Andy thought we'd been discussing *him*, which smacks of a guilty conscience in my opinion. 'How about you?'

'She's managed to get me on my own,' Becky replies. 'She was on about Marty as we were getting out of the taxi – the minute we arrived.'

'Asking what? Just so I'm prepared.'

'She wanted to know what my problem is with him.'

'She's not daft, is she?'

'She thinks I'm jealous.' Her face darkens. 'She couldn't be further from the truth.'

Their Last Days of Summer

'We should tell her the truth, really.' I fill a jug with water. 'Even if it *is* all in the past, she has a right to know.'

'But nobody *else* needs to know about all that, do they?' She drags a chair from beneath the large glass table at the far end of the kitchen. 'This was meant to be the trip of a lifetime, and—'

I turn from the counter. 'I just wish we could relax in the present and stop worrying about the past.'

'Or the future.' Becky's voice is so quiet, it's barely perceptible as she sits heavily onto the chair.

'I'm making a pot of coffee if you'd like some?' I load another heaped scoop into the machine, enjoying its scent.

'Did I hear the word *coffee*?' Zane arrives in the kitchen wearing a skimpy white towel around his waist. I force my eyes to stay above the height of his midriff. Really, I don't know where to look. The heat's rising in my cheeks, and I can only hope Becky doesn't notice. He's already tanned from his work as a gardener, making his eyes look bluer, and there isn't an ounce of fat on him. I wish I could say the same about myself.

'Do you have to prance around the villa like *that*?' Becky scowls at him as he stands beneath the archway dividing the kitchen from our sleeping quarters. I don't blame her. There's no way Andy would wander around wearing nothing but a towel in front of our friends – at least I hope not. He'd be more likely to emerge from our room dressed in shoes, shirt and trousers. But with the Aruban effect, who knows?

What if Zane's towel were to slip? *No, Tina, you cannot think this way.* I chase the thought of the husband of one of my best friends from my mind and slide more mugs from the cupboard. Wherever I end up, home or away, I always seem to be the tea lady. Well, in this case, the coffee lady. 'Do you take sugar, Zane?' I spin around as he pulls a chair from beneath the table beside his wife.

'No, I'm sweet enough, I reckon.'

'There's nothing like the scent of coffee to invite a man into the kitchen.' Marty is the next to arrive with his hair on end, wearing just a pair of shorts, displaying his perfectly toned *everything*. I might not like him, but physically, I can see why Siobhan's had her head turned.

She comes up behind him, her wavy red hair loose around her shoulders, and a transparent kaftan over her shortie pyjamas as she cuddles him from behind. It's hard to imagine Andy and I ever displayed that level of affection. I look down at the frumpy PJs I'm wearing over my size sixteen frame and wish I'd tried harder to eat less and exercise more. The PJs looked nice on the minuscule model on the packet in Tesco, but nothing looks good on me, and it probably never has.

'I thought we'd have a leisurely first morning,' Siobhan announces. By now, Cameron and Jo have also appeared in the kitchen. Cameron looks relaxed in jeans shorts and a crisp white t-shirt, while Jo's sporting a long chemise that leaves little to the imagination. 'Then we've got snorkelling and a boat trip booked this afternoon. I hope everyone's happy with this.'

No one would dare protest otherwise, which is the trouble – no one ever has. Siobhan always does the organising and we other three have always fallen into line with Jo putting up slightly more resistance than me and Becky.

As Siobhan's relaying our day one plans, I feel like introducing a new rule amongst us. *Please dress appropriately in communal areas.* But I'd get laughed at, after all, I'm still in my PJs, but at least they cover everything they need to. Andy's now joined the others at the kitchen table, dressed respectfully in shorts and a t-shirt. 'Nice one, Tina,' he calls across to me. 'I'll have a coffee if there's one going.'

'I'm starving.' Zane pats his stomach as he passes me the milk. I made a point of getting the taxi to stop at a shop as we travelled back to the villa last night, despite everyone laughing at me for prioritising milk instead of wine and beer. 'Did we get any food in?' He looks at me as if I have all the answers. I'm happy making brews, but if anyone thinks I'm doing any cooking or organising any breakfasts, they can think again.

I shake my head. 'As soon as everybody's *dressed*,' I glare at Jo, hoping she'll get the message that it's unacceptable to wander around half-naked, especially in front of *my* husband. 'We'll go out and find somewhere for breakfast.'

'Who put *you* in charge, Tina?' Siobhan gives me a funny look. 'How do you know I haven't already got something arranged for breakfast?'

'Have you?'

'Well, no, but—.'

'Surely we're not all going to be joined at the hip every second of every day while we're here.' The sun-dappled kitchen of our villa might have felt spacious and airy when I was in here alone, but with all eight of us now in here, I feel like I can't breathe. I can't cope this week without being able to have at least an hour or two each day of my own space.

'We're supposed to be celebrating our birthdays *together*, aren't we?' There's an edge to Jo's voice.

I look over at Andy to support me, but he's too busy watching Jo as she speaks. I wanted him to set my mind at rest about her last night, but he was already snoring by the time I returned from the bathroom.

'It's day one and already, Tina's trying to peel herself from the rest of us.' Siobhan sits heavily in the chair next to Marty and bangs her elbows onto the table. 'And I've worked so hard to arrange things this week – I wanted it all to be perfect.' Marty slings his arm around her shoulder. 'I've really looked forward to this.'

'Me too,' says Becky.

'And it *will* be perfect,' Jo insists. 'We all appreciate what you've done, Siobhan, and we're very pleased with our room, aren't we, Cameron?'

'Which was supposed to be—' Siobhan stops mid-sentence as Marty nudges her.

'Supposed to be, *what*?' Becky tilts her head to one side, her mousy hair splaying over the curve of her shoulder. There's a flicker of amusement in her eyes as we slip effortlessly back into our teenage roles – the ones we never fully outgrew. We adored each other, no question, but jealousy and irritation were always woven into the seams of our friendship.

Even now, Siobhan can't help but try to orchestrate everything, bending the group's plans to suit herself. And Jo – well, since marrying her millionaire and launching her little empire with his money, she seems to think she's risen above the rest of us. Becky might keep to the background, but she knows exactly what she's doing when she stirs the pot – setting us off against one another, then sitting back to enjoy the show. And then there's me. Give me a few hours in the company of my friends, and I can feel every nerve in my body start to fray.

Everyone was so dazzled at the prospect and promise of an Aruban holiday that nobody could see the wood for the trees. But I can sense already that things are going to unravel.

12

JO

'I CAN'T BELIEVE she's making us bloody walk.' I mutter into Becky's ear. 'It's not even a proper path.' I shake my feet, annoyed that all this gravel is finding its way into my Jimmy Choos. They're not the most sensible shoes to walk in, but I assumed we'd be getting a couple of taxis into the main resort like we did last night.

'Oh, I don't mind,' Becky replies. 'Besides, the fresh air's clearing my head.'

'From what? Last night's cocktails – or something else?'

She doesn't reply but keeps her eyes fixed on the back of Zane's head as he wanders in front with Siobhan. I've noticed him hanging around her like a lap dog, so Becky will have noticed too. It's difficult to tell how much or little this might be affecting her. Becky's one who keeps her cards very close to her chest.

'I guess we see more while we're walking.' I glance across the road to the shuttered white villas, their pools protected by mosquito nets and their walls adorned with colourfully painted murals. But it's the designer boutiques I've heard about here that I most want to visit. However, I can't imagine the others will want to join me.

I turn to see how far behind *my* husband is. Cameron is lagging at the rear of our group, waving his hands around as he engages in animated conversation with Marty. I've caught the words *investment* and *opportunity* before he dropped back, so I'm not getting involved. He's probably spotted a chance to increase our wealth even further with this new person who's entered his sphere of influence. As he always says, *money flows to money, and you can never make too much.* Either that or he's doling out financial advice that if Marty were to successfully follow, Cameron would have even more to crow about than he already does. However, he has every reason to be proud of himself and all he's achieved. Apart from his bitchy daughters, that is. They've always been the main flies in the ointment of our lives since we got together ten years ago.

'How much further is it?' My back is slick with sweat, and I can't believe I didn't fill up a water bottle. I didn't realise how hot it was going to be today. 'Has anyone got some water?'

Immediately, Andy stops in his tracks, pulls his bottle from his bag and waves it in the air. Tina looks around at me with an expression I know only too well.

'You should have left that handbag at the villa,' she remarks as I pass the water bottle back to Andy. 'Talk about making yourself a target for thieves.'

'Yes, mother.' I give her a funny look as she points at my Louis Vuitton.

'Jo's got us four neanderthal males for protection.' Zane also turns back to us before beating his chest, Tarzan style. I steal a glance at Becky. If the look she gives him could kill, he'd drop dead onto the top of one of the cacti lining this so-called excuse for a path. And I don't welcome Zane's comments either.

'How do you know we're even going the right way, Siobhan?' I want to divert the attention from myself. 'We seem to have been walking forever.' In these shoes, every step feels like ten, but there's nowhere to sit and hunt in my bag for plasters, nor am I bending over in this skirt.

Siobhan waves her phone in the air, so I have to presume we're following her maps app. She's dropped back behind us now, probably to find out what Cameron and Marty are discussing so exclusively. Zane falls into step with Tina while Andy starts walking with me and Becky.

'At least Siobhan's got data on her phone.' Becky studies the ground as she continues to walk. I used to always remind her to hold her head up high when we were young, but I've given up now. 'My network charges through the nose for roaming data, so Zane and I have had to switch ours off.'

I do feel sorry for Becky and her lack of resources, but if she were to put the energy she expends bemoaning her lot into fixing her life, she wouldn't have nearly as much to complain about. Judging by the glance Zane throws her, he'd prefer her not to have told us all about having to switch off their data.

A silence hangs between us all. We four friends used to be so comfortable in the company of each other that whenever conversations lapsed for a few minutes, no one minded. Nowadays, the quiet between us is not so companionable. Pauses must be filled with *something*, however mundane, perhaps to ensure someone doesn't bring up one of our taboo subjects.

13

JO

'Do you remember the time we were first allowed into Leeds to go to the cinema?' It doesn't matter whether or not I say I remember, Siobhan will trot the same memories out whenever we all meet, her eyes shining as if she's reliving our teens for the very first time. The rest of us usually indulge her reminiscences.

She looks back to see whether Marty's listening, possibly believing that with him being new to our group, he might be interested in her old tales. I glance around to see him still hanging onto Cameron's every word. Everyone's in awe of my husband and all his success, at least in the beginning.

'Is Becky's sense of direction still as poor?' Siobhan laughs. 'She was the worst out of the lot of us.'

'The problem with Becky.' Zane joins in now. 'Is that she exudes such an air of confidence, she convinces me that she's certain of where she's going.'

'I even convince myself.' It's good to hear Becky and Zane bantering. They've been pretty distant from each other since they arrived, but not as distant as Tina and Andy.

'What are you on about?' Tina asks.

'I was just reminiscing,' Siobhan goes on, 'about the first time we were allowed to the cinema on our own, you know, when we went to see Dirty Dancing. We spent all our bus fare on pop and Opal Fruits, so we decided to walk. Then Becky led us in the wrong direction from town.'

'I honestly believed we were going the right way.' Becky is indignant. 'I *had* cycled it with my sister.' The second part of what she says is drowned out by a passing car.

'We walked for miles and miles,' Siobhan goes on, 'singing *Hungry Eyes* and *The Time of My Life* until we realised it was nearly dark.' She pulls a face. 'Then we got scared.'

Not as dark and scared as another time I can remember. But obviously, I don't say a word about this particular memory. It's always the biggest elephant in the room. Out in this glorious sunshine, so hot that the heat is shimmering above the tarmac, and surrounded by the scent of hibiscus, it's difficult to imagine a night as dark as the one we all experienced.

Marty's sped up to listen to *our* conversation, leaving Cameron walking alone. I can tell from the square of my husband's shoulders that he's not happy about no one giving him any attention. He hates us going on about the past, saying we resort to being silly, giggly schoolgirls instead of acting our age.

'What about that time Tina went missing?' Siobhan's clearly on a roll now. 'Do you remember that, Andy? Not long after the two of you got together – when she got rip-roaring drunk?'

'Are you talking about New Year's Day again?' Andy rolls his eyes. 'I must have heard this story a thousand times.'

'We spent the entire day searching for her.' I don't know who Siobhan's directing her tales at, but she seems happy in her own little world. 'Her mum was on the verge of calling the police.'

'No one even *thought* to check her room where she'd been

asleep and hungover *all* day.' She laughs like it's the funniest thing ever. She brings up the same stories whenever we get together. Every. Single. Time. It's like we've nothing else left to talk about. Marty's attention, however, is flitting between us as we speak. He genuinely seems interested in our conversation.

'I didn't know whether it was 6am or 6pm when I woke.' Tina pulls a face. 'I've never felt so terrible.'

'Well, that's not strictly true, is it?' The four of us exchange loaded glances but leave it there. Every single one of us has done or said things we regret over the years, things the other three know about, but that we're all sworn to secrecy over.

Now's not the time or the place to drag the skeletons out of our teenage closets. They need to be left safely to rest with our rah-rah skirts, stonewashed jeans and fluorescent belts. I have worried, however, since the planning of this holiday began that *anything* could come tumbling out once the drink starts to flow. But so far, so good, and we all had a fair amount to drink yesterday.

'And then there's Jo.' Bloody hell – Siobhan's still going on. I might have known her trip down memory lane would eventually lead to me. 'What can we say about her? Well, there's her lateness for starters.'

'Really?' Andy laughs, and he looks at me with an intensity I rarely see from Cameron anymore. No matter how much I try to slow down the hands of time, I'll never be able to compete with the pretty young things who work for him. But in the company of my three former schoolfriends, I can definitely hold my own.

'Jo's late everywhere she goes,' Tina replies.

I force a laugh as I shake more gravel from my shoe. She's right, of course – I always try and squeeze just *one more thing* in before I'm supposed to be *anywhere*. Articles I've read suggest I must value *my* time more than anyone else's, which I suppose *is* true to a certain extent. *Time is money*, as Cameron always says. And because we've got way more money than anyone we know, it stands to reason that our time *must* be more valuable.'

'Jo was even late to my wedding.' Tina is, no doubt, glad of an opportunity not only to remind me that she's *married* to Andy, but also to rub my nose in my past faux pas. 'Right at the point where the vicar says, *does anyone know of any reason, blah, blah,* well that's the moment Jo burst into the church, looking incredible, of course.'

'Everyone dresses up for a wedding.' I load my voice with indignation. 'What did you want me to do, turn up in a tracksuit?'

'Just not in a long white, flowing dress.' Tina's eyes narrow as I recall the beautiful summer dress I found in C&A. I guess it *was* slightly bridal, but it serves her right for not choosing me as one of her bridesmaids. 'Talk about trying to upstage me.'

When we were at school, Tina was my *best* friend out of the three of them. I loved them all, of course, but I *did* look better beside Tina and was always the one people picked or boys chose. I'd be described as *the pretty one,* or *the thinner one,* or *the fair-haired one.* I know that's a shallow belief to have held, but growing up, that's who I was.

Tina would step to the side, a perma-smile fixed on her face, trying not to look hurt. We were all happy when Andy came along when they were at university. He was so nerdy and uptight, I don't think anyone other than Tina would have looked twice at him at the time. But like Cameron, he's aged incredibly well in so many respects.

'Speaking of Tina's wedding.' Becky glances at Siobhan. 'Do you remember how drunk Caleb got?'

Siobhan gives her a funny look. Her ex-husband will be the last person she wants to talk about in front of Marty, but Becky clearly can't resist.

'We had to stop him getting into a car with a bunch of

random strangers at the end of the night. Who knows where he'd have ended up?' She laughs, but she's the only one.

'Happy days, eh?' The smile fades from Marty's face and his voice is laced with sarcasm. He won't like hearing a memory associated with Siobhan's ex. After all, it was probably *him* who broke up their marriage. She hasn't told us this was the case, but it must have been.

I lift my eyes from where I'm watching my step for a moment to look around at my friends and our partners. Outwardly, we look like four pairs of happily married people with perfect lives.

Inwardly, we all know that *anything* could happen this week – and I have a sinking feeling that it probably will.

14

BECKY

'Well, this is the life, isn't it?'

I twist in my seat to look at where Siobhan is gesturing. Unfortunately, I'm sitting with my back to the straw-topped palapas and the crystal blue ocean.

Jo, Cameron, Siobhan and Marty jumped straight into the seats with the stunning view, leaving the rest of us to sit with our backs to it.

'Move it or lose it.' Marty grinned as he reached the final seat a millisecond before I did.

I guess someone has to sit with their back to things, and I shouldn't complain after travelling here in business class. But I'm sick of nearly always being the one forced to have my back to it all, the one who's usually the last in line.

The differences between us four friends are telling in our choice of breakfast. I choose, as I always do, the cheapest item on the menu – omelette, and glare at Zane when he orders *three* pastechis, whatever they are.

'Well, I have to try the local cuisine,' he explains.

I can't remind him in front of the others how we need to go easy, and how the dollars we swapped at the post office need to last us all week. However, the look I throw him should convey what I'm thinking. Perhaps I *should* have accepted Siobhan's offer of a loan before, but I can't stand feeling like a charity case. I seem to have gone from being the most bullied person as a child to the most pitied person as an adult. Zane doesn't respond to me, so I stare down at my cheap flip-flops instead, imagining from the foreign words drifting to us from the next table, what they might be saying.

'I'll have the stack of pancakes with maple syrup,' Tina says to the waiter. 'Well, I *am* on holiday.' She pats her midriff. I know exactly where she'll be heading when she's eaten *her* pancakes, and it won't be pretty. Just about every time we all meet up for coffee and cake, she always has two or three times more to eat than everyone else and usually ends up in the loo. We've all heard her throwing up on several occasions over the years. She might think she's being quiet, but no one can be *that* quiet when they're retching. Ugh.

Zane's sitting opposite Jo, which, no doubt, *he'll* be happy about, but I'm facing Cameron. There's something about the man which always makes me nervous, and he's so good-looking, I'm almost scared to make eye contact with him. It's worse than that – I don't know where to look, which is why usually, unless I really can't get out of it, I don't speak to Jo's husband.

'You OK, Becky?' Cameron's looking straight at me with eyes that seem to pierce through to my soul. I hate the effect he has on me.

'Why wouldn't I be?'

'It's just – you seem really jumpy.' His voice is filled with concern, and I'm struggling to put my finger on how this is making me feel. 'Relax - you're supposed to be on holiday.'

'I'm fine.' My face heats up even further in this thirty-degree heat. Why Cameron would suddenly be taking an interest in *me*, I have no idea. Probably because we're all stuck together for the week. Or maybe it's to piss Jo off in some way. I try to focus on the carnival music that's being carried towards us on the breeze. I don't want Jo to notice my blushes.

I don't know what to say to my friends anymore, and feel even less comfortable around their partners. These women might be my oldest friends, but these days, we have little in common, apart from the past and the secrets we've kept for each other over the years.

Siobhan taps her glass with a spoon and gets to her feet, her floaty summer dress crinkling with her motion. I wish I had more clothes like that, I wish I could dress up so I look pretty. 'If I may have your attention while we're waiting for our food.'

'She's off again.' Marty cups his hand over hers, looking at me as he does, as if silently telling me that he belongs here more than I do. Marty shouldn't be anywhere near our holiday, and if I could have foreseen his involvement at the planning stage, I'd have never agreed to come. Nor will I be the only one who feels this way. Caleb should be here, not *him*.

'When we've had breakfast,' Siobhan begins, 'We can head up the beach to walk it off, and then I've booked us in for a boat trip and some snorkelling. You've all got your swimming gear like I mentioned back at the villa, haven't you?'

'Sure have.' I turn to look at Zane just in time to catch him winking, though I'm unsure whether it's at Siobhan or Jo. He shouldn't be winking at either of them, but I reckon he'll be doing more than just winking when we get on the boat. Jo's already shown us the expensive white bikini she's treated herself to. There's nothing wrong with my figure, but all I've got is my Primarni special. Jo has to be the best and have the best – it's always been the case, like she's got something to prove. At least I know now from Tina that Jo has a little extra help to achieve as much as she does. I thought her days of snorting cocaine were long behind her, and I can't believe she still does it. I wonder if Cameron knows.

'Wow, I knew I was in for a treat this week when Siobhan

invited me here.' Marty slaps his thigh. 'But snorkelling in the coral reef.' His grin widens. 'I've always wanted to meet a sea turtle.'

He *is* a creep, but I wish I had an ounce of his excitement. I've never snorkelled in my life and have more chance of drowning than encountering a sea turtle. Only Zane knows that this is my third time abroad. To say I'm fifty, I really haven't lived. Instead, I'm trapped in a dead-end job – I've no legacy in any way, shape or form, and even if I had, I haven't got anyone to leave it to. There was no way I could have ever brought a baby into my up and down existence. Nor would I have deserved to.

But with this milestone birthday, I've realised how much life's passing me by, and somehow, I've got to do something about it. I just don't know where to start. But by the end of this holiday, things have got to change.

'I saw a sea turtle in Australia.' Cameron smiles at the memory.

'I didn't know you'd been there.' Jo gives him a strange look.

'With my girlfriend's family when I was sixteen,' he replies.

'You must have been serious.'

'Ah, we broke up soon after that. Then I was onto the next one.' He winks at me, which feels seriously odd.

'How come you broke up?'

He shrugs. 'I can't remember. All I know is there were quite a few. I guess I was the school heart-throb back in the day.'

Everyone laughs, but it seems to be at him rather than with him.

After the safety briefing by the Peter Andre lookalike, who introduces himself as the captain of our boat, another man waves at a bottle before announcing unlimited 'Ariba Aruba,' the island's cocktail, which will be freely available for the duration of the trip.

Marty and Zane let out a cheer as the captain dances about, adding how, theoretically, the more we drink, the cheaper our snorkelling ticket price will become.

'Can't argue with that.' Marty grins around at everyone, his final gaze resting on me. I want to tell him to piss off and to look at someone else.

'Surely it can't be safe,' Cameron exclaims.

'What can't?' Zane turns to him. 'Don't tell me you won't be partaking in a little Ariba Aruba.'

'To go snorkelling under the influence.' Cameron's frown deepens.

'Give over.' Jo slaps his arm. 'Don't be boring.'

I lean back into my seat as the boat sets off, trying to enjoy the mesmerising Caribbean view, so blue, it's unclear where the sea meets the sky. I need to shove my worries to the back of my mind and focus on the music that's being blasted from the boat's speakers. I may not understand the words, but it has a catchy tune and a good beat.

Jo and Siobhan strip to their bikinis as the boat distances itself from the shore, but like me, Tina will, no doubt, be keeping herself under wraps until the last moment. I don't feel comfortable enough in front of the men we're with to get undressed in front of them. Plus, I couldn't be more ashamed of my pasty and skinny body alongside the others, namely Jo and Siobhan, who have enviable tans from already having been abroad this year. Nor can I cope with being told how I need to put on some weight, which usually comes from Tina. She, of all people, should realise that to be berated for being underweight is as offensive as having excess weight commented on.

And Marty's still staring at me. He's making me seriously uncomfortable.

15

BECKY

By the time we arrive at our snorkelling destination, our group is pretty well oiled, all apart from me and Cameron – as we've declared ourselves, *the sensible ones*.

'Come on, my fellow sensible one.' He nudges me.

'I hope your life-saving skills are up to par.' Cameron pokes his head into his life jacket. 'I think they might be needed out there.' He gestures towards the bay in which we'll be snorkelling. Sunlight dances on the waves, and I can see why people liken this group of the three Caribbean islands to paradise, the ABC islands as they're known. Aruba, Bonaire and Curaçao. If only I had the looks and the lifestyle of my friends, I'd perhaps feel as if I deserve to be here.

'What the hell have they put in this stuff?' Marty peers into his paper cup at the ice cubes rattling within the bright orange liquid. 'It's dynamite.'

It smells good though, sweet, fruity and boozy. I'm looking forward to getting my money's worth after I've been snorkelling.

'Don't you be drowning out there.' Siobhan's also slurring her words. 'I've only just found you.' She glances at me as if she's affirming ownership of her new boyfriend, her unanswered questions still resting on her lips. How she'd like the opportunity to grill me properly. She'll get it eventually, when I'm good and ready. There's no way I can go into detail without spoiling the holiday for *everyone*.

I turn my attention back to Cameron. 'How many times have you tried snorkelling?' At least my one Aruba Ariba has given me the confidence to speak to him.

'Oh, a few – nowhere as amazing as *this*. How about you?'

'Just once or twice.' It's a total lie, but I don't want Cameron knowing how little life experience I have. But I'm sure he suspects.

I wait for the others to begin making their way across the deck before tugging my shorts and t-shirt off and quickly threading my head into the life jacket I've been given. I just don't want anyone seeing the line of my non-existent breasts beneath my bikini. I'd normally favour a black all-in-one swimsuit, but my friend from work persuaded me to choose this green bikini when we went shopping together.

Even Jo looks daft in her orange lifejacket, snorkelling goggles, and mouthpiece as we follow one another down the steps to the water, in a heady haze of sweat and suncream. We've been told to be extra careful not to trip when walking in our flippers while still on the boat. That would be all I'd need right now – to faceplant and end up in some Aruban hospital. Especially when we haven't even taken holiday insurance out. I thought Zane had sorted it, but as always, he was full of excuses on the journey to the airport as to why he hadn't. We're both healthy enough, touch wood, so I'm sure not having it won't be a problem, as long as we don't get bitten by a mosquito or end up having any random accidents.

As I hang onto the rail at the bottom of the steps, Marty

brushes past me on his way into the water. Our skin touches, and an electric shock sensation shoots through me. It's not pleasant, far from it. He must feel it too, for he pulls his arm sharply away from me.

'Come on, Marty.' Siobhan, however, is smitten with the man.

The water is strangely cold as I find myself submerged, and my goggles fill with water. I return gasping to the surface to find Cameron laughing at me as he treads water at my side.

He tugs his mouthpiece out. 'There's only me and you who haven't drunk much, yet you're the first one to be trying to drown themselves.' It feels weird having Cameron's hand beneath my armpit as I splutter for breath. 'If anyone wasn't able to stay afloat, my money would have been on Marty or Zane after the amount of drink they've consumed.'

'Where *is* everyone?' As my breath returns, I glance around, expecting to see that Zane, at the very least, might have waited for me. But all I can see is Jo's white-bikini-covered backside as she swoops beneath the blue waves, mermaid style.

'They're all heading for the shore - evidently powered by Ariba Aruba.'

'OK – I'll be honest – I've never done this before,' I admit. 'And I was expecting more of a demo from the captain back there.' I gesture to the boat. 'It looks like everyone else knows what they're doing though.'

'You need to wear your gear like *this*.' Cameron points to how his mask is also tight over his nose as he gets his mouthpiece ready to reinsert. 'Then just relax as you put your head under, breathe through your mouth and just swim along the surface.'

After this much welcome instruction, I kind of start to get into it, until...

'But obviously, you need to look where you're going.' We both surface at the same time, seconds after I crash into him.

For the next twenty minutes, I almost forget everything. The world above melts away each time I dive beneath the surface of the sun-dappled, cobalt sea. The water envelopes me – cool, silky, and weightless – muffling sound and thought alike. Sunlight filters down in shimmering ribbons, catching the glint of scales as shoals of fish scatter and swirl around me. The stripy ones – bold yellow and inky black – move with hypnotic grace, drawing my gaze again and again. I hover above the ocean floor, conscious of every movement, careful not to let my feet brush the sand. *Step on a sea urchin and your holiday's over,* the captain had said, and his voice still echoes in my ears. The memory sharpens my awareness, making the thrill of this underwater world all the more vivid. Above, the sun scorches my back between dips, the salty breeze tickling my skin as I come up for air.

Out of the many eventualities that *could* result from this holiday, a spiky sea urchin might turn out to be for the best.

16

SIOBHAN

'Is this what it's going to be like for the entire week?' I point at Jo, her hair now hanging in clumps around her face after the snorkelling. 'You four and us four? We're supposed to have come away *together*.'

'It's just a taxi journey.' She pauses with her hand on the taxi door. 'We'll be back at the villa in ten minutes.'

'But you always go with Tina.' The words slip out, and I instantly hear the sulky fifteen-year-old version of myself in them. Pathetic. Back then, all I ever wanted was to be Jo's chosen one – whether we were walking to class, picking seats, or pairing up for anything. But it was never me. Tina always got there first. Always.

'It's just habit,' she replies. 'And *you're* being daft.' She closes the car door, signalling the end of our discussion.

But I don't think I *am* being daft. I'm certain Jo's been off with me since we all met at the airport, and I'm convinced it's something to do with Marty. They're all being civil enough to him, but I'm sensing that's only the case so the holiday isn't spoiled. I didn't realise their loyalty towards Caleb ran so deep.

We've agreed it's too hot to walk back to the villa, plus

everyone's squiffy from the plentiful, not to mention superstrong cocktails. Becky's been complaining about feeling queasy from the motion of the boat, but then Becky wouldn't be Becky if she wasn't complaining. It's more likely to be because of the free cocktails she began knocking back after we'd been snorkelling.

'How are you feeling?'

'I just need to get some food down me.' Becky slides into the back seat beside me. 'Wow, that air conditioning is nice.' Like the homes, many of the cars are white, probably to deflect the heat. 'We haven't eaten since that breakfast on the beach.'

I check my watch. The day's passed in a breath. I reach into the front seat to Marty, and as he grabs my hand, Becky looks away. I've concluded that she's jealous because of how far apart she and Zane seem to be. *He's* cheery enough, but it's like he's here with his friend or his sister instead of his wife. I had a stale marriage like theirs when I was with Caleb. He'd have probably gone on like we were forever – comfortable but bored. However, life's too short to be written off like that. Caleb would have never ended our marriage – after all, men rarely do unless another woman is waiting in the wings. They seem more content to be discontent than women are.

I never set out to have an affair, and to begin with, Marty was just my personal trainer at the gym, albeit my incredibly attractive personal trainer. I was amazed that he remembered me from school, especially as he'd been three school years in front of me. I'd noticed him back then, but we'd never spoken – not like he seems to have done with my friends when I was on holiday. From the loaded looks I've noticed him exchanging with Jo, I'm convinced *something* must have happened between them back then, but no one wants to enlighten me. It might be that I have to wait until after the holiday, but I'll get my information, one way or another.

As the weeks wore on, I couldn't deny the chemistry between

us. I tried telling myself Marty probably flirted with *all* his clients and that flattery was just his way, but that still couldn't diminish how much I fancied him. I spent a fortune on gym clothes and started removing my wedding and engagement rings before our sessions and taking care with my hair and makeup. I mean, who does their hair and makeup *before* a gym session? It was all worth it, as within a couple of months, he asked me out.

'What's the plan for food tonight?' Zane pats his belly. 'Is it just going to be a quick turnaround at the villa? Shower, change and back out?' He peers beyond Becky at me.

I laugh. '*A quick turnaround?* You're with four women.'

He pulls a face. 'I hope we're not going to be hanging around all night – I'm starving.'

'You must have noticed how high-maintenance Jo is.' Becky's tone isn't lost on me. Things just aren't the same between us anymore. The traits and habits we all used to find endearing about one another have become irritations.

'I thought we'd relax at the villa tonight since it's our first full proper night since arriving,' I continue.

'*Relax at the villa?*' Zane echoes my words. 'I thought I'd come away with a set of party animals. Are *you* happy with that Becky?'

She shrugs. 'I'll go with the flow.'

'We've got the tub and the pool,' I say, 'we've just bought plenty of booze in, and there's an Italian restaurant in the town which delivers.'

I, for one, can't wait to jump in that hot tub and will be doing so the moment we get back, since I don't take as long to get ready as the others. I've been doing intermittent fasting for the last month, I've cut out bread, and I'm feeling pretty good about myself. So much so, I treated myself to a new bikini to celebrate. Jo can do her best to outshine me, but she's not going to succeed. Andy and Zane might not be able to take their eyes off her, but Marty's only got eyes for me. And I'll do anything to ensure it stays that way.

'Sounds a bit boring, but who am I to argue?' Marty kisses my hand before letting it go. He's already caught the sun right up to his dark hairline and is a bronzed adonis in his crisp, white shirt.

'While you girls get ready, we boys will get the food on order and set the table.'

Becky's face softens. Like me, she must like Zane referring to us *girls*. In my head, I don't feel any different to how I did thirty years ago when I *was* a girl. Until a couple of months ago, when the changes to my body and my energy levels have told me otherwise. However, since drawing closer to Marty, it's like I've been granted a new lease of life.

And I don't care what any of my friends might think or say. Or at this moment, even my daughter. Life's short, and I've struggled enough, especially in my thirties, when I got into so much trouble with money. I'm going to grab whatever's on offer with both hands.

～

'That pasta was bloody amazing – just enough garlic and plenty of herbs. A good choice of restaurant, Siobhan.' Zane reaches for his beer. 'And thanks for treating us all, Cameron.'

Cameron wipes his mouth on a napkin. 'You're very welcome.'

Nobody could ever accuse Cameron of not being generous. He stood the bill for breakfast this morning, the snorkelling trip and now the meal. It's hard not to feel guilty when he keeps reaching for his payment card, but like Jo said, Cameron can buy and sell each of the other men here many times over, even Andy. His generosity will be a Godsend for Becky and Zane, who I'm certain won't have a great deal of spending money at their disposal.

I turn my attention back to Marty, once again thanking my lucky stars that he wanted to come on this holiday. I wondered if it was too much like early days between us to be inviting him to an entire week with my friends. But so far, apart from the odd bit of rivalry and a couple of barbed comments between one or two people, everything's been pleasant enough. But I'll need to keep my fingers tightly crossed that they stay that way.

'Just look at that sunset.' We follow Cameron's gaze to the patio doors. 'We should be out there, enjoying it, instead of being stuck in this kitchen.'

'Yeah,' Zane echoes. 'I suggest we get ourselves out in the jacuzzi.'

I don't know who looks more glum at the prospect – Tina or Becky. 'Come on, you two – we're on holiday.'

'I'll just sit here for a while before going in the jacuzzi.' Tina pats her belly. 'Give this food time to settle. I'll follow you out shortly.'

'Yeah.' Jo gives Tina a pointed look, knowing as well as I do why Tina wants us to go ahead of her. 'We don't want anyone throwing up in there.'

'I agree with Tina,' I say. I'm not leaving her in here to make herself sick again. 'We *should* let our meals settle. Let's just sit around the sides of the swimming pool. Go on Tina, get your cozzie on.'

17

SIOBHAN

'I RECKON an ice-breaker game could be in order now we're all out here.' Marty lets go of my hand and waves both of his around with enthusiasm, sending droplets of water over me. 'Not only will it get us more into the holiday mood, but I can also get to know you all better.' I glance at him – he looks as excited as he does when he announces how many pounds I've lost at my weekly gym weigh-ins. But he also looks like a man with an agenda.

'Well, I'm up for a game – as long as it's not strip poker.' The words come from Jo, but the mischievous glint in her eye tells a different story. She's slurring slightly, her voice loose around the edges as she leans back and stretches out her long, tanned legs, letting them drift lazily on the surface of the pool. She barely touched her dinner, so it's no surprise she's already a bit squiffy – all the Aruba Aribas and the wine have clearly hit her hard.

'What do you want to play then?' Cameron's voice is laced with amusement as he downs the rest of his Jack Daniels and allows his gaze to flit among us. 'Monopoly? Scrabble?'

'In a swimming pool?' Becky giggles, the sound echoing

around the high walls encasing the patio of our villa. They're beautifully painted with flowers, grasses and birds. I stare up into the peachy sky, watching the palm trees sway in the warm breeze against it. If we were to stop talking, it would be still and quiet, apart from the buzz of the cicadas and the chirp of some other insect. Either our neighbouring villas are empty or their occupants are out for the evening.

'Something *way* more fun than Monopoly *or* Scrabble.' Marty sets his beer at the side of the pool and hoists himself up onto the ledge. 'Have you got pen and paper in that enormous bag of yours?' He taps my arm before pointing at my bag on the patio table. 'As well as the kitchen sink?'

'Why, what have you got in mind?' Really, in this heat and with the amount of drinks I've put away today, I just want to relax amidst the scent of frangipani and listen to the slap of the pool against its edges. I haven't got the energy to play a game, but since Marty's my boyfriend and he's new to our group, the least I can do is to support his suggestion.

'*Two truths and a lie.*'

'What?' Oh God, I don't like the sound of this.

'OK, listen up.' He looks around at us all from his vantage point above us. 'For this game, we need to come up with some forfeits, no lame and boring ones, mind.'

'For *what* game?' Cameron stretches his arms along either side of the pool ledge and leans back, staring into the sky, which is as colourful as the walls surrounding us. Like me, he looks like he can't be bothered with playing a silly game either.

'Everyone writes two forfeits down.' Marty mimics writing using his left palm as the page and his right hand as the scribe. 'But they need to be kept from the others, so fold your paper up when you've written them.'

'Can I remind you that we're in a swimming pool?' I laugh. 'Wouldn't this game be best played another time?'

Marty reaches behind him and raises a towel into the air.

'Funny things, these.' He rolls his eyes. 'They dry your hands so you can write.'

I can literally feel the smile fade from my face. I hate it when he's sarcastic. He's perfect in so many ways, but I don't like his sarcasm.

'What sort of forfeits?' Zane raises an eyebrow. Marty's not doing a great job of selling *Two Truths and a Lie* to the rest of us.

'Well,' – he grins, – 'this isn't the time for anything naff, like drinking a shot or running around the block.'

'It depends on what you're wearing to run around the block.' I wink at Marty. All the time, Becky's watching us with an expression of disdain. This has gone too far – I'm going to collar her later and demand to know what's wrong. Because *something* is.

'So, have you got a pen and some paper?'

Sighing, I hoist myself up and out of the pool, drying my hands on the towel before heading across the still-warm terracotta tiles for my bag, leaving a trail of wet footprints behind me.

'Grab that ashtray to put the forfeits in.' Marty points at it. 'Since none of us smokes.'

'Right, two pens and notebook.' I hold everything in the air. 'Now what?'

'Rip two sheets out for everyone.' Marty gestures to the notebook. ' Me and you can write our two forfeits first, and then the next two people can get out of the pool and write theirs.'

'Yes sir.' An unsmiling Cameron mock-salutes him. Jo's husband likes to be the centre of attention. Marty and, to a lesser extent, Zane, are stealing that attention away from him. What he has in wealth, they have in charisma, and he's probably realising he can't compete. He's probably also sensed the attention Jo seems to have for my boyfriend, and that she's not the only one. But it's a strange kind of attention, one I'm struggling to put my finger on.

'I still don't get how this game is going to work.' Cameron rolls his eyes.

Maybe it's the drink which is bringing something out in us all. We've all had a skinful today with the cocktails we were drinking on the boat, and not one of us is showing any sign of slowing down this evening. Not even Tina now we've persuaded her to come out here.

'We need to sit boy, girl, boy, girl around the pool,' Marty announces as a lull occurs in the buzz of conversation that's risen up. I'm still perched on the edge of a sunlounger, trying to think of interesting forfeits. 'No one should be sitting next to their partner, and no one should be sitting next to one of their friends. While Siobhan's writing her forfeits, everyone else should be thinking about what they're going to write.'

The others begin to organise themselves around the edge of the pool, with a load of giggling and splashing. As they settle down, I notice a space has been left for me between Andy and Zane. They might think I barely know anything about the two of them, to know whether they're being truthful or lying, but they don't know how much the four of us friends have conferred and divulged over the years. I could probably tell them both things they don't even know about themselves.

'Oh look, a gecko.' I point at where it's arrived at the side of my foot. Indy, my daughter, used to have a pet gecko she called Steve. I rise to my feet to get my phone for a photo to send but as I do, it scuttles away. Oh well, I'm sure I'll see many more of them before the week's out.

Two forfeits. Right, Marty asked for something that's not lame, so I'm going to write what's just popped into my head.

Show everyone what you've got in your handbag by tipping it out, but if you're a man, show everyone inside your wallet and pockets.

OK, maybe that one's a bit lame – the next one has to be better. However, Jo might be in trouble if she's brought a stash of her trusty white powder along. I click the pen on and off, on and off, as I wonder whether I can write the second forfeit which has leapt into my mind. I stare at Jo, whose long eyelashes dust the tops of her high cheekbones as she inspects her scarlet nail polish.

Second forfeit. OK – I've got to write it.

Be honest about whether you've ever had sex with someone in this group who isn't your partner.

Folding the paper into quarters, I drop it into the ashtray, and return to the pool. Marty does the same.

'You next?' He seems to be enjoying his role, directing this game. He's used to being in charge at the gym.

Andy hauls himself out. I only hope Jo or Marty pick that last forfeit, and I'll be watching very closely for looks that pass between them or obvious signs of discomfort.

Jo follows Andy out of the pool. 'Just going to the little girl's room,' she announces. As she passes Andy, she tries to steal a look at what he's writing. He slaps his hand over his scrawl, and she giggles. 'I'll write mine when I get back.'

'No one will be able to read Andy's writing.' Tina tries to disguise her scowl by rolling her eyes. 'Even his secretary can't.'

'More drinks anybody, when I come back?' Jo calls from the patio door.

'Another glass of wine for me,' I call after her, staring into the swiftly darkening sky. Drink might make the next hour or so more palatable, as I have a feeling that *anything* could happen between us as a result of this game. I dread to think what forfeits the others will write.

Or what truths or lies will be divulged.

18

THIRTY-FOUR YEARS AGO

'COME ON. Young, fit whipper-snappers like you lot should be up these steps in record time!' Miss Smith's voice rises above the cawing of the seagulls, her hands braced against the small of her back. Her tone is teasing, but there's a flicker of concern behind her smile. 'What on earth's up with you all?'

She's got a point – our straggling line is trailing further and further behind. Her concern makes my throat tighten unexpectedly. I'm not used to adults noticing me, let alone caring. It catches me off guard, especially from someone who might be able to help. But I can't tell *anyone,* although my friends have repeatedly begged me to. I just wish they understood that it's pointless. Hopeless.

'Just keep moving,' she calls back over her shoulder. 'We'll have lunch when we get to the top.'

I lift my eyes toward the ruins of Whitby Abbey, silhouetted against a sky so blue it looks painted on. The crumbling arches tower above us, distant and unreachable, like the summit of Everest. The air smells of seaweed and damp stone, and my legs are already trembling. I've forgotten what it feels like to be normal. What it feels like not to ache. Not to dread every next step.

And I know—when I *do* stop feeling like this, it'll only be because everything has come to a head.

Miss Smith probably doesn't realise just how hard it is to climb 199 steps with another human on board. Not after we've already trudged across the beach all morning, collecting shells, seaweed, and God knows what else for our geography project. I tried to get out of the trip. I begged Mum. But she couldn't get me out of the door fast enough. Or rather, *he* couldn't.

My stepdad. Mr 'Nice Guy' when she's around, but cold as stone when she isn't. He didn't even look up from his newspaper when I left the house. He just muttered something about it being 'character-building.'

I was grateful when we finally stopped at the whale bone archway. The view out to sea was beautiful, but all I could think about was hiding my bump in the group photo, ducking behind my friends, hoping no one would notice. But it's getting impossible to hide.

I push myself up another dozen steps, the stone cool and gritty beneath my palm as I lean against the wall to catch my breath. The sea breeze brushes the sweat from my face, but it does little to cool me down. Above me, pairs of legs move steadily onwards, disappearing from sight. But at least my friends are still waiting.

'It's an amazing view at the top.' One of them mimics Miss Smith's singsong voice, and despite everything, I let out a hoarse laugh.

'Who cares about a stupid abbey anyway?' I gasp, dragging one foot in front of the other. 'Or some pathetic ghost walk. I just want to be normal again.'

'Are you having another pain?' Her hand lands gently on my shoulder, and I nearly lose it right there. Kindness cuts sharper than cruelty. Tears spring to my eyes, and I blink them back fast.

'They're not really pains,' I whisper. 'They're just... all tight. Like everything's squeezing inwards.' I press a hand to my belly. I try not to do it where people can see – it draws attention.

Mum hasn't noticed a thing other than I've put some weight on. She's too wrapped up in her work, her diet, and her husband. She keeps offering me gym memberships like that's the answer, lamenting my 'puppy fat' and telling me salad is the way forward. As if a bowl of lettuce is going to fix my life.

And him, my stepdad, he's already counting down the days until I leave home. He keeps joking about how he'll throw a party the day I go off to uni. As if that's ever going to happen. I'll be lucky if I make it through my GCSEs.

'Your tummy tightening means it won't be long until the baby comes.'

I flinch at the words. *The baby.* I can't even say it. I call it *it*. I won't read the books in the school library like the others have. I don't want to know how developed it is, or what fruit it's the size of this week. I've spent the last eight months pretending it's not real. That I'm not about to go through agony. And that I won't be kicked out of my house when it happens. Because I will. And Mum won't be able to stop him.

The only people who truly care are these three girls. They're up ahead now, glancing back as Miss Smith calls down again, impatient but well-meaning. They'd do anything for me. But this – this is too big, even for them.

I'm in serious trouble. And I'd give anything to make it all go away. But it's too late for that. Way too late.

19

TINA

WE'RE two rounds into *Two Truths and a Lie*. Siobhan's statements were dull and forgettable. Marty's weren't – one of his truths or lies made the air around the pool feel sharp and uncomfortable.

'When I was young, I fathered a child I never got to meet.'

I held my breath. Everyone laughed, waiting for the reveal. He claimed it was the lie – but the way he looked at me, then Becky, said otherwise. A flicker of something passed between the two of them. It tightened in my chest like a fist.

I should have said something then, instead of letting the chance pass.

I feel lighter tonight. And better. I devoured my dinner earlier, but even more satisfying was slipping away to quietly purge it in the bathroom while the others were getting ready for the pool. With the weekly weigh-in looming the day we get home, I can't risk any shocks. At least now I've earned myself room for the pastries and crisps I smuggled back from the shop while the others were preoccupied with alcohol.

But here, in the warm night air, tipsy and waist-deep in the lit-up pool, I almost feel normal. The Aruban breeze – constant and calming – threads through my hair, lifting it gently off my damp skin.

'Your turn, Becky. Andy's guessing.' Zane's voice is thick with drink. He's sunburned and half-cut, just like the rest of us.

Becky pauses, setting her wine glass down on the stone patio. The pool lights bleach her limbs to pale porcelain. She gives a little smile. Thoughtful. Calculated?

'Okay.' She clears her throat. 'Firstly, I've moved house twenty-nine times. Secondly, I've delivered a baby. Thirdly, I've had two black eyes at once.'

'Wait,' Marty's face darkens. 'What do you mean by delivered a *baby*? Your own, or someone else's?'

'She can't mean her own,' Zane snaps. He spits the words out like they're venom. 'Which is a sore bloody subject. Seriously, Becky – what are you playing at, bringing up this crap?'

Silence falls among us, broken only by the rustle of the overhead palm leaves.

Becky doesn't flinch. She doesn't even look at anyone. One glance at me and she'll see exactly what I think of her dragging this out into the open. Drunk or not, this is a betrayal.

'I'll go with the baby one.' Andy slaps the water with a lazy hand. 'That's the lie.'

'Wrong.' Becky casts a look at Zane that's unreadable. 'The lie is that I've moved house twenty-nine times.'

My stomach twists.

'So who gave you the black eyes?' Cameron asks, concern etched across his face. He glances from Becky to Zane—who looks ready to leap across the pool and knock his lights out.

'She got bullied,' I say quickly. 'At school. Before the four of us started sticking up for each other.' I shoot Becky a look. *We're going to have words.* Babies are off-limits.

'It's Andy's turn for a forfeit,' I say. Hopefully, it will be one which will sober him up a bit. One that will encourage him to put his tongue back in his mouth and stop drooling over Jo.

Siobhan passes him the ashtray. 'That's one of mine,' he laughs. 'I can't even read my own writing.'

'Draw another one.'

'OK, oh, this one isn't too bad. Who wrote this? *Theatrically shout 'I love myself as loud as possible from the garden gate.*'

'It's not exactly a garden.' Jo rolls her eyes. 'Besides, I thought we agreed, nothing lame.'

I stay quiet. It was one of mine, but nobody needs to know. I'd hoped Jo would draw it as it would have amused me to hear her declaring her undying love – to herself.

'It'll do for me.' Andy hauls himself from the pool, his taut torso rippling in its lights.

Jo's eyes sparkle with a bit too much interest as she watches him. She used to call my husband a bore. She said we were well-suited like it was a curse. Since we arrived here, though, she's been circling him. And he's been wagging his metaphorical tail in return.

'I love myself,' he yells into the dusk as everyone falls about laughing. Everybody apart from me. 'I really do.'

'Again.' Jo claps her hands together.

'I *really* love myself,' he shouts again. I think he really does these days. Far more than when I met him when he was confident, yes, but it was more quiet and unassuming.

'I truly, madly and deeply love myself.' His third declaration is even louder, and so is the laughter. 'There, was that good enough?' He closes the gate and struts along the patio back towards the pool.

I grab the drink Jo brought me from the villa. If I drink enough, maybe I won't care.

Andy's visibly swaying as he tries to straighten himself up. 'Alright, alright. My three...' He pauses, eyes gleaming like he's on stage. 'My first one is that I've skinny-dipped more than once.'

'No way,' I snap. 'Not with me you haven't.'

'Tina.' Siobhan gives me a look. The schoolteacher look. 'It's Jo's turn to guess.'

Jo smirks. 'It's a lie.'

Andy continues, slurring slightly. 'The second one is that my wife didn't want to come on this holiday.'

The way he looks at me, so slow and deliberate, makes the others shift. He wants them to believe it. The bastard. He's been cold since we got here, and all but panting after Jo.

Siobhan's mouth tightens. Even if it's not true, the damage is done.

'Thirdly,' Andy says, his voice dropping. 'I've often wondered what it would be like to sleep with someone else's wife.'

A collective gasp ripples through the group. Even Jo blinks.

Above us, the stars are out, scattered like pinpricks over a velvet sky. But all I can feel is rage rising in my throat.

'Go on then, Jo.' Zane is clearly enjoying the chaos. 'Which is the lie?'

'The one about Tina not wanting to come,' Jo replies, quickly. Evidently, she's attempting to appease me.

'Wrong,' Andy says, sitting up straighter, his eyes avoiding everyone. 'The lie was number three.'

'Really?' Becky and Siobhan say in unison, looking at me as if I should be reassured.

'Forfeit time,' Zane says, clapping.

Jo hops out of the pool and retrieves a folded paper from the ashtray. She waves it dramatically. 'I'll try not to get it soggy.'

Why is no one addressing what Andy just said? I know number three was the truth for him. Why am I the only one spiralling?

'Read it then.'

'I'm not doing that.' Jo scrunches the paper and tosses it back.

'Why? What does it say?' I snatch it and read it aloud, though the words are blurry.

Rate everyone in the group out of ten, for sex appeal, intelligence, and how much you like them.

'Zero for Marty,' Becky mutters behind her hand.

'Hark at the supermodel there.' Marty shakes his head.

'What is *wrong* with you?' Siobhan snaps, now turning to Zane. 'What's going on with your bloody wife?'

What about my husband?

'She's drunk, that's what.' Zane swipes at Becky's drink. 'Time to stop.'

'I don't think so,' Becky shifts her glass out of his reach.

'See what I'm dealing with?' Zane sighs. 'Honestly, I'm done with this stupid game.' He grabs the Jack Daniels bottle and refills his glass as if it owes him something.

'What now then?' Andy glances at his watch like he's not the grenade in the pool.

'Maybe we *should* call it a night.' I shoot him a look. 'You and I need a word.'

He chuckles. 'I've been in this pool so long, I'm practically pickled.'

'You're fifty, not a hundred, Tina.' Becky shoots back. 'It's a holiday. Nobody's turning in.'

'Let her go,' Jo snaps. She's probably still smarting from Andy's comment about me not wanting to come, and maybe a little from my glare.

Then Andy, with that glint in his eye I don't recognise anymore, says, 'if we're going to play something, let's make it memorable. Let's raise the stakes.'

God help us.

'Oooh, strip poker,' Jo laughs, waving her hands in the air. Cameron scowls at her.

'I'm with Tina,' Zane says suddenly. 'Time to call it.'

'Because of what I said?' Becky looks uncomfortable.

He looks at her, his expression flat, and unreadable to start with.

'No. Because if we're going to pair off for the night...' His voice slows, his eyes glinting. 'Let's not stick with our own partners.'

Silence cloaks itself over us.

And just like that, the air shifts. Our game isn't a game anymore.

20

TINA

ALL REMAINS silent for several beats. Even the wind through the palm trees seems to pause.

'What?' Becky looks from Zane to Siobhan, then to me – her face pleading for someone, anyone, to shut this down. 'You've got to be joking.'

Zane shrugs, not quite meeting anyone's eye. 'It's something different, isn't it? A bit more exciting than *Two Truths and a Lie*.' He lifts his glass to his lips. 'No offence, mate.' He nods at Marty, palm raised in mock surrender.

'Erm, none taken,' Marty mumbles, but his face says otherwise.

'There's absolutely no way.' Siobhan folds her arms across her chest like she's protecting herself. 'We came away to celebrate our birthdays, not launch a bloody swinging party.' The horror in her voice is almost comical – almost.

'He's not being serious,' Marty says, uncertain. 'Are you?'

But Zane doesn't laugh. He doesn't smirk. He just sits there.

Siobhan hauls herself out of the pool and wraps a towel around her body like she's suddenly naked. 'Well, there's no way me and Marty are getting involved.' She slams herself down on a sun lounger with such force that it groans beneath her.

What's unsettling is the absence of protest from the rest of the group. Not even Marty shuts it down, yet he and Siobhan are supposed to be in the honeymoon phase of their relationship. There's a current in the air – an undeniable charge – something forbidden has been spoken aloud, and no one knows how to un-hear it.

'Tell them, Marty.' Siobhan jabs her finger towards the group. 'Tell them to bloody count us out.'

'Well, erm...'

'Hypothetically,' Andy forms air quotes with his fingers, 'how would this *game* play out?'

'Andy!' Jo slaps his shoulder playfully – for the second time tonight. My stomach tightens.

I glance at him. He's not joking. He's interested and suddenly, I want to see what he'll do next. Zane's suggestion was no joke – and judging by the looks flickering between us all, no one's treating it like one.

'I'm game if everyone else is,' Becky says softly, placing her glass down. Her voice wavers as her eyes drift to Zane. 'If my husband wants this, who am I to argue?'

She's slurring, like the rest of us – but I've sobered up. Completely. The world hasn't stopped spinning, but the cold reality of this moment is a standstill slap.

Andy chimes in again. 'It could be fun – if we all follow some rules.'

The man I married would never have been interested in something like this. But the man on holiday with me now... I don't even recognise.

He wants it. He wants to sleep with someone else. Drunk or not, the truth seeps out when the walls come down. My instinct is to refuse outright. But now – watching him lean towards Jo like a lovesick fool – I snap.

'I'm in.' I yank the wine bottle towards me, my teeth gritted in resignation.

I don't say it, but the words are right there on the tip of my tongue, *maybe I'll get to be with someone who doesn't leave his socks on.*

My stomach churns, heavy with alcohol and disgust. I want to purge – body and soul – but the bathroom window is too close to the pool and it's become too quiet out here now. Everyone thinks I've moved on from what they call *Tina's former problem* therefore, it's too risky right now to give into things.

'You're joking, aren't you?' Siobhan crouches behind me, sounding desperate. 'You'd throw away your marriage over some idiotic game?'

'What's good for the goose...' I say, locking eyes with Andy. But he's not looking at me. He's looking at Jo, of course he is. Everyone always looks at Jo. No wonder Siobhan won't risk letting her boyfriend anywhere near her.

'So that's five of us in?' Zane glances at Cameron.

Cameron hesitates, then nods, his eyes on his lap. 'Only if this stays between us. It can't leave this group.'

'Actually, don't think I can do it,' Becky breathes. 'We *can't* do this.'

'It's just a bit of fun, love,' Zane says, too quickly. 'It might even spice things up.'

'Oh my God,' Siobhan mutters, burying her face into her towel.

'What happens in Aruba stays in Aruba,' Marty pipes up.

My eyes flick to Siobhan. For a second, she looks shattered – but then her face hardens.

'You take part in this, Marty, and we're done. You can leave this villa tonight.'

'What? Just you hang on a minute. I never said I *wanted* to. I just said—'

'So it's just you, Becky.' Zane's voice cuts through the pool's echo.

All eyes turn to her.

'If *he's* having sex with someone else.' Becky points at Zane, 'Then so am I.'

I can barely follow this. It feels like a dream – or a nightmare dressed in swimwear and alcohol.

'You'll regret this tomorrow.' Siobhan jabs a finger into the cushion of the sunlounger. 'All of you will.'

She's right. But the current is already pulling us under.

'It's a bit of fun,' Zane insists. 'Just like Andy said. Tomorrow, we go back to normal – but with an extra spring in our steps.'

Cameron eyes Jo. 'Do *you* want to do this?'

'Only if *everyone* is in.' She looks at Becky, who shrugs.

'I'm not going to sit here filing my nails, am I?'

Zane grins. Whether it's power or sex he wants, I can't tell. Probably both. 'We should set some rules,' he says. 'So things don't get messy.'

'Why do *you* get to set the rules?' Jo snaps. Her voice is trembling now. 'We'll go around the group,' she says. 'And each set one rule.'

The water suddenly feels colder. Or maybe that's just me, shivering. 'If we'd gone out tonight, none of this would've happened,' I murmur, but no one seems to hear me.

'Fine,' Zane says. 'You start then, Jo.'

She swallows. 'We stay with our 'new' partners until the morning. No switching rooms halfway.'

'Fair enough,' Zane agrees.

'When it's over, we don't talk about it,' Andy adds. 'Not to our partners. Not to *anyone*. Ever.'

'The men must wear something,' Becky mutters.

Zane glares at her like she's ruined his fantasy.

'I've got that covered.' Marty gestures toward the villa, presumably, where he's already stocked up.

'You *heard* me earlier, right?' Siobhan shouts, her voice echoing off the walls. For a moment, I wonder if anyone's listening from a neighbouring villa. I bloody hope not. 'We're not taking part.'

'I know.' Marty climbs out of the pool, his voice brittle. 'I was only offering supplies.'

Siobhan glares at him. 'Let's go to our room, shall we? Let them rot in their little sex swamp.'

'I agree with Andy,' Zane says, grinning. 'What happens in Aruba—'

'No one would believe it anyway,' I glare at my husband. 'Conservative Andy playing sex roulette? It's not exactly on-brand.'

'I haven't got anything to add,' Zane says. 'Since I'm the one who *started* it.'

What if everything changes after this? I stare into my glass, wishing it would blur it all away. 'We're miles from reality, I know, but—'

'Nothing will change,' Zane interrupts. 'Unless we let it.'

I catch Becky's eye. She looks as unsure as I feel. But underneath the fear, a tiny ember sparks – *excitement*. The kind I hate myself for.

I wish I'd lost more weight. I wish I felt desirable. But there's no undoing anything now.

'So,' Zane says. 'How do we pair off?'

'We women will go to our bedrooms,' Jo suggests. 'And the men draw names from the ashtray.'

'What if someone draws their wife?' Andy asks. There's real disappointment in his voice. My fists clench under the water.

'Then we redraw.' Zane shrugs.

And just like that, the thought hits me like a slap, *What if no one wants me? What if everyone draws my name and tosses it back?*

I've always been the fat friend. The backup dancer. The shadow.

But I'm doing this. Whether I regret it or not – I'm already in.

21

JO

'I'VE GOT A CONFESSION TO MAKE.' Andy lands in bed beside me, still wearing his boxers, and moves the satin strap of my nightie so it's off my shoulder, which he kisses.

'What?' I turn to look at his face, bathed in the moonlight which is filtering through the skylight above us. What could he possibly have to confess when most of what he's been doing 'wrong' lately involves *me*.

For the last three months, to be precise.

'I drew Tina's *and* Becky's names before I got to yours.' He rolls himself closer to me, and the scent of woody aftershave I've come to associate as 'my happy smell' fills my nostrils. 'I just pretended that I kept choosing the same scrap of paper with *Tina* written on it.'

'I'm pretty certain she suspects us, you know.' My friend's face fills my mind as I close my eyes. Since we met at the airport, every time I've looked up, she's been watching me through narrowed eyes. Either that, or she's been watching Andy, watching me. I shouldn't be thinking about Tina – not now that I've *finally* got Andy on his own for the first time since we arrived here, but I can't help it. I'm not proud of my behaviour of late, but being married to a man who barely notices I exist anymore has pushed me into Andy's arms.

'I know I can't stop looking at you.' Andy's teeth almost glow in the faint light as he smiles, 'so it's little wonder that people are going to notice.'

'I can't stop looking at *you* either.' I feel almost shy saying this – it's totally out of character for me to say nice things to a man. Tina might think her husband is dull and ordinary, but she couldn't be further from the truth. I never thought of Andy as my type when they met in their late teens, but he's so different these days, and I've never wanted anyone more. 'But I feel so guilty - I *never* wanted anyone to get hurt.'

'I don't think Tina suspects us – all she really cares about these days is our boys. Besides, we've been so careful.' Andy rolls away from me and sits up against the pillows. He used to be fairly tubby when we were all young, but these days, he's pure muscle. He goes everywhere on his bike, and their dog is so well walked, it's a wonder she doesn't file a complaint. As is *my* dog in the last three months.

'We women are very perceptive,' I reply. 'Especially Tina.'

If I'm not careful, I'm going to kill our impromptu night of passion before it's even started by going on about Andy's wife.

'Has she said something to you? Gosh, it's boiling in here – surely you've got aircon, given that you've got the best room in the villa. We've got it in *our* room.'

I'm not keen on his use of the words *we* and *our* in relation to Tina. Not when we've only just jumped into bed together. 'Tina hasn't said anything *directly* – I'm just getting a sense that she knows something. She's been a bit sharp with me.' I point the remote control up at the air conditioning unit. At least it's generating a whoosh of noise now. At this rate, we're going to be subjected to squeaking bedsprings and possible moans and groans from the other bedrooms before we get around to immersing ourselves in our own action.

'I think she'd have confronted me if she knew.'

'Perhaps you don't know your wife as well as I do.' I reach for a band from the bedside cabinet and twist my hair into a ponytail, enjoying the sensation of the cold air from above on the back of my neck. Though I'd prefer Andy to be kissing it again.

'What do you mean?'

'Tina's far more shrewd than you give her credit for. If I know her correctly, she'll be plotting something. We should probably both be on our guard from tonight.'

'Well, right now, she's in another room with either Cameron or Zane, so it'll be a case of pot, kettle and black if she gets on her high horse about *me* sleeping with someone else.'

'Is that all it is between us?' I tug the sheet up over my bare legs. '*Sleeping together?*'

'It can be whatever you want it to be.' He reaches for my chin, tilting it so we're facing each other directly. He's looking at me with the same intensity Cameron did once upon a time. Before he became complacent in our relationship. I can't quite believe I've ended up in this bed in our gorgeous room with Andy – and *with* Cameron's blessing. I wonder which of my two friends *he's* gone to bed with, but I guess I'll find out soon enough.

'*Whatever I want it to be?*' I echo Andy's words. 'What do *you* want it to be?'

22

JO

I stare at the angle of Andy's jaw in the semi-darkness, longing to run my fingers through his chest hair, but for now, talking's more important. Things have definitely shifted.

'It's just that the more we've been meeting up, the more I've been realising how fast life's slipping by.' Andy's whispering, his words barely perceptible as if he's scared someone might overhear him. 'And we're not getting any younger, are we? Perhaps it's time to just go after what makes us happy. Which is each other.'

'Are you saying what I *think* you're saying?' I tear my eyes away from Andy's face and glance towards the shape of Cameron's wallet on the bedside cabinet at the other side of Andy. If I were to leave my husband, so much more would change, aside from the man I lie beside every night. I love being with Andy and the way he makes me feel, and part of me would love to throw caution to the wind and choose to be with him.

Cameron, however, has given me *everything* I've got and could just as easily take it all away again. He bankrolled my business. I live in his house. He bought my car – in fact, there's not a great deal I've had to pay for myself. Even my dog was a gift from him.

However, Andy's right. There can be no denying that over the last three months, since we bumped into each other while out with our dogs and got chatting, Andy has offered me something which Cameron no longer can. However, I'm not sure what we've got is worth me risking my marriage and my entire lifestyle for. Not to mention the three friendships that have endured since I was eleven years old.

'I'm saying we should just come clean.' He cups my face with his hand. 'Getting away with *you* like this has shown me how bored I am with Tina. My boys are almost grown up and gone now – I can do what I want.'

'You said in that crappy truth and lie game that Tina didn't even *want* to come to Aruba – what was *that* about?'

'Because she's probably just as unhappy as I am.' He waves his hand in the air and then slaps it down onto the cool bedsheet.

'No shit.' She's agreed to this 'game' after all – something no *happily* married person would in my opinion.

'I just wish these doors had locks on them.' He points at the door. 'I can't shake the feeling that either she or Cameron could burst in here at any moment in a pique of jealousy.'

'Of course they won't.'

'I hate seeing you around him, you know.'

'I reckon *my* marriage is pretty dead in the water too – it's become one of convenience more than anything.'

'Perhaps it's normal,' Andy says with a resigned sigh. I suppress my own sigh. We're getting further and further away from the reason he's come into my bedroom.

'*What's* normal?'

'That once you're in your fifties and you've been together as long as we all have, the rot inevitably sets in.'

'I haven't been with Cameron anywhere near as long as

you've been with Tina.' A vision of their wedding floods my brain. It's funny that Tina was talking about that yesterday. Thinking back, there *was* a sharpness to her voice as she was going on about it.

'Siobhan and Marty have only just got together.' He gestures in the direction of their room, further down the corridor. 'Which makes it interesting how they're the *only* ones who didn't want to be involved in this swinging business.'

'Don't call it that.' I shudder.

'What else can we call it?' He laughs.

'It makes it all sound so sordid.'

'It would be, under normal circumstances. But what me and you have got is *way* beyond normal.' He reaches for the bedsheet and peels it back from me. 'Anyway, I think we've done more than enough talking, don't you?'

'I don't know what I'd have done if anyone else instead of you had walked in here tonight.'

'Do you think I'd have allowed that?' Andy leans in closer. 'Not in a million years – you're *mine*.'

He pounces on me, rubbing his stubbly chin on my collarbone, making me squirm with laughter. 'Shush,' I tell him. 'Let me put some music on. We don't want anyone to hear us.'

I let a long breath out as I hold the phone away from Andy's ministrations to find a music channel. Someone's raised their voice in the next room. It sounds like Tina. I don't know how I'm going to look her in the eye tomorrow. It will make it easier that she, too, is currently in bed with a man who isn't her husband.

Though for her and whoever she's with, it will be the first time. For me and Andy, well, I've lost count.

23

BECKY

I TURN to face Cameron in the emerging sunrise. We haven't had a lot of sleep, but surprisingly, I'm quite well rested. He's given me more attention in one night than Zane has in the last year.

'You OK?' His eyes crinkle in the corners as he opens them and smiles. I feel almost like Cinderella, lying in this bed in this lovely bedroom beside this powerful man. Before the holiday, I'd have sworn he barely knew my name, but things have changed now – *everything's* changed.

He's not taking his eyes off me. I can't believe this. Broke Becky, the mousy one, whose husband only stays with her because he's too spineless to do anything else, is in bed with a sexy, handsome and intelligent millionaire. God, do I wish we could make this a permanent arrangement.

'I just can't believe we've – you know – me and you – normally I'm so nervous around you.' Suddenly, I feel nervous again. The wine and shots I drank last night, not to mention the cocktails after the snorkelling, turned me into someone I barely recognised. She was confident, sassy and sexy, and I much preferred her to the version of myself who can hardly bear to look in the mirror.

'Do you think I hadn't noticed these nerves?' He smiles and brushes his hand over my hair, an affectionate gesture which Zane would never dream of doing. Jo doesn't know how lucky she is, being married to him.

'So how do I measure up to what you're used to?' Cameron moves so close I can smell the sourness of his breath. However, I don't mind – not like I would if Zane were breathing in my face. *Familiarity breeds contempt,* as they say.

'You're asking me if you're better in bed than my husband?' I grin back at him and glance towards the door. It's as if Zane's going to suddenly burst in and hear me say the worst thing I'll have ever said against him. 'Well, of course you are.'

'I'm pretty sure Jo's having an affair, you know. What's good for the goose and all that.'

I swallow, excitement bubbling within me. If she is, well, it could change *everything.* 'With *who*? No, I'd know if she was – she hasn't said a thing to me.'

But then we're not nearly as close as we all once were, especially Jo, who's become harder than ever to pin down for our yearly meet-ups. Siobhan said when she first put forward the idea of this holiday that she wanted us to recapture the closeness we had in our teens. But maybe we were *too* close back then. Perhaps our friendship has only lasted because we all know too much about each other.

Cameron taps the side of his nose. 'Let's just say, I have my sources. But I have to box clever, as no way will I allow Jo to take half of what I own. I'm planning to watch her carefully while we're on this holiday, and take it from there. Knowledge is power.'

Oh my God – he's talking about them splitting up. My heart's suddenly hammering faster than ever in my chest. I *could* end up with Jo's perfect life. Everything about her that I've ever coveted – well, it could be within touching distance. Cameron even showed he felt protective towards me last night during the game when I was talking about the black eyes I once had.

'Do the two of you have a prenup?' Here I am, trying to act like I know what I'm talking about when I've barely got a clue.

He shakes his head. 'My two daughters, they're grown up now, were so opposed to our marriage and trying to force me to have one drawn up that they became the main reason I didn't.'

'What, to spite them, you mean?' I recall it like it was yesterday. Jo was so relieved when they decided not to attend the wedding. They'd have probably sabotaged it if they had. It was a lavish affair, so different to the shoestring register office Zane and I settled for. I was just happy to be with someone, *anyone*, that I snapped up the chance of marriage without properly thinking it through. I've always believed the wedding and then the life I've had with him was all I deserved, but after the last few hours, I'm becoming convinced of something else. I *do* deserve better.

'It was more to show them who was in charge, much as they tried to be. Along with their bloody mother.' He closes his eyes as he leans back against his pillow. 'All she could think about was my daughters' inheritances.'

'I don't think there's anyone on this holiday who married at the right time for the right reasons. When we're young, there's a risk of growing apart as the years go on, and when we're older, we're all carrying a ton of baggage into new relationships.' I turn my head towards the heavy curtains with the early sunshine seeping around them. I wish I could stay here with Cameron all day. It's been the fastest night of my life.

'You're fairly wise for someone normally so quiet.' He's staring at me with those clear blue-green eyes as if he's only just seeing me for the first time. I feel like I'm in a dream. At any moment, I'll wake, and then I really *will* be too frightened to speak to Cameron for the rest of the day.

'You're so different to Jo.' Cameron rolls onto his side without taking his eyes off me. 'You pay attention when I'm speaking, you respond when I touch you, you *look* at me like you see something she doesn't.'

24

BECKY

'Perhaps because I *do* see something Jo doesn't.' I turn slightly away from Cameron, my heart beating like it might explode. This wasn't part of the plan. He isn't supposed to be saying these things. 'You're not still drunk, are you?'

'What makes you say that?'

'Because the two of us are poles apart and until last night, you barely registered my existence.'

'*Financially* poles apart, you mean? Is that a problem?'

'It's just that I live paycheck to paycheck, and I've spent my whole life—' I stop myself from continuing. Cameron doesn't need to hear my sob stories, nor is he probably even interested in my tales of how victimised I've always been, most of all by myself, how lonely life has been so far and how my lack of confidence holds me back from *everything*.

But this morning, he's looking at me like I'm *someone*, and even if that's just to wind Jo up if he's suspecting her of having an affair, I don't care. I'll take whatever I can get. 'I wish I could stay all day in here with you.' I turn to wrap my arms and legs around him, suddenly needing a repeat performance of what

I've found with him. Then we both jump as there's a crash from the kitchen. 'What the hell was that?'

'It's probably just someone having dropped something,' he replies, sitting himself up.

I tilt my phone towards me from the bedside table. 'It's just after seven.'

'It's noon in the UK,' Cameron replies. 'I doubt any of our body clocks will have adjusted yet. Everyone's clearly starting to get up.'

'We're supposed to be on holiday – surely we can stay here as long as we like.'

'It's not as if anything's normal this morning, is it?' He smiles and I realise for the umpteenth time just how good-looking he is, but in a manly way. Even though he's fifty later this year, Zane still acts like a boy. I often think we wouldn't be in this financial mess if he didn't leave *every* aspect of our lives to me. But Cameron's a *proper* man.

'Do you think you and Zane will carry on as you were, after, you know,' – he points from himself to me. I don't want him to be asking me this – I want him to be asking me a *very* different question. He seemed to be going that way before.

'I really don't know.'

'He could make so much more of himself,' Cameron says. 'Like I was telling him yesterday – he has his own gardening business. He—'

'He doesn't know the first thing about business,' I cut in. 'It pays him pocket money more than anything. It funds his gaming addiction, his nights out with the lads, his—'

'It sounds like you've shouldered the burden for long enough.' Cameron's voice is gentle, and my eyes fill with tears. I've had a lifetime of people looking down their nose at me, so for someone in Cameron's league to be treating me like this really means something.

'Hey, come on, I didn't mean to upset you.' He turns me towards him, just as there's another crash from the kitchen.

'Becky?' Zane's voice echoes through the door. Any moment at all, he's going to burst in here. I bet he's regretting what we all did last night. But I'm not and I never will.

'Are we all getting up or what?' Tina's voice is shrill along the hallway. Cameron and I exchange glances.

'Becky?' Zane calls again. 'I'm having a shower and then I'm coming in there for some stuff. So make sure you're ready.' We both know what he means by that. *Make sure you're on your own.*

'Neither of them sound very happy this morning.' Cameron pulls a face.

'Tina and Zane must have ended up together. He'll be gutted it wasn't Jo. *Everyone's* always gone after *Jo*.'

Cameron gives me a funny look. 'Since when?'

'Since *always*.'

'You sound a little resentful if you don't mind me saying. Don't be – you've got plenty going for you, you know.'

'Me – no, I'm not resentful.' My nose has probably just grown by three inches.

'Listen, I know all this has happened between us, but I'm not ready to jump into something else. Not yet, anyway.'

A flush creeps over me. 'Wow, this is all seriously messed up, isn't it? I don't know if I can even go out there and face everyone.'

'Well, we're going to have to, sooner or later.' Cameron sits up straight and swings his legs over the edge of the bed. 'We might as well get it over and done with.' He reaches onto the chair beside the bed for the clothes he so neatly folded before joining me in bed last night. I watch the muscles ripple in his shoulders as he pulls his t-shirt over them.

'Wait, is that it?' I reach out for him, but he's already got to his feet. 'I thought – I mean.'

He tugs his shorts on, still with his back to me, but saying nothing.

'What happens now?' My shoulders are chilly under the air conditioning unit, but I feel even colder now that he's got out of bed.

'I guess we go on as normal,' he replies as he strides to the door. 'Whatever *normal* is going to look like after this.'

I want to ask him if he meant anything he's said to me. Whether *I* could mean anything to him in the future. And if he does find out that Jo's having an affair, will he definitely leave her?

I'm confused. He went from being all attentive to suddenly upping and going. Damn Zane. He had no right turning up at the door like that. Everything was going great until *he* showed up.

Perhaps Cameron was just being kind to me before. But now, he's probably looked at me properly and has seen what everyone else sees. Once, I was the ugly duckling who others took pity on. Nowadays, I'm a saggy, craggy old duck with nothing going for it whatsoever.

Back then, I could tell myself that one day things might improve. But nowadays I know that far more sand in my timer has passed through than is yet to come. This is my lot. Being temporarily wanted for a few hours for revenge sex is as good as it's likely to get.

Soon, I'll be back to my mostly empty home, nursing an eternally empty heart, living an always-empty life. Even when Zane's at home, I never know which version of him I'm going to get. The fun and attentive version – or the polar opposite.

Even being in a place as amazing as Aruba can't shake how miserable I feel now that Cameron's left me alone. In the last ten minutes, I've gone from walking on air to crashing back to the ground.

Really, I might as well not be here anymore.

25

SIOBHAN

'Sit down for goodness sake, Tina. I'll make you a drink.' Knotting my dressing gown around my middle, I flick my hair behind my shoulders, then reach beyond her for the coffee jug. 'You need to calm down.'

'I need for none of this to have ever happened,' she hisses, spittle flying from her mouth. 'We've got our two boys at home. I don't know what we were all thinking last night.'

'*Everyone* was so drunk.'

I'm beyond thankful that Marty and I opted out of the stupid game they all played, a scenario I wouldn't have predicted in a million years when I was planning our holiday. I discussed it with him when we went to bed, and he said that while he thought the whole thing was amusing, he'd have *never* joined in. Still, part of me thinks I should have given him the chance to show his true colours instead of putting an immediate stop to him potentially wanting to be involved.

I've risked *everything* for Marty. I've thrown away my marriage of over thirty years and have really upset my daughter, who's always been a daddy's girl. Indy's my North, South, East and West, and the last thing I ever wanted to do was hurt her. I haven't told her about him yet, but I imagine she'll hit the roof when the time comes for me to confess.

Many of the friendships I've had, aside from Jo, Tina, and Becky, have also slipped away since Caleb moved out of our marital home. One *friend* told me to my face in Tesco that I should have moved out instead of him. She was one of our many mutual friends to have sided with Caleb, who all now believe I'm the wicked witch of the west. So, I don't want to end up with more egg on my face, with my new relationship falling apart after just a few months. Besides, I'm besotted with Marty – far more than I'd like to be, but I can't seem to help it. The prospect of him ending up in bed last night with one of my oldest friends would have torn me apart.

'I don't know how we're going to all face each other after this.' Tina rocks herself forwards and back in her chair, her hands gripping her arms as if she's hugging herself. Last night's debris still covers the patio – empty bottles, half drunk glasses and strewn scraps of paper, probably the ones with my friends' names on. There's a smashed glass of red wine right by the pool which is no doubt going to stain like blood. That's the sort of thing I'll end up being charged for.

'Once we've all been together again for a few hours,' – I fill the coffee machine with beans, – 'everything will settle down and last night will fade away.' So far, I've resisted asking her who she ended up with out of Cameron and Zane and whether...

'Good morning.' I have part of my answer as Cameron emerges from Becky's room with his normally groomed blonde hair standing on end. 'There's nothing I wouldn't do for a coffee.'

'You could use a better turn of phrase, mate.' Marty claps him on the back as he comes up behind Cameron, showered, dressed for the heat and shining like a new pin. He's wearing the Birkenstock sandals I helped him pick out. He has nice feet, which is unusual for a man. All four of us have good-looking men on our arms, but reading between the lines, I'm the only person out of us who's appreciative of what I've got. 'Since you've shown us already what you're capable of *doing*.'

'Alright, alright.' Cameron holds his palms up as he staggers across to the table. 'Ugh, I won't be drinking a drop today.'

'Normally I'd ask you if you slept well, but that wouldn't be an appropriate question this morning, eh, Cameron?' Marty cackles as he reaches into the cupboard above me for a mug, slides it in front of me and then leans in to kiss me on the side of my neck. The tickle his gesture creates makes me shiver.

'No – it really wouldn't be.' Cameron sits heavily at the table, wearing the same shorts and t-shirt as yesterday, as he sits two seats away from Tina. The oldest of our group, Cameron looks even older this morning with his lined face and his blonde stubble. I've never seen him unshaven before. He nods in acknowledgement to Tina, but seems not to notice, or else he ignores the fact that she's fighting back tears. I got the impression that she only went along with the 'game' last night to spite Andy, who was surprisingly enthusiastic. She was right when she confided in me that her husband's changed – he certainly has.

'Just give me a minute, will you?' I whisper to Marty. 'I need to have a quick word with Tina.'

'Just leave her alone - she's a grown woman, isn't she?'

'She's my friend.' I jerk my head for Tina to leave the table and to come and stand with me while I make these coffees. She's in enough mental turmoil at the best of times without what's taken place between everyone last night. But she was a willing participant in it all too, even if she looks to be bitterly regretting it this morning.

'You're really struggling, aren't you?'

She nods, fresh tears seeping into her eyes, which she brushes away furiously with the sleeve of her dressing gown.

'Just let me finish up with these coffees, then we can have a proper chat.'

'I'm fine, really. A chat isn't going to make it all go away.' Her words emerge through gritted teeth.

'What happened last night?' I rest my hand on her arm. 'Just tell me. I might be able to help.'

26

SIOBHAN

'I HONESTLY DON'T WANT to talk about it.' She tugs her arm away.

'We could go outside or to your room.' I don't want to give up on her – not in her current state. 'Where no one else can hear.'

She shakes her head. 'I don't want to.'

I let out a long breath, unsure where to go with this next. If she won't talk to me, there's not a lot I can do. 'Why don't you go for a shower and get ready for the spa?' I nudge her in the direction of the main bathroom. 'I'll bring your coffee to you when the machine's finished brewing.' I nod towards where the machine is dripping fresh coffee into the jug below. It smells divine. 'If you change your mind about speaking to me, you know where I am.'

'How can I get a shower? *He's* in the bathroom.'

'You mean Zane?'

She nods, with fresh tears spilling from her eyes. I wonder if he rejected her last night, if that's what's upset her so much. I hate to think this, but if she was waiting for him in the baggy floral pyjamas she's wearing beneath her dressing gown, she won't have done herself any favours.

'I'm sure that if I were to knock on the bathroom door and tell him to get a move on—'

'Oh, what a nightmare.' She drops her elbows onto the counter beside me and lowers her head into her hands.

'Did you go through with — you know?' I nod to the bathroom.

'Please Siobhan – just leave it, will you?'

'I thought we all agreed not to discuss last night?' Marty's voice drips with sarcasm as he calls out from the table. I thought we were keeping our voices low and that he was busy talking to Cameron. I didn't realise he was listening into *our* conversation.

'Were we even talking to you, Marty?' Tina's voice is uncharacteristically snappy.

'Leave it, eh?' I put my hand on her arm. I agree that Marty needs to button it, but it's important to keep the peace this morning, and *he* doesn't deserve Tina's hostility. There's enough weird stuff floating about between everyone.

'I'm going outside – I want to be on my own.' She shakes my arm off. 'Just let me know when *he* comes out of the bathroom, will you?'

'Marty's right, Siobhan.' Cameron shrugs as Tina storms across the tiled floor and slides the patio door after herself. 'She *did* know what she was letting herself in for, and we all heard her agreeing to take part.'

'Hopefully, Zane might shed some light on what's upset Tina so much when he comes out of the bathroom.' I glance at the still-closed door. The shower is in full force behind it, where Zane will be washing the night away. The whole thing

Their Last Days of Summer

makes me feel sick, and I can hardly believe they all went along with it.

'What is it *you're* all doing this morning then?' Cameron accepts a mug from me. 'We've got our plans, haven't we – assuming everything is civil when the others join us.'

'We girls are going to the spa, then we're supposedly meeting you guys for lunch.' It's a relief to talk about something normal. 'And then, we've *all* got the jet skis booked for this afternoon.'

'Have you booked one for *each* of us?' Marty sits up straighter, his face filled with anticipation. 'This is the main reason I came.'

This isn't what I want to hear in the slightest. I want him to say that he wanted to spend the week with *me,* that he couldn't bear to be apart for seven days.

'There was a special offer for group bookings – book four, get one free, so we can take it in turns riding on our own if we want to.'

'How long have we got them for?'

'An hour.'

'I can't bloody wait.' Marty clasps his hands over the top of his head as he stretches. 'I've always wanted to have a go. How fast are they?'

'They only get to about forty-five miles an hour,' Cameron replies. 'But they're fast enough to make some serious waves.'

'Or to cause some serious damage.' Marty pulls a face.

'Marty's not the most careful driver.' I laugh as I fill my cup. 'Hence why *I* drove us to the airport the other morning. Let's hope he's safer on a jet ski.'

'Are *you* still up for a few rounds of golf this morning, Marty?' Cameron's talking as if his wife *isn't* still behind that bedroom door with Andy, and as if he hasn't just left Becky in her room after spending the night with her. If I could have foreseen them all wanting to get involved in this partner-swapping arrangement, I'd have never suggested this holiday. It's turned into utter madness.

Maybe I should check on Becky – she hasn't shown her face yet. But first, Tina.

Shielding my eyes from the harsh morning sun, I step out onto the patio. The heat hits me like an opening oven door, baking the air after the cool cocoon of the air-conditioned villa. Tina sits hunched at the table, surrounded by the wreckage of last night – empty glasses, crumpled napkins fluttering in the breeze, and a couple of stray flip-flops.

If I asked anyone whether last night's chaos was worth it, I'm pretty sure the answer would be a hard no.

I cross the patio, a coffee in each hand. 'Mind if I join you?'

She doesn't look up. 'Listen, I'm not being rude, but I just need to be on my own right now, OK?'

She's so strung out she hasn't noticed the trail of ants weaving across her bare feet.

I nod toward them, glad I'm wearing my flip-flops. 'You've got insect repellent on, I hope?'

'That's the least of my problems.' But she brushes them away anyway, lifting her feet onto the opposite chair.

'What's going on, Tina?' I set the coffee down and rest my hand gently on her shoulder. 'Come on—you'll feel better if you just let it out.'

She exhales, slow and flat. 'I'm just trying to figure out how to deal with everything.'

'I can help if you'll let me. You know I'm a good listener.'

She lowers her head into her hands. 'Honestly, Siobhan, you'll be the first person I come to when I've made sense of it all. I promise.'

'Alright.' I step back, giving her space, though part of me wants to demand answers. Maybe she's reeling from Jo and Andy still being holed up together. Or maybe it's something to do with Zane.

Their Last Days of Summer

'You know where I am,' I remind her.

As I walk back towards the villa, I catch my reflection in the glass of the patio doors. I look drawn, puffy-eyed – like someone who's aged five years overnight. Not a good look when you're with a gym instructor who's surrounded by tight bodies and bright smiles all day. I need to pull myself together if I want to keep Marty's attention, especially now that our so-called friends are blurring lines and boundaries left, right and centre.

One thing's for sure – I'm not drinking like I did yesterday again. Not this holiday. Today, I'll suggest we stay on the beach after the jet skis. It's easier to pace yourself when you have to wait for a bartender, not just pour yourself another glass in the heat of the moment.

I close the door behind me and feel it, that thick, creeping dread settling over everything. Normally, I'd be excited about a spa day, and about sun and sand and little to do apart from relax. But today? Who knows what tension we're walking into? And once the four of us arrive at the spa together, I doubt it'll stay hidden for long.

I could be just like the rest of them this morning – waking up hungover, wracked with guilt after sleeping with someone else's husband. But even if I were still with Caleb, I'd never have gone along with that ridiculous game. Some lines just shouldn't be crossed.

'That feels better.' Zane's the next one to join us, rubbing at his dark hair with a fluffy white towel as he emerges from the bathroom in a cloud of steam. At least he's got dressed this morning instead of parading around in next to nothing like he did yesterday. I glance again at the patio doors just as Tina moves seats so she's now sitting with her back to us all.

'I take it things went wrong between the two of you?' I slide a coffee in front of Zane and sit with him, Marty and Cameron at the table.

'Cheers – you're a good 'un, Siobhan. You'd make someone a good wife.' He nudges Marty, who pulls a face. Zane knows I'm still technically married to Caleb, so it's a crass thing to say. Marty's told me he's not the marrying kind anyway, which suits me fine. He's got *his* home, and I've got mine. We both have our own lives, but we also have our lives together now. We've both got the best of both worlds, and long may it last. I *really* hope it lasts.

'Never mind your matchmaking.' I jerk my head in the direction of the patio doors. 'What the hell's wrong with Tina? What happened between you?'

'She slept in here.' Marty points at the L-shaped sofa in the far corner of our kitchenette, and for the first time, I notice the crumpled sheet and two bed pillows on the floor beside it, stacked next to Tina's sandals.

'Oh, right. How come? You didn't say something to upset her, did you?' I can't imagine he did. Zane's lovely. A little immature and irresponsible, but lovely nonetheless.

'I'd better not talk about it.' He looks apologetic. 'Really, it's not fair on Tina.'

'Come on, you've got me intrigued.' Marty peers at him from beneath his floppy fringe as he wraps his fingers around his mug.

'I just wish I'd gone to bed with my own wife, alright?' Zane gives Cameron a pointed look, then stares down at his hands as he twirls his thumbs around and around each other. 'I'd better go and see her, hadn't I?' He glances at the door which Becky is still behind.

'Listen, no hard feelings, mate. Remember what we all agreed last night?' Cameron claps him on the back, and I resist the urge to say, *I told you all so.*

'What's Tina had to say about last night?' Zane looks up from his hands.

'Nothing much,' I reply, glancing out at her. 'She just seems really upset.'

'She's blown something I said out of proportion, that's all.' He follows my line of vision.

'What?' We all look at him. I'm even more intrigued.

'If Tina hasn't told you, we'll leave it at that.' His face and his voice are suddenly etched with relief, which is weird. Whatever he's said, I'll get it out of her sooner or later – I've just got to be patient. 'Right.' He gets back to his feet without looking at Cameron. 'I'd better go to Becky and face the music, hadn't I?'

Cameron's face darkens as he watches him walk along the corridor. He's probably wondering about his own wife and why she hasn't yet emerged. Today, as I suspected it might, is shaping up to be a pretty fun day.

27

THIRTY-FOUR YEARS AGO

'It hurts,' she gasps. 'It really hurts.'

The three of us look at each other, each petrified pair of fifteen-year-old eyes searching the others for possible solutions, before turning our gazes back to our friend, red-faced and dripping with sweat. She's writhing on the narrow bunk bed, which creaks beneath her weight.

'What are we going to do?' Just as I'm about to reach for her hand, I tug mine back. I'm scared to touch her. 'These aren't just tightenings anymore. The baby's coming this time. It's finally happening.'

'Ow-ow-ow. Please help me.' Her face is twisted in agony. It's worse than any of the videos we were forced to watch in Biology. I don't know how to help her.

'Should we get Miss Smith? Which room is she in?'

'No!'

'The teachers are right at the other end of the corridor.'

'No – no you can't.' Her words are laboured and pleading. 'She'll call my mum. Oh my God,' Her knuckles whiten as she scrunches the white sheet within her fists. 'I can't do this.' She arches her back in agony.

'What if she starts screaming and wakes all the other dorms up?'

It seems none of us can offer her any comfort – we're just too frightened. We've known about this all along and haven't told a soul but it was never our secret to tell. It was hers and we had to respect that.

'We've got to get her out of here if we don't want anyone to hear.'

'Where to?'

'I can't move.' Her voice is a yowl, and I shush her. It will be a miracle if she hasn't woken everyone else yet.

'The storage shed.' I jerk my head in its direction. 'You know – where all the walking boots are kept.' It will be pitch black in there, but we've got our torches. They were on the list of things to pack. 'There was that long bench we could put pillows and towels for her to lie on.'

'It'll be locked.' The contraction must have passed as her voice has returned to normal.

'I saw where Smithy hooked the key. Come on.'

'I can't walk.' She begins moaning softly again. Another contraction must be already building. As the night has worn on, her pain's been getting worse, and there is less time between her contractions, just as I read about at the library.

'We'll all help you.' I smooth my hand over her damp brow. 'You can lean on us. Just as you always have done.'

I nod at the other two. 'Fill my rucksack with some towels and grab your pillows.'

They look at me as if I've gone mad.

'But what about... you know – after?'

'I haven't thought that far ahead,' I reply. And I really haven't. Even as her belly has swelled in recent months, she's been able to wear my older sister's school skirt from last year to disguise it, and she just looks a bit chubby to the unknowing eye.

Somehow, I never believed this would really happen – that a baby would be born – I don't think any of us did.

Even if we can keep *her* noise down while she's in labour, we can't stop the baby from crying afterwards. As soon as Miss Smith hears it, that will be that. We have no choice other than to get her out of here.

28

TINA

'Yes, it's for me, and my three friends. We've also got treatments booked. Two massages and two facials.'

I stand beside Siobhan as she checks us in – the only person in our friendship group I don't mind being associated with this morning. I certainly don't want to stand next to the woman who's had sex with my husband, nor next to the woman who believes I've had sex with *hers*. It feels uncomfortable to continue describing them as *friends*.

'Who wants the treatment first?' The woman behind the counter asks. I like the way the locals speak here. Their English has a Dutch lilt but is mixed with a Caribbean rhythm.

We all look at each other. I shrug, and Becky looks away from me. Yes, she definitely believes I've had sex with Zane. However, she couldn't be further from the truth.

'I'm not really bothered,' replies Jo.

'I give you a moment to choose, no rush.' The perfectly-groomed woman behind the counter looks taken aback. She'll be used to seeing women entering this ylang ylang-infused reception area with its piped music and screens of running water, relaxed and excited about some pampering, not looking as though they're about to throttle one another.

We assemble ourselves on the loungers which surround the pool, Siobhan thankfully inserting herself between me and Becky. Jo ended up being the first to go in for her treatment, and my booking is in half an hour. I can't wait to just go and lie in a darkened room where I no longer have to pretend I'm happy to be here.

Jo didn't appear until we were practically climbing into the taxi. Not a word of explanation, not even any eye contact. She slid in beside Siobhan like nothing had happened, like she hadn't blown a crater through my marriage. I sat in the front, wondering if she'd even acknowledge me. She didn't. Not once on the drive to the spa.

But it's not just *last night* I need to confront her with – not anymore.

Because ten minutes before we left the villa, I cornered Andy in the bedroom while he was pulling on his polo shirt. The air still smelled of chlorine and stale rum, and my voice was trembling so badly I could barely get my words out.

'Tell me the truth, Andy.'

'What about?'

'Jo. Was last night the first time?'

He didn't even look ashamed. He exhaled through his nose, as if *he* were the one who was tired of *me*.

'You've been right all along,' he said, casual as anything. 'It's been going on for three months.'

Three. Months. His words hit me like a punch to the stomach. My brain couldn't catch up. I'd suspected flirtation, the beginnings of something ugly. But three months?

'We're both leaving our marriages,' he added, like it was an admin update. Just like that.

Their Last Days of Summer

I didn't cry. My throat closed around the sob, but my mind was already scrambling, trying to recall the last three months in slow rewind. Every argument. Every cancelled plan. Every time I'd caught him texting and he'd flipped the phone screen face-down. Every single time I'd defended him to our sons.

'Andy—' I started, but I wasn't even sure what I was going to say. Maybe something about our home. Our history. The family he was leaving behind.

But before I could speak again, Marty called his name from the kitchen. Andy didn't hesitate. He grabbed his sunglasses, muttered something about being late for golf, and walked out of the door. He just walked out.

Like our marriage didn't even deserve any further discussion. Like the truth he'd dropped on me was an afterthought. Something to deal with *later*.

And now we're here. After our treatments, I'll be forced to be in *her* company. The woman who's been smiling in my face, sitting by my side, sharing wine and stories and *secrets*, while screwing my husband behind my back. The one who hasn't even had the guts to look me in the eye this morning. I don't know whether I'm going to scream, or shatter. Or both. I feel hollowed out. Frozen. Like if I move too fast, I'll fall apart completely.

Everyone thinks this is a spa day. A detox after a messy night. But for me, this is the day everything's changed. Because now that I know, *she's* going to find out what I'm capable of.

'You OK?' Siobhan peers at me as I pluck the book I was trying to read on the plane from my bag. I might as well try to escape my own drama by attempting to immerse myself in someone else's. Perhaps what I read about will be so terrible that my circumstances will become favourable by comparison.

'I'm thinking about going home,' I reply. 'I'm sorry, Siobhan, but with what's going on—'

'You *agreed* to be part of things last night.' Becky leans forward on her lounger, her voice snappy. 'So don't start playing the victim now.'

'Look, both of you.' Siobhan lowers her voice to a hiss. 'People are watching us.'

I glance up. She's right. A couple of women whose loungers are at right angles to ours are peering, probably wondering what there could be to argue about in a spa as sumptuous as this. Under normal circumstances, I'd be luxuriating by now, either in the pool or the jacuzzi, but I can't even begin to enjoy myself at the moment. Like I said to Siobhan, I just want to be back in my familiar surroundings, with the bass of my boys' music echoing from their rooms. I want to be away from these women I used to believe were my friends. I should have listened to my gut. I should never have come on this holiday.

I turn the page of my book, but my eyes don't move. The words blur. All I see is white space.

'Is it any good?' Siobhan asks, glancing over as Becky disappears with her therapist.

'Oh... erm, it's alright.'

She raises an eyebrow. 'You've been stuck on the same page for the last five minutes.'

'I'm struggling to concentrate.' I force a small smile. It's the truth. If Siobhan asked me to summarise what I've just read, I wouldn't have a clue.

She nods, accepting that, and returns to her magazine. Beside us, two women erupt in quiet laughter, the kind that bubbles up easily when life feels light. I'd give anything to be able to laugh like that.

But I can't. Not today. I'm watching strangers smile and wondering what it even feels like.

The truth I learned this morning presses against my ribs like a rising tide, begging to be let out. I want to tell Siobhan everything – about Jo, about Andy, about their months of betrayal. But if I start, I'm scared I won't be able to stop. That my misery will all pour out in one messy, uncontrollable flood.

And it's not just *me* Jo's betrayed. Siobhan and Becky deserve to know the rest of it, too. They need to understand who she *really* is – and what she's capable of.

But not yet. I'm not ready. Not until I can find the words. Not until I can breathe without them sticking in my throat.

∽

'Any sickness or injury I need to know before we start?' The therapist leads me into a candlelit room.

Yes, I'm fat, I'm depressed, my husband is sleeping with one of my best friends, and I make myself vomit to cope with my awful life. Instead, I shake my head.

'I let you get comfy now, okay? Take off your things, lie face down, and just breathe and relax. I come back in a few minutes.'

Relax. That's a joke.

'You like that pressure, or too much?' The sensation of someone's hands on my skin invites the familiarity of tears back to my eyes. Andy hasn't laid his hands on me for months, and even before that, it was in a perfunctory way. Jo will no doubt have enjoyed a very different experience last night.

It should be easy to relax, to drift off after my endless hours of lying awake on the sofa, chilled to the bone beneath the air conditioning unit. I was too drained to find the control to turn it off, yet too wired to drift into sleep. With my noise-cancelling headphones stuffed into my ears, I listened to sleep-inducing meditation after sleep-inducing meditation until I accepted there was no way I was going to escape from everything my brain was turning over.

It's no wonder I'm so exhausted.

29

TINA

I'M SPRAWLED along one side of the steam room, no longer caring how much my belly protrudes between the two pieces of my plus–sized bikini. Nor do I care if anyone else wants to sit down alongside me. I am not moving. I'm sick of being Mrs Nicey-Nice. Look where it's always got me. Precisely nowhere. Here I am, thousands of miles away from home with a husband who doesn't love me anymore and two so-called best friends who can't even look me in the eye.

The glass door into the steam room opens and closes. I'm tempted to part my eyelids to see who's arrived or left, in case it's one of our lot, but I keep them tightly shut. I don't want to move, and I don't want to talk to anyone. If I keep my eyes closed, perhaps no one will disturb me. My back feels slimy with the combined effect of steam and the massage oil from my treatment, but the eucalyptus is relieving my blocked sinuses, stuffed after an endless night of tears.

Rather than being soothed throughout my massage, I found it aggravating. The therapist kept telling me to relax, but it was impossible. I lay there, feeling like I should be taking action or doing *something*, not just lying there like everything was normal. But *what*? I don't know. I haven't a clue how to handle any of this.

The air is thick with steam and silence.

'Now that the four of us are alone in here.' Siobhan's voice is slightly hoarse from the heat. 'We need to talk about last night and clear the air.'

Becky snorts. 'What's to discuss? Besides, I thought we'd agreed – no 'morning after' chat.'

The defensive edge in her voice tells me everything. She slept with Cameron. I've seen the way she's been looking at him since we arrived, like she's starving and he's the last decent meal on planet earth. But at least she didn't conduct a *three-month affair* behind her friend's back. Not like Jo.

'I can't stand this atmosphere,' Siobhan says, her voice cracking with strain. 'I don't want the whole holiday poisoned.'

'Like I said earlier – I'm looking into flying home early.' The words spill from me before I can stop them. So much for keeping it to myself. What I don't say – what I *can't* say – is that after I leave Aruba, I don't want to see any of them again. Not even Siobhan.

'Don't be daft, Tina.' I feel a hand – Siobhan's, warm and damp – rest on my shoulder. 'We can get through this. We've been through worse.'

Becky cuts in, her tone brittle. 'Go home if you want, I won't stop you.'

I turn to face her, my words ready – but I catch myself. She'll have enough to stew in shortly.

'You say *I'm* the one who's always miserable.' Her voice rises. 'But *you're* the one dragging everyone down. Andy said you didn't even want to come.'

I swing my legs around, the slap of my wet skin on the

plastic seat echoing through the hiss of the steam inlet. 'You've always been jealous of me, haven't you, Becky?'

Her laugh is sharp and humourless. 'Why the hell would I be jealous of *you*?' She drags her eyes over me – my body, my hair, my everything—and I feel it like a slap. Even through the mist, the sneer on her face is unmistakable.

'You should take a long, hard look in the mirror.' My voice is low and shaking. 'Before you go hurling insults. You might finally see what the rest of us already do.'

'What's *that* supposed to mean?' She leans forward, her eyes blazing. For a moment, I think she's going to lunge at me. Wouldn't that make headlines – *Brawl in Boutique Spa*.

If anyone walked in now, they'd either bolt or call management. The tension is thick enough to drown in.

'It means I can hold my head up high,' I reply. 'I don't live beyond my means. I don't accept loans for holidays I can't afford.'

'Tina – *enough*.' Siobhan's voice is hard now.

'Who borrows money to lie on a beach?' I throw my hands up, the heat pounding at my temples. 'You can't even pay your rent!'

Becky's face twists. 'Who told you that?' Her gaze darts to Siobhan. 'Oh, I see. *You*.'

'I'm sorry.' Siobhan shrinks behind Jo.

'I mentioned that in *confidence*, Tina.' Siobhan steps forward. 'You had no right—'

'There *is* no confidence between us anymore,' I snap. 'Last night proved that. Friends don't screw each other's husbands.'

Siobhan sits up straight. 'I didn't.' Then she stands, steam clinging to her limbs like a second skin. 'Not because of you lot. But because I still respect *myself*.' She points at each of us, one by one, her finger trembling with rage. 'I'm done.'

She yanks the door open and storms out, the glass slamming behind her with a crack that feels final.

'I need to get out of here as well,' Becky mutters. 'I feel like I'm suffocating – and it's not just the steam.'

'If only you *were*,' I shout after her, as the door slams again.

And then there were two. Me. And Jo. And the truth I haven't confronted her with. Yet.

'We'll get chucked out of here if we keep slamming that door.' Jo's tone is oddly pleasant – like we're still friends. Her hair hangs in dripping, rat-tail strands after dunking herself in the plunge pool, but no doubt she'll be back to full, preened glory before long. Anything to impress *my* husband. But she's got more to worry about than her hair.

'I think we need to talk, don't you?' I fold my legs up onto the slick plastic bench, my hands clasped in my lap. I'm calm and controlled. For now.

Jo's brows lift. 'About what?'

'Don't insult me. You know what. Were you *ever* going to tell me?'

'If this is about *last night*,' she starts. 'We were all drunk and no one's proud of what happened, but we agreed to move on.'

She's still lying and still hiding. The coward.

'It's gone *way* beyond that, Jo – as you very well know.' Rage is bubbling beneath my skin like lava.

'We can get past this, Tina.' She reaches out and lays her hand on mine. 'Come on—how long have we been friends?'

I wrench my hand away. 'You're no friend of mine. Not after what Andy told me this morning.'

Her body stiffens. She'll know what's coming. Her hands brace against the bench, ready to stand.

'Not so fast.' I move first, my hand slipping on her slick skin as I shove her back down.

'You're not going anywhere until you admit what you've been doing with my husband.'

'Admit *what*?' She gasps as her back hits the tiles.

'That you've been screwing Andy for *three months*.'

She bows her head. Her voice is low now, more careful. 'Is that what he told you?'

'He said you're both leaving your marriages. Said you're going to 'start afresh' and sail off into some glorious bloody sunset.' My voice breaks. 'Well, over my dead body.'

'I didn't *agree* to it,' she whispers. 'I told him I'd *think* about it. Cameron doesn't even know anything yet.'

She tries to stand again. I shove her harder this time, and her head knocks the mosaic wall with a thud. Good. I want her to feel it. I want her to feel even a fraction of the pain she's causing me.

'He's ready to throw away thirty years – his family, his *children*. For *you*.'

'They're hardly children anymore,' she mutters.

'So you're *considering* it?' I spit the words out. 'Don't you care what this will do to them?'

'They *like* me, Tina.'

'Don't you *dare* think you can have anything to do with my sons!' I'm almost growling now. 'They're *mine*. I won't let you drag them into your dirty little fairytale, you slut!'

She shoots to her feet. 'What did you call me?' She grabs my arm – hard. Her nails dig in, sharp and unforgiving.

'You heard me. Once a slut, always a slut.'

She tightens her grip. 'You have *no* right to talk to me like this.'

'Like hell I don't. You've spent three months screwing my husband. So who's next? *Zane*? Oh wait—' I pause, letting my silence sting her. 'He's already told me everything.'

Jo freezes. 'What?'

'He told me what you got up to when he first started seeing Becky.'

She doesn't deny it. And her silence is everything.

'What's the matter? Cat got your tongue?'

'It's not—'

'Zane even joked that after me, only Siobhan would be left for him to go to bed with out of the four of us.' My voice splinters. ' But *you* – you've now worked your way through every man in our group, haven't you?'

'Is *that* why you slept on the sofa last night?' Jo flops back onto the bench like the air's been knocked from her.

'How do you know where I slept?'

'Siobhan told me. Zane must've loved twisting the truth.'

'He told me *enough*. Just like Andy has.'

'Have you told Becky or Siobhan?'

'Not yet. But I *will*. Becky also deserves to know what kind of a friend you've been.'

'It was *years* ago, and it meant nothing. Becky doesn't have to find out, and certainly not from *you*.'

I rise to my feet and loom over her, the heat rising with me. 'It isn't in the past with Andy, though. Is it?'

'He came after me,' she whispers, shrinking back.

'Bullshit. You're not some innocent little doe. You've been clawing for male attention since the moment we met at the airport. I just hope Cameron gives you what you deserve after this. I hope he strips you of everything.'

'It was *ages* before I gave in to Andy. You've got to believe me.'

'That makes it alright then, does it?' My laugh is hollow yet furious. 'Three bloody months, Jo. Three months of lies and betrayal. How could you?'

'I'm so sorry, Tina. What else do you want me to say?' Her eyes dart to the door like she's hoping someone – *anyone* – will walk in and rescue her.

'You're sorry *I've found you out*.' I take a step closer. 'Did you really think you could run off into the sunset with my husband and I'd smile and wave you off? I've been with him since I was *nineteen*. He's the father of my children.'

'People can't help who they fall in love with.'

My vision tunnels. How *dare* she mention the word *love*? 'You *bitch*.' I lunge at her before I know what I'm doing, my hands gripping her hair, which I yank as hard as I can. We hit the floor in a tangle of limbs and steam, and she screams as I drag her scalp-first across the tiles towards the steam inlet. I'm going to shove her face in it – I'm going to burn the skin right off her face.

'Get *off* me!'

She thrashes around, but I've got years of fury fuelling me. Fury of being constantly overlooked and now replaced.

Suddenly, an alarm shrieks overhead, piercing and metallic. The glass door slams open, and hands – multiple hands – grab my arms and haul me back. Jo slips from my grip like seaweed and curls herself, panting, into the corner.

She's lucky there was nothing in here to smash over her head. Because right now, if I had the chance, I'd end her.

30

JO

'You're both lucky you didn't get arrested after that little performance.' Siobhan falls into step beside me. She's effortlessly chic in a white shorts jumpsuit, her hair swept up like the spa drama never touched her. Of course. Siobhan never lets chaos crease her edges.

Tina's storming ahead, still in the same crumpled vest top and shapeless shorts she arrived in – rage fuelling her stride. Behind us, Becky trails at a distance, eyes fixed on the ground. No wonder she's avoiding me this morning. It's hard to make eye contact when you've spent the night wrapped around someone else's husband.

'I know.' I lift a hand to my scalp. My fingers come away with more blonde clumps. The bitch actually *ripped* my hair out. Who does that? What are we – still fifteen?

'But just so we're clear,' I add, 'it was Tina who went for me. I didn't lay a finger on her – not until I had no choice.'

Siobhan casts me a sidelong glance but says nothing. Her silence is heavy. Not judgmental, just loaded.

I can't help but wonder if she's questioning who the real villain is. Because the thing no one wants to admit is that there's no single villain in all of this. We're just a bunch of women –furious, betrayed, and exhausted for different reasons, all tearing each other apart under the weight of our secrets.

But Tina was bang right about Andy. He really *does* want to leave her for me. However, he had no right to come clean about me and him without my blessing. I only told him I'd *think* about leaving Cameron. Really, I'm so confused about what I want to do. Since all this shit has hit the fan, the prospect of leaving Cameron isn't an attractive one. I can't help but worry I'll be giving up more than I can afford to lose.

'Tina reckons she's got way more on you than just your affair with Andy.' Siobhan smooths her hand down her sideways plait. 'So what's she on about?'

'I've no idea,' I fib. Yet I know it's only a matter of time until Tina spills the beans about my history with Zane. Yes, we *did* have sex all those years ago, but not in the circumstances she's cooked up in her head. I was never trying to break Zane and Becky up – that's not how it happened at all. But Tina wouldn't give me the chance to explain, and Becky won't either.

'Who's *she* on the phone to?' I point towards Tina, who's waving one hand around as she walks along. The streets are relatively quiet as we follow the signs towards the beach. We were told yesterday that only tourists and those who *are forced* to be outside for their jobs risk the sun between midday and three o'clock. It's the time when most locals take a siesta.

'I don't know,' Siobhan replies. 'But she looks pretty upset. It's difficult to tell, but she looks like she's crying.'

'She'll be begging Andy not to leave her.' I sound catty, but I don't care anymore. Not after the way she attacked me in that steam room. I'm lucky someone raised the alarm, as she really had the better of me.

'I can't believe how you've treated her, Jo.' Even beneath her sunglasses, there's no mistaking Siobhan's cold and hard stare. 'Don't you think you should back off and give Andy and Tina the chance to fix their marriage?' She hoists her handbag back onto her shoulder. 'For their kids' sake if nothing else? And what about Cameron?'

I shrug and keep clomping along in my Jimmy Choos, each step louder than it needs to be. 'Shit happens – I should know.' It comes out colder than I intend, but I don't know how else to cope. Ever since we all met at the airport, I've felt caught in a tidal wave of tension and toxicity, pulled under by every look, every lie, every unspoken gesture. I don't know how to climb out of it. This trip is spiralling into a disaster.

Well, it's not *the* worst. Not quite.

There was another trip, years ago, when things were worse for our group. Much worse. And I can't help but think all that's about to come out too.

'I'd better catch Tina up.' Siobhan's always been the peacemaker throughout any of our spats over the years. 'We've got another five nights together in that villa, so we need to smooth things over. Talk to Becky, will you?' She jerks her thumb behind herself.

'I've got *nothing* to say to Becky.' I take my sunglasses off to wipe the sweat that's accumulated on the bridge of my nose.

'She'll be feeling dreadful about last night – but she'll be waiting for *you* to broach it.' Siobhan's voice is softer again, probably because she wants something from me. 'All you've got to do is to tell her there's no hard feelings.'

'But what if there *is*?'

'Last night was utter madness.' Siobhan rolls her eyes to the sky. 'But I was there when you *all* agreed to draw a line under things today.'

'It isn't as simple as that, is it?'

Cameron and I didn't even speak to one another this morning. I managed to avoid him by showering and getting ready in the main bathroom while he used our ensuite. But I've messaged him saying, *hope you're OK, hope we're OK,* when I was lying at the side of the pool earlier, and he responded with a thumbs up and a smiley emoji, which was a relief. For now, anyway.

I really don't feel ready to completely upend my life. However, just as Tina said something about *true* friends not sleeping with one another's partners; partners who love each other don't have sex with other people. If mine and Cameron's marriage had been strong enough, neither of us would have dreamed of sleeping with anyone else.

'The bottom line is that the four of us have been friends for a long time.' Tendrils of Siobhan's red hair blow around her face in the Aruban wind as she keeps pace with me. The taxi driver told us this morning that it's a dangerous wind, one that makes the sun scorch you faster. 'I know you three better than I know my own family. And after all we've been through…'

'Don't remind me,' I sniff.

I continue at my same pace rather than dropping back to match Becky's as Siobhan strides ahead to speak to Tina. I have no intention of smoothing things over with Becky. Instead, I'm steeling myself for how I'm going to handle Cameron when we all join up again for lunch and this afternoon's jet skiing.

A lot depends on whether Cameron has uncovered the truth about my fling with Andy. But even if he hasn't, he's going to find out soon enough, and the news is way better coming from me than anyone else, especially Tina.

I'm only too aware that Cameron's unlikely to forgive me once I tell him the truth. Then, this situation will become about damage limitation and me getting what's fair as a divorce settlement. My nasty stepdaughters will love that. They'll be glad to have me out of the picture, but won't want me to get my hands on a penny of their father's.

Andy was trying to convince me last week that I'd be fine

for money if Cameron and I were to separate. He also said there isn't a court in the land that would force me to hand my salon back to Cameron. *What should I do?* Yes, my lifestyle is cushy, but the older I get, the more time my husband has for his female employees. Plus, as Andy has also pointed out, why would I want a husband who allows his daughters to speak to me like I'm dirt? Oh God, I'm so mixed up.

I let a long sigh out. For Tina's sake, I know I should back off from Andy, but as her violent display in the steam room confirmed, it's too late for that. I tried to explain how Andy had come on to me to start with. I could also have told her that I only reciprocated when he told me their marriage had run its course. But she was too busy trying to shove my face in the steam outlet.

At the beginning of this holiday, someone made a joke about how well we'd know each other by the end of it. We were even laughing at the prospect of how a whole multitude of secrets could worm their way out. We're only on day two and everything's unravelling already.

I've been walking so fast to ensure Becky doesn't catch me up that I've almost closed the gap between me, Siobhan and Tina. But it seems Becky has also sped up, as I sense her presence right behind me. It doesn't feel comfortable. It doesn't feel comfortable at all.

The sea has come into view in the distance, the sparkling surface completely at odds with the darkness that's infiltrated our friendship.

'No, you *can't* talk me out of it.' Tina twists herself out of Siobhan's grasp as I follow from several paces behind. 'I've told my mum *everything* and she's looking at flights for me *today*. I'll be leaving the minute I can.'

'I bet you didn't tell your mother that you spent the night with the husband of one of your best friends, did you?' Becky calls out. Which is rich, coming from someone who spent the night with *my* husband. But for now, I'm going to keep quiet – it's a relief not to have the spotlight on me for a change.

'Actually,' – Tina stops and spins around on the heel of her sensible sandals to face Becky, – 'I spent the night on the sofa. And you can ask Zane if you don't believe me.'

'You still tried to have sex with him first, didn't you?' Becky's tone is acidic.

Tina stands firm, her dark curls now dry and frizzy from the sun. 'You can't say that. You don't know *anything* for sure.'

'Zane told me *himself,* actually. He told me you're being a bitch with him today because he *rejected* you. He'd sobered up by the time you got in the room together and told you he couldn't go through with it.'

'Is that what he's been saying?' Tina's mouth drops open. 'It's absolute rubbish.'

'I know who I believe out of the two of you.'

Who you want to believe. But I don't say a word. I've got enough problems of my own to deal with.

Tina sets off again, at an even faster pace than before. 'I've had enough of the lot of you. After I leave, none of you will have to see me again.'

'Thank God for that,' Becky shouts after her, then she turns to me. 'I'm meeting Zane for lunch now. The rest of you can do what you want.' I thought for a moment she might broach what's gone on between her and Cameron last night, but no – she probably daren't.

Siobhan has set off at a jog in an attempt to keep pace with Tina. 'Come on.' She grabs her arm. 'We can sort this out – I'm sure we can. We've not even had two full days here.'

'Just leave me alone and give me the keys for the villa to get in for my stuff.'

'You've got no chance.'

31

JO

> Yeah, Tina stormed off in one direction and Becky in the other. We don't know exactly where either of them has gone. I'm just in a cafe with Siobhan.

> Becky's with Zane – she rang him and he went off to meet her, and I'm with Marty. We haven't a clue where Cameron went after golf. He said he needed some space.

I RELAY the information from Andy's text to Siobhan as the waiter sets our lunches on the table. I'm usually ravenous after a visit to the spa, but the combination of nerves churning in my stomach and the hangover which still has me in its grip, is conspiring against my appetite.

> Are you going to let Tina get a flight, or will you try to stop her from leaving?

> I'll have to stop her until I've spoken to our boys. I can't risk her poisoning them against me. They're always more for her.

> I doubt you'll be able to stop her, you know.

> In fact, how do you know Tina hasn't spoken to them already?

> > She wouldn't tell them something like this over the phone. Not when she's not at home.

> What if she leaves? Will you go after her?

> > She can't leave. Her passport is in the safe at the villa, and I've set the code.

> > Anyway, when are you going to speak to Cameron?

> What were you playing at, telling Tina—

Siobhan tugs the phone from my hand and lays it down on the table. 'Leave it alone and eat your lunch.' She sounds haughty.

'I'm not all that hungry, to be honest.' I raise my fork from the table and turn over a cucumber slice. 'How can I be? I've still got Cameron to face. I think I need to speak to him before anyone else beats me to it.'

'This is all *such* a mess.' Siobhan's eyes moisten with tears.' I really don't blame Tina for wanting to go home. I can't believe how everyone's been behaving. And after all my careful planning. This was supposed to be the holiday of a lifetime.'

'The demon drink and too much sunshine took hold – that's what went wrong yesterday.' This doesn't explain the ill-advised affair Andy and I have been having, but it certainly explains the stupid wife-swapping game we ended up embroiled in.

'Listen Jo, I need to tell you about something else.' Siobhan lifts her eyes from her plate to meet mine, the expression in her face telling me I won't like whatever I'm about to hear.

'What now?' As if there could be more. I put my fork down. I can't eat this salad. I can't eat *anything.*

'It's not just what you've got going on with Andy.' She dabs at her mouth with a napkin.

'What isn't?'

'Tina's got something else over you, Jo.' She looks back at her plate as though checking in with herself that she's doing the right thing by imparting whatever she's about to say. 'Something she found out last night.'

'Tell me then.' As if anything could be bigger than my affair with her husband.

'While you were getting dressed after the spa, we had a coffee.'

'Who, you and *Tina*? And?'

'She told me something about Zane. What he said to her last night.'

'It's OK – I already know all that.'

'You do?' She looks confused. 'She never told me you did.'

'Tina confronted me in the steam room after we'd had a set to about Andy. I take it she hasn't said anything to Becky yet?' I'm certain that if she had, I'd be fighting Becky off with a big stick too.

'I don't think she has, but it's only a matter of time.' Siobhan closes her eyes for a moment. 'Anyway, you should know that I've spoken to Marty about it and—'

'What the hell's any of this got to do with *Marty*?' Great, this just gets better.

'He's going to warn Zane that Tina's told us all.'

Wonderful. What's Andy going to think of me *now*? I can't imagine him wanting to run off with me in quite the same way once he hears something happened between me and Zane even if it was many years ago. And Cameron will just be disgusted.

'Zane's probably regretting getting so drunk now.' Siobhan

shakes her head. 'Fancy him spilling to Tina that he slept with you behind Becky's back.'

'It was bloody years ago.' I pick my fork back up, not that I'm intending to eat anything, but I need something to do with my hands. 'I can't believe what he's been spouting off to Tina.'

'I still don't know what's gone on in the past between you and Marty.' Siobhan's voice is low and even. 'And I want to know, Jo. Don't you think I've got a *right* to know if my new boyfriend and one of my best friends once slept together?'

She's taking full advantage of having me cornered, just the two of us. But our attention's diverted by my phone lighting up on the table.

> You haven't answered my question, Jo. When are you going to tell Cameron you're leaving?

> I don't know – like I've told you, I need to think.

> You should tell him now, then the two of us could take off together for the rest of the holiday and leave the others to it.

'Never mind *Andy*.' Siobhan doesn't take her eyes from me as she turns my phone face down again. 'I'm not leaving this cafe without the truth. How well do you know Marty?'

Perhaps in the wake of everything else, it's time to be honest. It's time to tell the *whole* truth.

32

BECKY

'There should be eight of you, yes?' The bronzed activities assistant in white shorts and a red t-shirt starts unhooking life vests from the overhead rack.

'That's right. Five jet skis – the special offer on your website.' Siobhan steps forward. Always the organiser.

I stare down at my pink toenails. I shouldn't be queuing for a jet ski. I shouldn't even be on this holiday. I still owe Siobhan money for booking this activity – just another chunk on top of what I already can't pay back. And now she's gone and told Jo of all people. Which means it'll get back to Cameron soon enough.

When the tension exploded back at the spa, I'd wanted to run. To leave like Tina was planning, but I couldn't afford to. Cameron doesn't want me. The thread Zane and I have been hanging by has frayed even further, and it's a miracle we're all still standing here together with how explosive things have become.

'Where's the other person?' The assistant frowns, counting us again.

The sand burns the soles of my feet, so I slide them back

into my sandals and glance towards the shore. The sea looks cool and gentle, but standing on its edge with this lot is anything but.

There's Tina. Alone and small against the vast blue horizon. She hops from foot to foot in the shallows, avoiding families playing catch and couples walking hand-in-hand, as if they can't see her. And honestly? They probably don't.

She looks fragile in the sun, like something easily broken. A flicker of sympathy catches me unawares – until I remember how miserable I've been since Cameron left my room this morning. I can't afford to feel anything for anyone else right now.

'We'll just have to go without her,' Marty says. 'Wait – there she is. Tina!' He jogs down the beach, waving like he's found his long-lost friend. God, who does he think he is? Acting like he's part of our group, like he's one of us. Even with his arms around Siobhan, he's still an outsider. The only thing uniting me, Jo, and Tina these days is how much we don't trust him.

But I feel marginally lighter since I met Zane for lunch. We cleared the air, or at least, skimmed the surface of it. He swore he didn't sleep with Tina last night, and he didn't push me about Cameron either. Still, there was something off in his eyes, something unsaid. But I didn't dig and I won't until we get home. The atmosphere between us all is precarious enough.

Cameron's the one I really *can't* read. He's barely looked at me since we all came back together. Actually, he's barely looked at anyone. That distance he's always kept from the group has grown.

'Have the two of you spoken yet?' Siobhan's voice slices through my thoughts. She's staring at Zane with an expression I can't place.

'Who? Me and Zane? Yeah. We had lunch.'

'I know that.' Her voice is flat and measured. 'But what did he *say*?'

'Things are fine,' I reply. 'We agreed to put last night behind us and to try and enjoy the rest of the trip.'

Zane's noticed us talking. His body tenses, and his eyes seem to narrow as he walks over. The last thing I need is Siobhan poking him into one of his moods. He's subdued for now and easier to manage this way.

Siobhan and Jo share one of those silent glances I've grown to hate. Then Siobhan looks back at me. 'You and I need a word about Zane, Becky.'

'What about?'

'As soon as we get off these jet skis,' she says. Her eyes stay locked on Zane as he reaches us.

'Zane? What's she on about?' I turn to him. 'Why does Siobhan want a word about *you*?'

'I've no idea.' His tone is dark, the glare he throws Siobhan even darker. 'Let's just leave last night where it belongs, shall we?'

'A word about *what*, Siobhan?' I press her.

Zane opens his mouth to say something else, but the assistant interrupts.

'You still want this booking?' She gestures behind us, where another waiting group are starting to look impatient.

We all look at each other. Jet skiing was meant to be one of the highlights of our trip. Now, judging by everyone's faces, the only people still remotely enthusiastic are Siobhan and Marty.

'What's this about?' I hiss to Zane. 'Has it got something to do with Tina?'

He exhales heavily. 'I just said something I *shouldn't* have.'

The image of Tina's creased sheets and messy pillows on the sofa fills my mind. God knows what he said to her.

'Can't you just give us the vests and take us over there?' Cameron asks the assistant. 'We'll organise ourselves.'

'You need a safety brief,' she says curtly.

'We can relay it to the others,' he gestures toward Marty,

who still looks to be coaxing Tina. I don't know why he's bothering.

Try as I might to act unaffected, it *hurts* to be near Cameron now. A part of me still holds onto the fantasy that if Jo confesses to her affair with Andy, he'll come to me. He'll want *me*. My life would change overnight with him at my side. I know I'm deluded, I know it's desperate. But it's still there.

'We don't work like that,' the assistant says coolly.

'Marty, come on,' Siobhan calls out, starting towards him. 'We'll lose our booking if we don't get moving.'

Marty says something I can't hear, and somehow – miraculously – Tina laughs and starts following him back to our group. I have no idea what he said to make that happen, but I'm curious.

Still, not half as curious as I am about what Siobhan wants to discuss.

33

BECKY

Hopefully, getting out on the jet skis will take everyone's minds off all the negativity and provide something of a reset. Perhaps it will even soften whatever Siobhan said she wants to talk about with me. It could be something to do with money, but how it might involve Tina remains to be seen.

As Marty and Tina rejoin our group, Tina walks with Siobhan. I'm dying to ask them to explain things to me *now,* but there's no time.

'Ready to go?' asks the activities assistant. Without waiting for an answer, she sets off to the water's edge with the rest of us in pursuit.

Zane goes ahead of me. I can't make out whether he's speaking to Siobhan or Tina. But before I've had the chance to find out, we've reached the jet skis and the woman is waiting.

'Vests stay on, always. Wire clips here – see? You fall off, engine cuts.' In an exaggerated gesture, the activities assistant's hand slices through the air in front of her throat.

'What about the passengers?' Jo calls out, and Andy smiles at her. I glance at Cameron to see if he's noticed, but he doesn't appear to have done. Jo and Andy will no doubt wish they

Their Last Days of Summer

could ride together, but they've got no chance unless they want blood to be shed. 'Does the passenger have a wire?'

'Only the driver,' she replies. 'You have one hour. You see the blue hotel? Don't go past it, yes?' She points to a building in the distance to our left. 'And that one.' She points to a pink building way out to our right. 'You keep the beach in sight, always. If you can't see the shore — you've gone too far. And stay out the swim zone, yeah?' She points to a glittering expanse of water in front of us, its edges demarcated by bright green buoys.

'I remain until you go, then I will meet you here in one hour.' She counts us as diligently as a teacher would count children on and off a bus for a school trip, instead of the group of fifty-year-olds we've become.

'Who's going with who?' It's the million-dollar question, and in poor taste after last night.

'We're going together.' Siobhan points at Marty. As if anyone would think otherwise.

'We'll go together too.' Zane slings his arm around my already sunburnt shoulders. Really, I could do with spraying some more suncream on, but I don't want to hold the others up – we've already wasted some of our allotted time.

Perhaps while we're out there together, Zane might be able to shine some light on why Siobhan was looking at him so strangely when she announced her need to speak to me. And what the hell he's said to upset Tina? It's looking like I might owe her an apology after ignoring her so far today.

'You can swap out there, no problem,' the activities assistant tells us. 'Just make sure the engine's off first.'

'I'm going on my own, since there are five jet skis.' Tina's voice is sulky. I'm surprised she's even having a go, given the mood she's in. A couple of hours ago, she was adamant she was going home.

'I'll ride with Jo then.' Jealousy courses through my veins as

Cameron gives her a nudge towards their nearest jet ski. 'Come on, love, you've ignored me for long enough, don't you think?' I don't like the sound of this. But hopefully, he'll change his tune. As things stand, he has no idea about his wife and Tina's husband. And if he doesn't find out soon, I'll have no qualms in enlightening him. I'd *hate* to be the last one to know – like he is.

'I guess that's me on my own as well then.' Andy heads off in front of us all, evidently not happy that Jo's agreed to ride with Cameron.

Poor Cameron. Surely, he can't remain in the dark about their affair for much longer. And poor Tina. I had no idea Jo and Andy had been carrying on together for so long – it's little wonder she lost it like she did in the steam room.

'Who's steering then, me or you?' Zane grins like everything's normal between us. Like last night never happened. Really, I don't think things have ever been 'normal.' It's just been one long struggle to make ends meet, a never-ending blame game, and me being forced to tiptoe around his dark moods.

'You can sit at the front.' I usually let Zane drive whenever we go anywhere together. Besides, the thought of being in control of one of these jet skis as it bounces around the waves is pretty scary.

They could do a lot of damage.

∾

'Oh my God, slow down,' I shriek into his ear. I recall someone saying these things go up to forty-five miles an hour, and that's exactly what he's doing, but somehow, when on the back of one, it feels even faster.

'This is awesome!' He's ignoring my pleas to slow down. I glance back as we get further and further from the shore, gripping onto him for dear life. Tina, who was just pottering around on her jet ski around half a mile from the beach, is now a mere dot way behind us. She probably won't dare to get up to a speed much faster than ten miles an hour.

'You're going too far out,' I yell. 'You need to turn around.' Maybe this is his warped plan. He's going to ride as far away from the shore as possible, throw me into the water and then zoom away again.

Cameron rides up beside us, grinning from ear to ear as he bounces up and down on the waves. Jo's clinging on behind him, her blonde hair flying out in the wind. She and I lock eyes for a moment, then she looks away.

I've been trying to talk myself out of it, but it's no good. I've got to be honest about what, or in this case, *who*, I really want to be with. The truth is that I'd do *anything* to take Jo's place with Cameron. To be riding behind him, to be sharing a bed with him, to be going home with him.

I'd do *anything*.

34

SIOBHAN

'You still alive?' Marty calls back to me as he brings the jet ski to a halt. Gasping for breath, I loosen my grip around his middle. It feels good to be this close to him for the first time since this morning. He's felt somewhat distant since the 'games' in the pool last night.

'Just give me a moment before you go again, will you?'

He laughs. 'Why? Don't tell me you don't share my need for speed. Where's everyone else disappeared to anyway?'

I squint out to sea, where the other two couples – Becky and Zane, and Jo and Cameron are barely more than specks now. 'They've gone way further than they're supposed to.' My damp leg squeaks against the slick side of the jet ski as I shift. I can already feel the ache building in my thighs from gripping so tightly, and by the time I climb off this thing, my skin will be raw from holding myself upright.

Marty lets go of the handlebars and shields his eyes from the sun. 'Andy's also on his way out there by the looks of it.'

Searching for my other friend, I twist my neck in the opposite direction. 'Can we check that Tina's OK?'

'She'll be fine.'

'But she's all on her own, so I want to make sure.' I glance over at where she's just perched on her jet ski, staring pensively into the water. We're the closest people to her, but she still looks miles away.

'Do you want to have a turn at riding this thing over to her?' Marty twists in his seat to look at me more closely. He's already killed the engine and unclipped himself from the wire. He'll probably hope I'm as much of a daredevil as *he* is. Maybe I used to be, but at the age I've reached, I've become more aware of the fact that I'm not as invincible as I used to think I was.

'Oh, I don't know.' I glance at the handlebars. Driving it looks no harder than controlling a bike – so I *should* have a go, I'll only regret it if I don't. At the beginning of this year, I promised myself I would say yes to as many opportunities as possible. Well, to most things anyway. I wouldn't have said yes to last night in a million years.

'Don't be boring.' Playfully, he pushes my shoulder. 'I'll slide off at this side, then shuffle back so you can come forward.' As Marty begins to move, the jet ski wobbles on the water.

'No, no, you're tipping it.'

He laughs as he draws one leg over, then leans to the side to make way for me. But he loses his balance on the foot rest and then, splash. I bet even Tina's laughing if she's watching us. It's the most comical fall into water I've ever seen.

'Man overboard.' He splutters at the surface, gripping onto the side of the jet ski as I slide forwards in the seat, hysterical with laughter.

'I warned you, you were tipping it.'

'Actually, it's good to cool off in here.' He grins as he hauls himself back up, shaking water from his ears like a labrador.

'Aren't there sharks in this sea?' I sweep my gaze over the vicinity of where we're bobbing. The azure-blue sunlit surface looks so innocent, so picturesque. Beautiful on the surface, but an unknown entity beneath, like so many things in life.

'Erm, there *are* sharks, but they're not the kind that'll eat you.'

'All sharks eat you. Oh my God.' I grip the back of the seat I'm sitting on. 'I think I might go back to the beach and wait for you.' I glance back. The sun loungers in the distance *do* look incredibly inviting, as does the book I have tucked inside my handbag, back in our beach locker. I've hardly had a chance to read a word since we set off from the airport. I'd planned to read on the plane, but Zane barely stopped talking to me. Zane. We've still got *that* situation to confront.

'Don't be daft.'

'I'm not – honestly, I've got a thing about sharks.'

'Duh, duh, duh, duh.' He sings the Jaws theme tune as he swings his leg over to sit behind me. 'Start her up then, let's see what you've got.'

'OK, OK.' Gingerly, I twist the throttle as I feel his wet arms around me, but I must twist it too far as we lurch forward. I immediately let it go again and we stop dead.

Marty laughs. 'You need to be smoother than *that*. Just turn it gently until you get used to how it works.'

I start it up again. 'Oh my God, oh my God.' I'm driving the thing like I'm a seventeen-year-old out for a first driving lesson. It bunny-hops along.

'Faster,' Marty shouts above the engine. 'Smoother.'

I twist the handle some more and quickly have the hang of it. I'm really doing this. When I go home, I'll be able to tell the girls at work that I rode a jet ski – not only that, but I also controlled it.

'Woo-hoo.' We're bouncing around like tin cans on the back of a wedding car, but I have to admit, it's pretty awesome. 'I'm driving it,' I yell. 'It's all me.'

'Take it to the max,' he shouts back, nuzzling into my neck. 'All the way.'

I twist the handle towards myself, and we lurch forward at speed. Thirty, thirty-five – forty – forty-five miles an hour.

'Yee-ha,' yells Marty. 'Way to go.'

It feels more like I'm doing seventy on a motorway as we munch up the waves. We're not heading out to where the others are but remaining parallel to the shore. The truth is that I'd rather avoid the others until we go back. Apart from Tina, that is.

'I'm riding over to her now,' I shout as I slow our ride.

'Why? I thought you were enjoying yourself. You've got all day to talk to your friend.'

'But she's all on her own.' There's a spray of water as I turn us so I'm facing in Tina's direction. I know Andy's locked her passport away, but I'm sure I can persuade her to *want* to stay for the rest of the holiday. Yet how the situation will pan out once I've spoken to Becky about Zane, I really don't know.

It's a shame we got the free jet ski, really, as without it, Andy might have ridden with his wife. That way, the two of them would have been forced to spend some time together and could have perhaps sorted things out to some extent.

It's comforting to have Marty's arms tightly around me as I head at a more conservative speed of thirty-five miles an hour towards Tina. I feel safe with him behind me and far more loved and desired than I ever did when I was with Caleb. It feels weird to be with another man after all these years, but it's an exciting sort of weird. More so, perhaps, because I never a hundred per cent know where I stand with him.

As we approach Tina, I let go of the throttle, bringing the jet ski to a stop beside hers.

'You OK?' I call out, raising my voice over our idling engines, their sound thick and mechanical.

She doesn't answer straight away. She just sits there, stiff-backed and staring into the distance, her fingers white where they grip the handlebars. When she finally turns to me, her face is pale, her lips pressed tight. 'I'll have to be, won't I?' she says flatly, and for a moment, I wonder if she's talking to me at all, or just muttering into the breeze. She looks like she's on the brink of something – fury, fear, collapse. Maybe all three.

Then her hand jerks up, pointing out towards the horizon. 'Look.' Her voice is thin as it threads itself through the noise. 'Someone's in the water.'

I follow her gaze. At first, I see nothing but the rippling blue, broken by flecks of sunlight. Then I spot it.

She's right. Someone *is* in the water, and something doesn't look right.

35

SIOBHAN

I scrunch my eyes behind my sunglasses. 'Perhaps some swapping around is going on out there,' I tell Tina.

'So long as it's not the sort of swapping around that was going on last night.' Marty laughs.

'What?' Tina frowns, clearly unable to hear us.

I do the same throat-cutting gesture that the activities assistant was doing earlier, so Tina kills her engine too. We're far enough away from the shore for it to be silent out here. No longer is it possible to hear the whoops and enjoyment from bathers from the beach. I'm looking forward to relaxing among them when we go back.

'Jo's got herself behind Andy by the looks of it.' She points out to sea, then hangs her head, misery etched across her face.

'Gosh, your eyesight must be good.' I cup my palms over my eyes.

'Look, it's them. Can you believe it?'

'Jo and Cameron must have had a row out there.' Bloody hell – I was hoping we only had what we know about Zane to sort out.

'What the hell's going on?' Marty sounds incredulous.

'Someone else is in the water now. Is it Andy? I can't really tell. We'd better have a ride over and make sure everything's alright.'

'I hope the bastard drowns.' Tina turns her attention back to me. 'I hate his bloody guts.'

It's on the tip of my tongue to say Andy's hardly going to drown while wearing a life vest — but I bite it back. Because I get it, I really do. What happened last night was already pushing boundaries, a bit of reckless, drunken wife-swapping among them all, but this? A full-blown affair that's been going on for three months, with whispers now of Jo and Andy actually leaving their partners? This is a different beast entirely.

And if Tina's right, if Jo really has climbed on with Andy in plain view of everyone, then that's a whole new level of brazen. I squint out to sea, but without my glasses, it's all just a blur of bobbing blobs. Still, there's something about the way Tina's staring, rigid and silent, that makes me think she's seeing things a lot more clearly than I am.

'Will you be OK for a few minutes?'

'To be honest,' Tina says, 'I was on the verge of riding the thing back in and going to sit on the beach. I need to call my Mum back about these flights.'

'No, you can't.'

'You need to tell her, Siobhan.' Marty nudges me with his leg.

'Tell me *what*?' Tina's face darkens. 'What now? Surely there can't be anything else I need to know.' She looks pained, and I feel terrible for her.

'If Siobhan won't tell you, I will – Andy's locked your passport in the safe at the villa, so you can't travel *anywhere* and he's not planning to tell you the code either.'

Nice one, Marty. There's nothing like telling her straight.

'Why? I'd have thought he'd have *wanted* me out of the way so he could conduct his sordid little affair more openly.'

'The fact that he now seems to have Jo as his passenger tells me he's already doing that,' Marty says.

'Marty, be quiet.'

'Apparently...' I stop. I don't know if I should be telling her what Jo said over lunch just to stop Marty from saying anything else.

'What?'

I *am* going to tell her. She's got a right to know. 'He doesn't want you going home and telling everybody what's been going on without him being around to defend himself, namely your boys. He wants the chance to speak to them himself.'

Her face darkens. 'He's going through with this, then? What he mentioned earlier? He's definitely leaving me?'

'Shelve this for now, Siobhan,' Marty mutters into my ear. 'We've only got just over half an hour left.'

'Do you want me to talk to him? Andy, I mean?' I ask gently, shifting on my seat. I probably shouldn't get involved — technically, it's none of my business, but watching Tina like this, hollow-eyed and hurting, makes it impossible to stay on the sidelines.

She gives a half-hearted shrug, her gaze fixed somewhere beyond the horizon. 'I can't imagine it would make any difference,' she mutters as she fumbles with her life vest buckle. 'Listen, I'm going to head back to the beach. I'm not exactly having the time of my life out here.'

'Will you be OK?' I ask, though the answer's already written in the slump of her shoulders.

'I'll have to be, won't I?' She replies, not quite looking at me.

'I won't be long, I promise.'

She pauses, then gives me a small, strained smile. 'Look, sorry – I'll be fine.'

I turn to Marty, who I can tell is growing more and more impatient by the second. 'Right then, let's swap back over.'

He manoeuvres himself to the side of our seat, making us wobble uncontrollably again.

'I'm going to fall in, aren't I?' Fear washes over me. 'Please tell me I won't get eaten by a shark.'

'There's not enough meat on your bones.' Marty laughs again. Tina looks even more downcast, sitting pink-skinned with rolls of her belly protruding beneath her life vest and spilling over the waistband of her shorts. When we get home, I'm going to frogmarch her to the doctors to get help with this bulimia issue once and for all. Along with the way she feels about herself. In my opinion, the best thing she can do is kick her philandering husband to the kerb and then work on herself. The 'divorce diet' is renowned for wondrous transformations. She fires her engine back up and points it in the direction of the shore.

'Hold on tight.' Marty starts our engine too, and spins around to face the direction of the others. Then with the wind blowing his hair back, he sets off, spraying water behind us.

I'm incredibly thirsty after well over an hour without a drink. Plus, mixed in with the sun cream, the saltwater from the spray is stinging my eyes behind my sunglasses. I squint in the sunshine, trying to relieve the soreness.

'Oh my God, what's going on out there?' Sore eyes or not, we've got ourselves close enough to the others to see blood splattering into the sun-rippled air. It looks like either Cameron or Andy has pulled the other from their seat. Whichever one of them has done the ousting is repeatedly punching their adversary in the face. Meanwhile, Jo's screaming at them to stop.

'Get over to them,' I yell. 'Before they kill each other.'

36

THIRTY-FOUR YEARS AGO

I RUB my eyes as I swap the gloom of the storage shed for the glare of the early morning sun. I haven't got my watch on, so I've no idea of the time. I only hope the others get back to the dorm without anyone hearing or seeing.

I carefully transport my rucksack against my chest, only too mindful of what I'm carrying. It's no longer just a couple of towels we threw in to deal with the mess of amniotic fluid. It's now the mess of a tiny human. One we had to separate from its mother with nail scissors. I had to rush outside and throw up as the scissors snipped into the blood-streaked and slimy cord. It was gross. Bile rises in my throat again as the image forces its way back into my mind.

Loose stones crunch beneath my trainers as I lurch across the uneven ground. Oh my God, oh my God. I wish I could call Mum right now and ask her what we should do. But we'd be in so much trouble – all of us, especially now that we've let our friend give birth without calling for help.

This is terrifying.

I should be lying comfy in my squeaky bunk bed, fast asleep while the seagulls squawk out here amid the ebb and flow of the sea below the cliff. Instead, I'm out here on my own and can only pray I don't encounter anyone. I'm bound to be challenged, a fifteen-year-old girl, alone at dawn, still wearing pyjamas and clutching my rucksack as if I'm running away.

Maybe that's what I should do.

The church is getting closer, the one we were forced to look around and take photos of yesterday, after we finally made it to the top of the hundred and ninety-nine stone steps. I don't know which was more boring, the church or the abbey. We should be allowed to enjoy ourselves in the amusements or by playing crazy golf. Instead, we're forced to take pencil rubbings of wall carvings or write descriptions of how our surroundings make us feel.

Bored.

There's a strange chirping noise rising from the spongy grass I've swapped the gravelly path for. *Crickets*, I think. At least that's what Dad said they were when we walked in the Yorkshire Dales during the summer holidays. Something else that was boring, but at least it was normal.

Right now, I'm longing for normal.

The four of us have agreed that once we've done what we've got to do, no one will breathe a word of this, and we can somehow get back to how we should be.

But it's *me* who drew the short straw – *me* who the others voted to do *this*. To leave the bag at the church. And if I get caught, I don't know what I'll do.

The church gate opens with a click, and I creep between the crooked graves up the uneven path. Some of the gravestones are unreadable, their names eroded by decades or even centuries of being battered by wind and rain. Others, where the writing can still be made out, are in memory of people who died not much older than the four of us are. I remember Miss Smith telling us that women used to regularly die in childbirth, and I bet that's how some of them lying in these old graves were taken. We've been lucky that it hasn't happened with us. Three panicked fifteen-year-old girls aren't exactly equipped to deliver a baby.

It's well creepy being alone among the dead like this, all rotting away only six feet beneath where I'm standing. And if I get found out for my part in what's happening and for what I'm about to do, I'll be dead and rotting with them – *we all will*.

I shiver. We're in the middle of an Indian Summer, Miss Smith reckons, but it's chilly this morning. She says we're very lucky the sunshine has fallen while we're having our residential.

Just as I've grown good at when I'm slipping a Constance Caroll lipstick into my pocket in Chelsea Girl, or a pair of dangly earrings in Top Shop, I scan for overhead cameras without moving my head. If there are some, I'll have to find another place where there aren't any. But we've agreed that a church is the best place to dump this bag – perhaps it makes what we're doing slightly more forgivable.

There are no cameras. But as I enter the echoey porch, I sense the eyes of the last thousand years boring their silent condemnation into me. *What comes around, goes around.* Mum's voice floods into my brain. I feel certain that even if we're not caught today, I'll be punished in the future, but I can't let this fear change my mind. I'm doing this for my friend – as *any* good friend would.

It's fairly warm on the porch, but it's shaded from the sun or any rain, if it were forecast, which it isn't. I rest on the bench inside, next to an arrangement of flowers which look to have been laid on top of a coffin. I rest the bag at my feet, swallowing fresh bile. I don't want to be sick again, but I'll never forget when the baby's head first poked out. There was so much slime, and so much blood. I can't imagine how people would have more than one baby after going through *that*. Not to mention how much agony she was in.

After it came out, she didn't even want to look at it – none of us did. Straightaway, we agreed that we just needed to do what I'm doing now. I just can't believe it's fallen to me, and I hope I'll be able to live with myself after today.

I jump as the clock chimes seven o'clock above me. I need to get back before we're called to get up and get ready for breakfast at half past.

I take several deep breaths in readiness to leave. This is my final chance to change my mind about leaving my rucksack behind. But what else can I do? The only other option is to take it back to the youth hostel and confess to Miss Smith.

No, I can't do that.

We've come this far, so dumping the bag here is the only chance of my friend getting back to some kind of normal. At least she'll be allowed to continue living at home, to do her exams and to live the life of a fifteen-year-old. She'd do it for me – I know she would.

I rise from the stone bench and take a last look at my pink and black Nike rucksack. It's so ordinary looking. *Big enough for your books and lunch box,* Mum said at the start of the school year, only three weeks ago. What she didn't know was that it would also be big enough to hold a newborn baby.

~

'What are we going to do?'

None of us has had a wink of sleep. God knows how we're supposed to get through today. Any minute at all, Miss Smith's going to be calling us for breakfast, and I couldn't eat a thing after what's happened. I was so excited when this trip was first arranged back at Easter, but we couldn't have foreseen this. Never in a million years. We didn't even guess about the baby's existence until the end of April.

'I need to go home.' It's the first time she's spoken since we brought her back in from the shed. I wish we could tell someone what's happened – that our friend has given birth to a baby. But then what?

The next question would be, *Where's the baby?* Of course it would. No matter how much of a panic we were all in a couple of hours ago, nobody could ever understand or forgive what we've done. Part of me would like to go back in time and change things, but there's no going back now.

'What happens when someone finds the rucksack? If our teachers hear something and mention it in front of us, just one look at our guilty faces will put them onto us.'

'Where's she gone?' I point at the space where our fourth friend should be.

'She said she was feeling sick. I guess she must still be in the bathroom.'

'Her and me both.'

'I just want to be in my own bed. There's still so much blood coming out of me.'

'You *can't* go home.' I glance at my friend's stricken face. 'We're all stuck here until tomorrow, whether we like it or not. You're going to have to pretend you're ill when Smithy comes in.'

37

TINA

'As if things weren't bad enough.' Siobhan's voice is tight with disbelief as she turns her head and spots what I've been trying to keep my back to.

Marty kills the engine with a twist of his wrist, but neither of them makes a move to dismount. They just sit there, staring.

'Just look at them.'

I should storm across the beach and tear strips off Jo and Andy – shout, scream, make a scene. But I can't. The rage is there, coiled and ready, but right now I'm hollow and drained.

There they are — my husband, propped pathetically on the sand, and Jo, one of my oldest friends, crouched beside him like some makeshift Florence Nightingale, fussing over his wounds like they're lovers in a bloody war zone.

And neither of them even glances in my direction.

'I can't imagine what you must be going through.' Siobhan bows her head. Her voice is quiet and apologetic. 'I'll never be able to look at Jo the same way again, not after this.'

I exhale sharply, forcing myself not to cry. 'I take it Cameron went for him out there, then?' I gesture towards the open water. The sea sparkles like nothing's wrong – like it's too beautiful a place for this kind of emotional carnage. I never should have come. And now I know why Andy was so keen on the trip.

'You could say that,' Marty mutters, rolling his eyes.

I glance back at Andy, and a bitter satisfaction swells in my chest. 'Hopefully, Cameron landed one on him for me.'

'His face definitely caught a few.' Siobhan grimaces.

'Marriage doesn't mean anything anymore, does it?' The words leave me before I can stop them. Then I blink, realising who I've said them to. 'Sorry, Siobhan – I didn't mean—'

Marty slides from his seat and walks away without a word. I still don't know the full story of how he and Siobhan got together, but I'd bet good money he had as much to do with the end of her marriage to Caleb as Jo has with the demise of mine.

'I'll go and get our stuff from the locker,' he calls over his shoulder, heading towards the booking hut.

Siobhan nods towards Jo and Andy. 'Climbing on with Andy was always going to be like a red rag to a bull for Cameron. I reckon she came clean out there. Told him everything.'

I shiver, even though the sun is still blazing. 'Where's Cameron now?'

'He said he was heading back.' She slides her sunglasses up onto her head to scan the shoreline.

But it's impossible to tell. A new group is just setting off, making it hard to see who's returned. And if Cameron were back, surely there'd have been another scene by now, another explosion aimed at Andy.

The tall activities assistant approaches us, all bronzed limbs and swishing blonde hair. She reaches for the life vests with a breezy smile that doesn't reach her eyes.

'Jet skis, five there should be,' she says. 'And eight people, yes?'

'Erm, yes,' Siobhan says.

The assistant frowns, glancing toward Andy and Jo. 'What

happened to *him*?' She nods at Andy, then back at me. 'They will not say. We should fill in the accident book.'

I open my mouth, but nothing comes out. Tears sting my eyes. 'It's nothing to do with me.' My voice is barely audible. And for the first time, I know that's true. Andy stopped being mine the moment he let Jo into his bed, maybe even before that. And God, it hurts.

The assistant frowns again.

'I'm sorry,' Siobhan says. 'The others must have lost track of time.'

The woman still looks puzzled, like she doesn't understand what Siobhan's saying, or maybe she's just not used to this kind of drama among her tourists.

I turn away from them, my gaze drifting back out to sea. Two more riders are appearing on the horizon, gliding closer through the golden haze.

I should be sipping an Aruba Ariba on the beach right now, stretched out on a lounger with the sound of waves in my ears and the sun on my skin.

Instead, I'm watching the ruins of my marriage wash up on the sand. This holiday has turned into a nightmare.

38

TINA

THE TWO RIDERS we've been watching arrive back at the shore, but they have nothing to do with us. I'm getting increasingly jittery and looking at Siobhan as she hops from foot to foot, she clearly feels the same. Marty's still waiting at the booking hut to retrieve our things.

'Where's Cameron?' Jo calls.

'You're talking to *me*?' I swing around, pointing at myself. Andy's lying down on the sand now, holding a wedge of tissue to his face. I hope he's in agony.

'Cameron's *your* husband,' Siobhan retorts. 'How should *we* know where he is?'

'Great. *You're* cutting me off as well, Siobhan?'

'Friends don't behave like *you* have, Jo.' She shakes her head.

'Thanks.' I squeeze Siobhan's arm. She's right. I'm still reeling from the revelation that Jo and Andy have been carrying on behind our backs for so long – but what's also hit me was learning last night that it isn't the first time. That she once lured Zane away from Becky too. It can't just be blamed on a youthful mistake. It's a pattern. At least now I can see Jo for exactly what she is.

'If they don't come back soon — five minutes — I charge extra, okay?' The woman taps her watch.

'Could they have come in over there?' Siobhan points to the other side of the cordoned swim area where a row of jet skis are lined up.

'You bring them back where they were taken.' She points to where we vacated our rides. 'And I count only five vests.' Her finger is now redirected at the pile of five yellow life vests, one slathered in my husband's blood. 'I still need to know what happened for accident book.' She points at it.

'I need the loo.' Siobhan digs her sandals from the bottom of our piled up shoes. The glitter on Jo's heels sparkles in the sunshine, and I'm suddenly tempted to hurl her expensive footwear into the sea. 'I won't be long.'

'You must not leave,' the woman reiterates. 'There will be charges.'

'I'll just be a few minutes,' Siobhan replies. 'Stay well away from *them*.' She nods in Andy and Jo's direction as she slides her sandals on. 'Confronting them won't do any good. Don't stoop to their level.'

As she walks away, I sink to the sand, miserably listening to the excitement of the new group about to board their rides. I bet they weren't getting off their faces last night and swapping their partners for 'fun.'

I reach for my flowery Birkenstocks from the shoe pile, the sandals I treated myself to before the holiday. When I thought I still had a marriage worth working on, and when my sons believed they still had a father who wanted to live with them. I knew *something* was amiss with Andy, but he'd have been the *last* person I'd have suspected of having a full-blown affair. I've been putting the changes in him down to some sort of midlife crisis he might be experiencing.

'You might need stitches in that.' Jo's voice is filled with concern as it drifts over the whoops and enjoyment of the other group. I glance around as she sits beside *my* husband, resting her hand on his bare thigh, right in front of me. 'I still can't believe Cameron attacked you like that.'

Maybe it's because Siobhan's no longer here to stop me, or perhaps it's because it feels like I have nothing left to lose, a red cloak of rage drapes itself over me. She's brazenly fawning over *my* husband like I don't even exist, right in front of me. I've never hated anyone more in my life.

'How can you say that?' I leap to my feet and storm over to her with one of my sandals in each of my hands. 'You can't expect to carry on behind mine and Cameron's backs and for us not to react. You're cruel bastards, both of you.'

'We never wanted to hurt—'

Before I can stop myself, I swing my sandal into her face. I'm as shocked as she is when the wooden sole connects with her cheekbone. I've *never* been violent before today.

'Owww.' She raises her arms in self-protection as I go for a second blow.

'You're an absolute bitch.' I smack her again, then again. As Andy tries to get to his feet, presumably to stop me, I smack *him* around the head with the sandal in my other hand. I'm screaming and grunting as I continue to pummel them both, all the while as they're trying to get from the sand to their feet. Fury's clouding my vision, and I can't stop. I want them to hurt as much as I'm hurting.

'The police have been called,' yells a voice. Then another voice, which sounds like Siobhan echoes in the distance. If only I had something harder to hit Andy and Jo with. I should have picked up her heels and stabbed her eyes out. I'd like to permanently disfigure her for what she's done to me. My life's in ruins, and I don't know how I'm going to go on.

I feel the weight of hands on my arms and shoulders as I'm

dragged away from my so-called friend and the man who was supposed to love me forever. As swiftly as it arrived, the anger seeps from me like a deflating balloon, and I sink to the sand in floods of tears. I've always taught my sons that the biggest and best person walks away from a confrontation, yet here I am, battering their already injured father around the head with my sandal. I'm probably going to be arrested, and for what? *Them?* It's not as if they're worth it.

'You call the police, yes?' I hear the activities assistant ask her colleague, her voice low but urgent. 'I have no clue what's with these people.'

Siobhan arrives at my side, breathless, her hand shielding her eyes against the glare. Her voice sharpens. 'Is that... is that another one of our group coming in?'

I follow her gaze, my heart thudding. A single jet ski *is* slicing through the haze.

There's only one rider. But it's impossible to see who it is.

39

JO

THE OTHERS WATCH INTENTLY as the rider approaches, but as they come fully into view, we realise again, that they have nothing to do with us.

Marty's the first to step forward when one of the uniformed police officers approaches. He brushes the sand from his hands and clears his throat, but when he speaks, his gaze stays fixed on the ground.

'Martin Bell.' He replies when they ask for his name.

The officer scribbles in a notepad, his face unreadable behind dark sunglasses. 'And you were part of this group this afternoon?' He waves his finger around at the rest of us.

Marty gives a small nod. 'Yeah. I was on one of them, with my girlfriend.' He nods at Siobhan. 'But I wasn't involved in... any of that.' He gestures vaguely towards me and Andy, glancing at us briefly — just long enough to make eye contact with me before looking away again.

The officer doesn't respond right away. He just keeps writing. 'Did you witness any fight?'

'Not directly. I was—' Marty stops himself, then shifts on his feet. 'Look, I saw *something* happening in the water. But I wasn't there when it all kicked off. You'll have to speak to the others.'

The officer nods slowly, as if weighing the truth of it, then looks towards Tina. Marty exhales, rubbing the back of his neck as he sinks back to the sand. He's right – he wasn't involved in the fight between Cameron and Andy, but still, there's tension in his jaw.

He's acting weird, and I'm getting a sense that something else happened out there after we rode away. Something's *really* not right. Why haven't Cameron, Becky *and* Zane come back yet?

'Three jet skis and five people here, but two jet skis and three people still out there.' The officer hovers his pen over his notepad. 'I need the rest of your names.'

Tina gives hers next, barely disguising the contempt in her eyes as she throws a glance my way, like I'm something she scraped off her shoe. Siobhan follows, measured and composed, and then Andy and I take our turns.

My face still throbs from where Tina's sandal repeatedly struck me, but it's nothing compared to the state of Andy's face. He took a proper beating, fists flying from my husband, then a brutal slam against the side of the engine. But even then, Tina still went for him with her sandal.

I want him checked over at the hospital. But the police have been clear, no one's going anywhere until the rest of our group are found.

'The two of you rode together?' The officer points from Siobhan to Marty.

'Yes.' Siobhan nods, standing closer to him.

'I rode alone.' Tina points at herself. I've never once seen her lose her temper in all the years I've known her, but I guess I've deserved both instances of her losing it today. Perhaps I'd have reacted the same in her situation.

'And you two.' He gestures at Andy, still dazed on the sand, then at me.

'Yes.' I won't bother explaining that Andy and I never set off together and that I swam over to him from where I'd been with Cameron, after finally making my confession. It's getting into details we really don't need to.

'We need to talk while we're on our own,' I'd said to Cameron as I clung to his back. We tore across the waves, further and further from the shore. It was just us and the endless sea. It might be the only chance I had to tell him the truth.

But even out here, I could feel Andy watching us, keeping me in his line of sight. It made my stomach twist. My nerves were already frayed, and that gaze only added more pressure.

Cameron slowed the engine to idle, its roar giving way to an uncomfortable silence. He turned slightly on the seat, trying to catch my eyes.

'Is this about last night?' His voice was wary as if I was going to accuse him of something.

'Kind of.' My heart was hammering. 'But you need to hear this from me — before Tina or one of the others tells you.'

'Tells me *what*? Look, last night was just drunken stupidity, wasn't it?'

'No,' I said quietly. I was grateful we weren't facing each other head on. I couldn't have said what I needed to if I had to look directly at him. 'The truth is... last night wasn't the first time something happened between Andy and me.'

There was a beat of silence then his jaw clenched. 'What?'

In that split-second, I realised maybe he'd cared more than he'd let on. Or maybe it wasn't love. Maybe it was control – not wanting me, but not wanting anyone else to have me either.

'You're never home, Cameron. Your daughters can't stand me. I feel alone all the time. I—'

'Oh, so now this is my fault?' His voice sharpened. 'How long?'

'Three months.' There was no point lying.

'You absolute slut.' He twisted fully round on the seat and grabbed one of my shoulders, his fingers boring into my skin. 'After everything I've done for you.'

There it was — that word again. *Slut*. I'd heard it before, too many times. It didn't sting anymore. It just made me angry.

'Don't you dare call me that,' I snapped. 'You didn't seem to mind jumping into bed with Becky last night, did you?'

'You're leaving me for *him*? Is that what you're trying to tell me here?' His grip tightened. My thighs pressed hard against the sides. We were too far from shore and too isolated. My mind raced. What if he pushed me into the water before Andy could reach me?

'I don't know what I want, Cameron. I'm confused. I didn't mean for this to happen, but—'

'Then I'll make it easy for you, shall I?' His face was inches from mine.

'What's going on here? Jo, are you okay?' Andy's voice cut through the tension like a lifeline. He'd pulled up nearby and quietened his engine, concern written all over his face.

Cameron spun towards him, letting go of me. 'You can fuck right off. I thought you were my mate.'

'I asked if *Jo's* okay. I don't think she should be with you – not when you're in *this* mood.'

'Oh, you don't, do you?' Cameron snapped. 'Well, I'm warning you—'

I didn't let him finish. I couldn't. Andy was right – I wasn't safe. Not here. Without thinking, I threw my leg over the seat and plunged backwards into the water.

I swam hard, every stroke pulling me closer to Andy. I didn't look back – I didn't need to. I knew Cameron would be livid.

But I also knew someone else was approaching. I could

hear the engine, distant but getting closer. If things turned ugly, someone would see. Someone would step in.

I'd never known Cameron to be violent but as I reached Andy and looked back to see my husband sliding into the water after me, I realised there was a first time for everything.

And I was genuinely afraid of what Cameron was going to do.

40

JO

CAMERON MIGHT HAVE SNUCK past us on the beach without any of us seeing him, maybe while I was helping Andy to clean himself up. Becky or Zane could have sneaked past too? No, they can't have done – at least one of the jet skis and life vests would be back if that was the case.

The eight of us returning to that villa and continuing with any kind of holiday is unthinkable after all this. Perhaps we should follow Tina's lead and look at earlier flights home. On separate planes if possible. The prospect of us all sitting together on the plane is equally absurd.

Cameron rode away from the rest of us like he had the devil after him when he'd finished attacking Andy. I naturally assumed he'd be back at the shore before us, tending to his bruised ego with a glass of something strong in his hand. *But who knows?*

He certainly wasn't in his right mind. In fact, he completely lost it when I jumped into the water. Perhaps he's – no, I shake the thought away. My husband would *never* attempt to hurt himself, no matter how wretched he might be feeling. But neither is he the sort of person to vanish when something serious is happening. Normally, he'll stick around and face a situation head on.

I give Cameron's name and date of birth to the officer, while Siobhan gives details of our villa to the other officer. The feuding between us is beginning to feel less important now that people from our party are missing at sea. It's been over half an hour since they *should* have been back.

'It's Becky I'm the most worried about.' I wrap the towel around my shoulders. Even though I'm not cold, after all, I'm here in thirty-degree heat, I still feel shivery. No matter what tensions exist between us all, especially after last night, Becky's been part of my life for such a long time, I'd be devastated if anything's happened to her. But as far as Zane's concerned, I really couldn't give a stuff about him.

'You're not worried about your *husband*, then?' Tina scowls at me as if I'm harbouring a deadly disease.

She's right – of course she is, however, there can be no denying that it would solve a few problems for me if Cameron *were* to have been swallowed up by the ocean. There'd be no blame on my part when facing his family – it would just have been a terrible accident. And there'd be no question of my keeping the house and my business. As well as the lion's share of *his* business.

'I need descriptions of the three who didn't come back,' the officer says. 'We start with Cameron Burnley-Jones.'

Everyone looks in my direction. Evidently, it's down to me, as Cameron's wife, to describe him.

'You are related to Cameron?'

'I'm his wife.'

Being that I'm sitting so close to Andy, the officer is probably confused. 'Go on.'

'Cameron's got a beard.' I run my fingers over my chin, 'He's got blue eyes and dark hair with bits of grey.' The officer writes all this down. 'He's tall.' I point at Marty as if that might demonstrate how tall Cameron is. 'He was wearing his life vest with a white t-shirt and red shorts.'

I'm suddenly wondering whether the *three* of them being gone has anything to do with Becky spending last night with Cameron. Perhaps it's some sort of revenge thing. All I know is that it's seriously strange. People don't just evaporate into thin air. We should probably be telling the police the truth about the hostility between us all. But unless one of the others says something, I'm keeping quiet.

'*Red* shorts? Easy to see then. And, Zane Johnson? The husband of Becky Johnson, yes?'

The five of us look at each other as if silently conveying who our next spokesperson should be. Everyone around us is looking over, too. The police presence has brought a weird kind of hush over the beach.

'Zane Johnson?' The officer looks inquisitively at me, probably because I've just described Cameron. I look away, and Marty steps in. For the first time since I laid eyes on him two days ago, I'm grateful. Zane is the last person I wish to bring to mind and describe after what happened between us when we were young. I've just about managed to tolerate him since he turned up at the airport the other day, but only just.

'He's also around my height,' Marty begins, 'though maybe a bit taller with brown, short hair.'

'He has a beard too?'

'No, he's clean-shaven, and he was wearing black shorts.'

'Eye colour?'

'I haven't got a clue.'

'Brown,' I say, probably too quickly. Andy gives me a funny look using his eye which isn't swollen.

'Well, we've known Zane a long time, haven't we?' *Too long.* It was a relief to finally get things off my chest over lunch to Siobhan about him. Perhaps what I've told her *could* have something to do with him and Becky not coming back. But it still wouldn't explain anything about Cameron also disappearing into thin air.

'And Becky Johnson?' The officer looks at me again.

'She's got light brown hair down to here.' I point at my shoulder to indicate the length. I could say *mousy*, but I doubt he'd understand what I mean. 'It's tied up in a ponytail, I think.' I gather my hair into a ponytail to demonstrate.

'She has blue eyes and lots of freckles.' Siobhan dots them onto her face with her finger to show him.

'And she was wearing a blue, all-in-one swimsuit.' Tina smooths her hands up and down her middle. Andy looks the other way as she speaks. What a mess. I know how guilty he's been feeling about his boys, but now that our affair is out in the open, there's probably no turning back for either of us.

'One of you knows where those three are,' the officer demands, his voice stern and the eyes beneath the peak of his cap marble-hard. It isn't a question, it's a statement. 'We need them found. Right now.'

None of us speaks, but a few looks pass between us all, almost in silent condemnation of one another. The policeman is correct. One of us *must* know something. But what, and about *who,* is another matter.

'We need a statement from you all,' he says. 'And to begin a search. And we need to know what happened there?' He points at my fat lip.

'I banged it while I was out there.' I raise my hand to my face.

'And him?' The officer gestures towards Andy.

'There was a bit of a fight earlier today.' They don't need to know it happened while we were out at sea. 'But it's nothing – it's all sorted now.'

Tina snorts. 'Just hold—'

'Wait – over there.' I point into the distance at the flash of red shorts striding across the sand from one of the beach bars towards us. 'It's Cameron.'

～

Since my husband showed his face, having disembarked on the *other* side of the swimmers' enclosure, he's managed to convince the police that his only involvement in any problems is thumping Andy. Andy doesn't want to press charges, so it seems that will be that. However, Cameron hasn't convinced *me*.

'Becky and Zane must be *together*,' he says while the two officers are standing at a slight distance from us, conferring over something.

I stifle a laugh. *No shit Sherlock.*

'Maybe they're faking their deaths so someone can claim off their insurance and then pay it back to them?' Marty grins.

Tina glances at him in disgust, then immediately averts her eyes in the opposite direction. She's getting good at giving looks that could kill at the moment.

'They wouldn't be able to afford insurance.' Andy's hunched over himself, and his shoulders are starting to burn. I should tell him to put some lotion on, but I don't want to sound like his mother. Or his wife.

'Who asked *you*?' Cameron glares at him. 'Shut your fucking mouth before I shut it for you. Again.'

Both officers look over at us. 'Stop it,' I hiss.

'Look, we need to put the shit between us to one side before we make things any worse.' Andy raises his palm at Cameron. 'Two of our crew are missing. That's all that matters right now. Once they've been found, that's when we can iron out our differences.'

Cameron, with his face like thunder, doesn't reply. But there's more chance of plaiting fog than *him* ironing out any differences. God knows where we're going to go from here.

I avert my eyes in time to notice a look pass between Siobhan and Marty. Their unspoken communication is either because of the drama between me, Cameron and Andy, or else it's something to do with Becky and Zane. Has Siobhan repeated what I told her over lunch?

'What is it with *you* two?' I switch my gaze between her and Marty. 'What's with the loaded looks?'

Neither of them reply.

I need a drink. I shouldn't be thinking of alcohol while my friend's still missing, but part of me is inclined to agree with Marty. Becky *must* be up to something out there. It seems strange that both she *and* Zane are missing. Maybe they *were* planning something when they met earlier for lunch. Maybe it *is* some kind of scam.

She's always been so easily led, and I certainly wouldn't put *anything* past Zane.

41

BECKY

I LINGER among the crowd at the beach bar, continuing to watch as I have for the last twenty minutes. I can't believe the police are already over there, and reckon I'll have to get myself involved before too much longer. But with everything that's happened, I'm struggling to get myself back together.

'It's *Becky*.' Siobhan jumps to her feet with a gasp and throws her arms around me. 'Where the hell have you been? I've been worried sick about you.'

'Cameron dropped me at the shore earlier.' I point at him and he nods as if to confirm what I'm saying.

'When? So where have you bloody been?'

'Not long ago. I've only been in the toilet.' I jerk my thumb in the direction of the beach bar. 'I wasn't feeling well.'

'And you didn't think to tell us when we were worrying about her?' Tina snaps at Cameron. All eyes turn to him.

'Yeah, well, I guess I didn't know – I assumed she must have rode back out to sea again.' I've never seen it before, but

Cameron appears to colour up. 'I dropped her here well before our hour was over.'

'You are Zane Johnson's wife?' The female officer approaches me. She looks like something out of Baywatch with her blonde hair tucked beneath her *KPA* baseball cap and her flawless olive skin.

'Yes.' That I'd prefer to be with Cameron doesn't come into play right now. Instead, I have a part to perform. I *am*, after all, still Zane's wife.

'You tell us where he is please?' The officer arches one of her perfectly shaped eyebrows.

'He *was* out there.' I point out to the horizon, my emphasis on the word 'was' conveying my doubt. After all, as far as anyone knows, he *could* have also returned to shore unnoticed, like I did.

'Was he alone?'

'Yes. Like Cameron just told you, I came back here with *him*. But I thought Zane would be back by now as well.' I glance at my watch, however it's not like I need anyone to tell me we should have all been back here quite some time ago.

'Ride closed,' announces the activities assistant – the same one who organised our rides earlier – as she steps forward to intercept a group of eager holidaymakers.

They slow to a halt, frowning in confusion until their eyes drift over to where we're gathered. Their expressions shift from curiosity to what could be silent judgment. We're the reason their fun has been curtailed.

'Not feeling well, you say?' The other officer steps closer.

Marty's watching me like a hawk as I answer the questions being asked of me, as are Siobhan and Cameron and my heart's hammering against my ribcage. Whenever I'm in the presence of a police officer, I imagine I look guilty, whether or not I've done anything wrong.

We all turn at once as the unmistakable growl of engines

rises behind us, slicing through the thick, sunbaked air. The sound grows louder, urgent, out of place against the lull of waves and tourist chatter.

A young man in a matching t-shirt and shorts – part of the same crew as the blonde activities assistant – stands upright as he nears the shore. He throws an arm back towards the second rider behind him – a young woman.

'We have missing jet ski,' he calls, his accent thick. 'We bring it back — but no man.'

A hush settles over our group, followed by a sharp intake of breath from someone beside me.

'So he's missing?' The more senior-looking officer of the two narrows his eyes, scanning our faces before focusing on the young assistant. 'He's in the water?'

The man nods, his expression tight.

The officer turns away from us and raises his radio to his mouth. His voice is low but clipped as he speaks rapidly in Dutch. Only two words punch through the language barrier.

Zane Johnson. My husband.

Siobhan nudges me gently, her brow furrowed. 'Are you OK?'

I stare at the place where the sea meets the sky. 'I don't know.'

'Things will be fine,' she says softly. 'You'll see.'

The others are watching me, no doubt expecting hysteria, panic, screaming, and demands for the police to search the water. But instead, I feel oddly still. Like something inside me has gone numb. It hasn't hit me yet. Or maybe it has, just in a different way.

Zane is missing. But I'm sure the police will find him.

42

BECKY

THE HORDES of holidaymakers have just been ordered out of the sea, herded away from the shoreline like cattle. Even we weren't spared. Now we're waiting under the flimsy shelter of the beach bar awning, sipping at plastic cups of iced water.

The shade offers little relief from the sun. My head pounds with the threat of a migraine – part hangover, part dehydration, but mostly raw, consuming stress. I've never felt like this before. The air's too thin, the ground's too hot, and my heart's too loud.

Above us, a helicopter circles like an angry wasp in the sky. Out on the water, search boats zigzag over the waves with a sense of urgency. Every time one slows, I feel like I stop breathing.

Around me, the others sit hunched and silent. For a group usually incapable of shutting up, the stillness is unnerving. No one meets each other's eyes.

'How long has it been?' Siobhan whispers.

I glance at my watch. 'Well over an hour.'

I check my phone again. My stomach knots as I scroll to Zane's name – and there it is. The last message I received from him.

> Meet me for lunch, Bex. We can get beyond all this, can't we? Let's sort ourselves out and to hell with the rest of them. Zx

'Did Zane say much to you when you had lunch together?' Jo asks. At least she and Andy have put a more respectable distance between themselves since things became more serious.

'Nothing out of the ordinary." I frown at her before glancing at the officer who's been assigned to wait with us since the search began.

I probably need to watch every word I say with this being a missing persons investigation. I widen my eyes at Jo as if to convey, *let's leave the husband and wife swapping shit out of all this*. I still can't quite believe what we all did last night, but it pales into insignificance with all we've got going on today.

The officer's radio crackles, and he raises it to his lips, looking at us cautiously before speaking. I don't know what he's worrying about. It's not as if any of us understand any Dutch.

'How are you holding up, hon?' Jo asks gently, reaching for my hand.

'What does she care?' Before I can answer, Tina scoffs. 'She's never liked Zane.'

'Alright, Tina,' Siobhan warns, shooting her a sharp look.

But Tina's not finished. 'Well—apart from liking him a bit *too* much at the start. No wonder you got blind drunk at their wedding. Just like you did at ours, eh, Jo?'

Jo draws her hand back, her face stiffening. The sting of Tina's words hangs between us.

She's not wrong. Jo did drink herself into oblivion that night – Siobhan and Tina had to carry her out and pour her into a taxi. But that's not a memory I care to unbox. Our wedding is a day I'd rather forget.

'We've found a man in the water.' The officer's voice brings me back into the moment.

Andy's hand flies to his mouth. 'Oh my God. Is it—?'

An endless pause endures as a look passes between the two colleagues.

'Is he—?'

One of them nods at the other. 'The man is deceased.'

A stunned silence settles over us, dense and suffocating, as I let the words sink in. *The man is deceased.* Have they found Zane?

His name echoes inside me like an old song. At fifteen, he was my everything – my first love, my forever plan. I used to picture us growing old together, grey-haired and still laughing.

But that was a lifetime ago. And now, as the others shift uncomfortably around me, my face is still, my breath is even. I guess I'm in shock.

'Oh, Becky.' It's Jo's voice again. I'm biting back the words threatening to spill from me. *Don't talk to me. Please don't talk to me.*

Instead, I shield my eyes from the sun, trying to make out what's happening out to sea. I can feel Cameron's gaze on me. The horizon suddenly seems darker, and everything looks like it's gone into slow motion, or maybe that's just how my brain's working.

The helicopter rises back into the sky. Perhaps now that the discovery of a man has been made, it's no longer needed. The weight of someone's hand lands on my shoulder, Cameron's, I hope. Voices resume, but I don't hear a word of what they're saying. My husband is missing, and they've found a man dead. It doesn't take an expert to join up the dots.

Practicalities start marching through my mind like soldiers. What will happen to his body? I haven't got any money for him to be flown back to the UK. We didn't have insurance. I can't even afford a funeral.

More police officers have descended onto the beach as if from nowhere, and several of them are tying cordon tape between the two beach bars, sealing off the area as if it's a crime scene. Others push the sunbathers and swimmers even further from the shoreline, their cheerful beach day now soured by something darker.

Our group remains rooted in place, suspended in the unbearable stillness between not knowing and knowing too much. No one's telling us anything. But one thing is clear, we won't be allowed to simply wander back to our villa.

They'll want statements, more details and exact timelines. And probably a trip to the police station.

My stomach twists, the remnants of my last meal gurgling uneasily. The last meal I shared with Zane. The last time we sat side by side, our knees touching under the table. The last supper, I suppose.

I don't take my eyes away from the officer, still speaking into his radio. It seems to be all in his hands.

'What's going on?' Siobhan asks when he pauses his conversation.

'Everyone gives a statement at the station.' I was right. He looks around — maybe for backup from his colleagues. 'I organise the cars. You go one at a time.'

Oh my God. They're going to separate us. That can only mean one thing – someone here is being looked at. Once we end up at that police station, being interrogated under fluorescent lights, I have a nasty feeling that one of us won't be coming back out of there.

43

SIOBHAN

I DIDN'T EXPECT to end up somewhere like this on our 'holiday,' this sun-beaten building in Oranjestad, the capital of Aruba. I think Jo's been brought to this station too – but Marty, Becky, Cameron and Andy have all been taken to different police stations or Politie Bureaus, as they call them here. It's about the only Aruban phrase I've got a grasp of.

I'm not being held, I'm here voluntarily, but I have a sense that I wouldn't be allowed to leave even if I tried. I'm told this is an interview room I'm sitting in – at least they haven't made me wait in a cell. They keep bringing water, and they've offered food, which I've refused up to now. My stomach's too wound up to eat a thing.

Formal identification hasn't taken place yet, but we all know. None of us said anything out loud, but the weight of it was pressing down as we were led to our respective police vehicles. It's Zane they've found. Who else could it be?

I had a brief, clipped phone call with someone from the legal firm that's being dispatched to assist me – their voice professional and detached. They told me the body's been taken for autopsy and toxicology.

I don't know how long I've been waiting for them to arrive, but it feels like forever. The police confiscated our phones and our Apple watches from those of us who have them. Therefore, all I can do is sit here and go over and over everything in my head. And I'm driving myself demented.

Finally, footsteps beat their path to the door of the room I'm contained in. I hold my breath. Are things going to get underway? I can't sit here for much longer.

'You can talk now or wait for lawyer?' The officer who brought me in here, the lowest-ranked 'agent,' pokes her blonde ponytailed head around the door.

I shake my head. 'Like I've said, I'll wait for the lawyer, thank you.'

Outside, I hear a laugh which is far too light for a dismal place like this before the door clicks shut and the officer's footsteps fade away back along the corridor.

She's asked me this question three times, but there's no way I'm speaking in a foreign police station about a suspicious death without a lawyer by my side. *Anything* I say could be misconstrued, so it's not worth the risk. I told Becky and Marty to do the same before they were led away, but I bet they don't. I was shot a filthy look by the female officer leading me as I said it. Becky will be of the mind that she can't afford a lawyer, and Marty won't want to hold things up. He'll want to get back out of the police station as swiftly as possible. Who wouldn't?

I'm also waiting for an interpreter, and I've asked for the British Consulate to be notified of our whereabouts. It's a precaution – or at least that's what I'm telling myself.

But the truth is, I don't know what's coming next.

Are they just taking statements, or will we have to give full, recorded interviews?

When Zane was simply missing, it all felt procedural and routine. But now that a body has been pulled from the water, a huge shift has taken place. This isn't routine anymore.

Their Last Days of Summer

Whatever it's turning into, my stomach seems to know it, and it coils more tightly with every passing minute.

44

SIOBHAN

I TAKE A SIP OF WATER, its chill sliding to my stomach. All I want to do is to be able to lie down. Perhaps it would have been better if they'd locked me in a cell, at least I *could* have had a lie down, rather than sitting here, as if waiting to be hung, drawn and quartered. I wonder if the others are still waiting, like me, and whether they're managing to stay calm.

The room's smaller than I would have expected, to say that it will hold me, a couple of officers, my lawyer, interpreter and maybe someone from the British Consulate. And it's chilly, as if the air con has been cranked up deliberately to persuade me to speak to the police in a more timely way. Even in the chill, my skin's burning from the extended time sitting outside at the hottest part of the day. I don't mind this time on my own, though. Not after being with the others non-stop for almost seventy-two hours, including the time at the airport and the flight.

At least now I can gather my thoughts, keep myself calm and ensure I'm speaking with confidence when I run the officers through today's events. They'll be disappointed with my statement when I say I was with Marty the whole time. When I confirm, that to my knowledge, there were no issues with Zane, not between him and his wife, or between him and anyone else. I can let them know about his money problems, about how *they* might have driven him to the edge of something drastic. But that's all I can say. The police might be suspicious now, but eventually they'll have to chalk Zane's death up to either something self-inflicted or to some terrible accident having taken place. At least I bloody hope so. The alternative doesn't bear thinking about.

A camera blinks silently in the corner. Is it switched on? Are they watching me? Are they allowed to watch me when I'm not even under arrest? The table beneath me is pitted with age, its corners softened by years of elbows and anxious fingers. It smells of disinfectant in here, but there's something fainter underneath. Maybe the stench of fear.

What happens to criminals in Aruba? Is the death penalty in place here? I know so little about the tiny island I chose for us to celebrate our fiftieth birthdays on. One thing is for certain – this is a 'holiday' which won't be forgotten in a hurry.

I wonder how Becky's holding up and hope the police are taking decent care of her. She went rigid when the news broke that a man's body had been found, and barely spoke a word. They were pretty up and down, her and Zane, but no matter what, all this is going to take her some serious coming back from.

'You still want to wait?' It's a male officer this time – dark and good-looking, almost with a look of Marty. 'Your friends have spoken – Jo? She did not wait. She back in sunshine.'

Why doesn't this surprise me? 'How much longer?'

'We just had call on the phone. Your lawyer will be sixty minutes.'

I've waited for this long now – it wouldn't make sense to give up after all this time. 'What about the consulate and the interpreter?'

He shrugs. 'We wait too. It's your choice.'

'Is there any more news on the reports? The man?'

'I can't tell you. We can say soon.' The door falls closed again, leaving me alone with my anxious thoughts.

I wonder what Jo said for them to let her go so quickly. Perhaps I should have just made a statement and got myself out of here as well. But at least by waiting, I might find out more about what they learn from the body they've found.

The walls of the station are thick – suffocatingly so. Whatever noise might exist beyond them can't be heard. There's no hint of the sea breeze, and no echo of island life. It's hard to believe this grey, soulless building sits in the middle of a Caribbean paradise.

Outside, the sun will still be shining. The sky will still be postcard blue. But for us, paradise has rotted from the inside out. This place, this trip, has become the backdrop for something unthinkable.

And not for the first time.

Since I spoke to Jo at lunchtime, I can't stop replaying that other sun-soaked day. Whitby. The air was just as warm, the tourists just as carefree — all laughter and fish and chips and seagulls overhead.

But not for us. Not then. That day was bright on the surface, but underneath it all, we were carrying a different kind of storm. Not death this time, but the opposite. A beginning. The birth of a baby.

Jo's baby.

As I sit, waiting to be questioned, I realise that everything was unravelling long before Zane's body was pulled from the water.

The truth didn't begin in Aruba. It began with the secret we left behind in Whitby.

45

THIRTY-FOUR YEARS AGO

'The other three of you still need to get ready.' Miss Smith stands over Jo's bed with her hands on her hips, looking from her to us with a puzzled expression. 'She seemed right as rain yesterday.'

'Well, she wasn't last night.' If guilt is written over our faces, Miss Smith doesn't appear to be reading it. 'Anyway, Mrs Lawson is going to wait here with Jo until we can reach her mother.'

'Isn't she answering?'

'Not at the moment,' our teacher replies.

'The story of my life.' Jo's head lolls to one side, and my heart goes out to her. Once, during a sleepover, she was throwing up, but ended up having to stay with us anyway when her mother couldn't be reached.

'The rest of us need to be on our way.' Miss Smith taps her watch. 'We have another full itinerary today, starting with a boat ride.' She strides to the door. 'Come along girls, it's beautiful out there.'

'You can't leave me on my own.' Jo reaches for my hand as I

begin to rise from where I've been slumped on her bed. 'Please, Siobhan.'

'You know I've got to. But you're going home to your own bed, which is what you wanted, isn't it?'

Jo closes her eyes, clearly beaten by her ordeal, as she turns her head away from me. Part of me is relieved that her mother will pick her up shortly, as we've shouldered far more responsibility than we ever should have done. Jo might not be close to her mum, but the rest of us are close to ours, and we're all being forced to stay quiet even when what's happened is massive. The truth can *never* come out. I dread to think what would happen to us all.

'It isn't over yet, is it?' Becky nods at the door as Tina reappears, her eyes appearing shrunken in her pasty face after yet another bout of throwing up. No one replies. We all know exactly what she means.

They've yet to discover the rucksack.

∼

'What happened to the towels?' I hiss at the others as they walk slightly in front of me. Both their faces are downcast, and their hands are thrust deep into their pockets. We've dropped back from the rest of the group as we head down to where Miss Smith has booked an evening meal for us all. We don't tend to mingle with the other girls in our class at the best of times, but for obvious reasons, we've kept ourselves to ourselves even more lately. Especially today – I don't know how we've kept it together. It wasn't so bad on the boat ride, where we were all sitting in pairs and able to face forward and not talk to anyone else. But after lunch, we had to take part in a load of 'team building' exercises and games on the beach. How were we ever supposed to forget what we've done and act like we were having fun?

'One towel's stuffed down the side of my bunk, and the other was wrapped around the–the—' Tina can't say the word, I don't think I'd be able to either.

I've been wrestling with the urge to go to the church, but I'm terrified of what I'll find if I do.

'They're going to find it sooner or later,' Becky whispers. 'And what if they trace the towel back to the youth hostel? What else was it wearing?'

Tina falls back in line with us. 'Just the towel.' Her voice wobbles.

Seagulls soar around, holidaymakers saunter in and out of shops, and everyone's wearing sandals, sunglasses and a smile. Everyone, apart from the three of *us*, that is. I've never felt more terrible in my life.

'Oh God.' Becky's sandals slap against the concrete as she stops dead. 'The bag.'

'What about it?'

'It's bound to be shown on the news.' She clutches at her chest. 'All this *won't* end up on the news, will it?'

'It probably will.' My insides sag even further. 'But maybe only in Whitby.' I glance up at the Abbey and the church at the top of the steps. 'I've seen this sort of thing before, and they'll be wanting to find out who the mother is – in case she needs any medical help.'

'And what if she does – we've just left her in that bunk on her own. She said she was bleeding—' The end of Tina's sentence is drowned out by a raucous seagull.

'Mrs Lawson's with her.' I'm trying to keep us all calm, but it's getting harder. What we've done is massive.

'What if Mrs Lawson realises what's happened?' Becky's becoming as panicked as Tina.

'How can she if no one tells her? She's no reason not to believe that Jo isn't just having bad period pain, has she?'

'I want to know who the lad is that got Jo into this mess,'

Becky says. 'The person who's walked away scot free, leaving *us* to sort it all out.'

'Me too,' Tina agrees. 'But she just won't tell us, will she? I must have asked her a dozen times.'

'Get a move on. We'll be late for our booking at The Magpie.' Miss Smith's voice is shrill as she waits for us to catch up. 'I don't know what's been up with you girls since we got here.'

No one replies. What could we even say?

'Jo will be fine, you know.' Her tone quietens. 'It's probably just a bug. So long as it doesn't go round us all, as I'm not letting *anything* spoil my fish and chips.'

It's the best fish and chip restaurant in Yorkshire, according to *my* parents, but I couldn't eat a thing. Imagining that poor baby zipped inside the school bag is making me feel ill.

But it's too late to change a thing.

'It doesn't bear thinking about – the poor little mite.' Miss Smith shakes her head as she points at the headline on the sign outside the newsagents. The early evening newspapers are out, and the baby is the top story.

'Oh my God,' Becky hisses. 'Look.'

'Try to stay calm,' I hiss back. 'We need to act normal.'

'What's going to happen to us?' Tina's voice is faint.

'Just stop it,' I whisper.

What's happened is a nightmare. I'm not sure how we expected it all to turn out, but it wasn't like *this*.

'I'm just going to the loo, Miss.' I point to the toilet block at the other side of the cobbled street from our queue into The Magpie.

But Miss Smith isn't listening. She's too busy replying to our other teacher. 'I can't believe how near to here it's been left. I wonder if they're anywhere close to finding the mother – I bet it's a young lass.'

'What's happened, Miss?' Someone shouts from further down the line. I need a few minutes on my own. I can't breathe. What if she puts two and two together and relates this news story to Jo being ill in bed?

~

The other dorms have quietened down far earlier than they did last night, when it sounded like everyone was in party mode. It's as if a more sombre air has descended after the discovery of the baby in a rucksack so close to the youth hostel.

'You still haven't told us who the father is.' Perhaps now that the baby is no longer inside her, Jo might be more willing to say. Out of the four of us, she's the only one who's dared to have sex with a boy, and I can't believe she never even told us about it at the time.

Becky's got a steady boyfriend, Zane, who she's been with for over a year, and he keeps going on about how he wants them to go all the way, but she says she's not ready. I hope he doesn't keep trying to pressure her and carries on being patient. I'd hate for Becky to end up like Jo has.

'I can't tell you.'

Poor Jo. Her blonde hair is matted with tears as she turns away from our three expectant faces. Despite repeated phone calls, her mother hasn't phoned to arrange to collect her. Miss Smith even sent someone from the school to knock on the door of their house, but there was no reply. Maybe it's just as well. Perhaps the three of us will take better care of her than Jo's mother would.

'I don't see why whoever's done this to you shouldn't take some of the blame and the guilt.'

'Why can't you tell us? Why are you protecting him?' I can't understand why she's keeping his identity to herself. The four of us usually tell each other *everything.*

'It wasn't that guy from the youth club, was it?' Becky narrows her eyes. 'The older one?'

'Who do you mean?' I look from Jo to Tina.

'*You'd* gone away to Ireland when they were flirting all the time,' she replies. 'He was in the upper sixth form. We had to pretend we were sixteen to get in, using fake IDs.'

'Oh yes, I know who you're on about.' Tina nods.

Jo closes her eyes. I can tell Becky and Tina are getting warm, whichever lad from the upper sixth form they're talking about.

'You know *exactly* who I mean, Jo.' Becky persists. 'The nice-looking one that wouldn't give me or Tina the time of day. He only had eyes for *you.*'

Jo might not have much recognition at home, apart from a mother who spends a ton of money on her to make up for it, but the attention she lacks from her mum and stepdad is made up for with the number of boys who are always after her.

'What's his name?' Becky scrunches her face up as if she's trying to remember. 'Was it *him* who did this to you?'

'How come this is the first *I'm* hearing about this lad?' I look at Jo. 'I can't believe you haven't said anything about going with someone from the sixth form.'

'It *was* him, wasn't it?' Becky tugs at Jo's shoulder. *He* got you into this mess.' She exchanges a glance with Tina.

Jo's silence says it all as she scrunches herself into a tighter ball beneath her sheet.

46

TINA

'Is SIOBHAN *STILL* AT THE STATION?' Becky looks up from where she's nursing a glass of wine at the patio table.

'I can't understand why she's been this long.' Jo shakes her head. 'The rest of us made our statements and were allowed to leave straightaway. Why should *she* be any different?'

I stare at Jo. How dare she act like she hasn't done anything wrong? That she's been enjoying a three-month affair with my husband seems to have paled into insignificance after the discovery of what is more than likely Zane's injured body, two miles from the shore. The others might have put what Jo's done to one side, but I can hardly stand breathing the same air as her.

Andy's lying down in our room, so I can't go in there to escape her. I haven't a clue what to say to my husband right now. We've yet to thrash out a way forward after what he's admitted to – what they've *both* admitted to. If I were to try speaking to him, I'd either make a fool of myself by begging him to reconsider, or I'd lay into him again. I'm dreading telling our boys. I haven't done anything wrong, but I feel like they'll still blame me. Our home life, as we've always known it, is about to be blown apart – because of *her*.

'I'm starting to get worried,' I say. 'Why the hell has she been so long?'

'It's not as if *Siobhan* would have had anything to do with Zane's death.' Jo frowns, but her voice is too nonchalant, as if she doesn't even care that he's dead. And after how he treated *me* last night, I'm finding it hard to be upset too, but I'm still sad for Becky.

Zane's death. Becky visibly sags at Jo's words. I think it's starting to sink in with her. It's inconceivable to think both she and I began this holiday, only two days ago, as married women. Now look at us.

'We still don't know that it's *Zane*.' But I can tell from the look on her face that my well-meaning words have had little impact.

'How are you doing?' As I reach for Becky's hand, I glance through the open patio door to where Marty and Cameron are sitting inside at the kitchen table, also clutching glasses.

We've agreed to only drink one or two to take the edge off things. After all, the police could turn up here again at any time to ask us more questions, so we need to keep clear heads. We've been told none of us can leave the island without their permission.

I can't even let Mum know to hold off on organising tickets for me to return home, since the police still have our phones. I can't imagine what they might hope to find on them, but like I was told, they have a protocol to follow.

'I'm just numb, I guess,' Becky replies. 'It doesn't feel real yet. And until I can identify him, I probably won't believe it's even *him*.'

'You won't have to face that on your own.' Jo clasps her hands in front of her on the table.

'No, *I'll* be there with her,' I retort. 'And she doesn't need an entourage.'

'Look, I know I've done wrong, Tina, but you don't have to act like I'm something you've stepped in.'

As if she's bleating like this after how she's treated *me*. And, as I now know, Becky as well. I couldn't believe it when Zane admitted last night to sleeping with Jo when we were teenagers. 'After you, I've just got to get Siobhan into bed and I'll have had all four of you.' Then he'd grinned. 'It's just a shame *she* didn't want to be part of our game. Instead, I've drawn the short straw with you, haven't I?'

Then he wondered why I couldn't bear to be anywhere near him and went to the sofa in the kitchen to sleep there.

'We've been through so much together, the four of us, haven't we?' Jo goes on. 'Just think about it. How many friendships last for as many years as ours?'

I can't reply. Nor can I imagine our friendship lasting much longer.

'Tina, *please.*'

Jo's so self-centred, she seems to think we're going to sideline the fact that she's been sleeping with my husband, that Zane is missing, presumed dead, and that Siobhan's still stuck at the police station. Instead, she thinks we'll turn our full attention to how *she's* feeling.

'Look, your friendship means *way* more to me than any man, Tina.' Jo's turned to *me* now, but has lowered her voice as if she doesn't want Andy to hear.

'What are you saying? That you've caused all this trouble, then—'

'I'm totally confused.' She drops her head into her hands. 'I never said I wanted to leave Cameron. I don't know what I want right now.'

Does this mean that she'd choose my friendship over her affair with my husband? Not that I'd suddenly want to stay married to Andy just because Jo's suddenly become acquainted with her conscience. It's too little, too late.

'The last thing I want is for you to hate me, Tina.' Jo's voice is small. 'Not after all our years of being friends.'

'I think we've got more important things to worry about right now, haven't we?' The vision of the scene on the beach fills my mind again. The emergency services swarming like bees, and the glint of their vehicles in the bright sunlight. Then the deathly hush that fell over the formerly fun-filled sands when it became apparent that a body had been found.

I wasn't there when the boat containing the body arrived back at the shore – I was in the back of a police car by then. But Marty's was the last car to leave the beach. I overheard him saying to Cameron that he'll never forget what he saw – the body, shrouded in a white sheet, being stretchered from the boat into the back of a private ambulance.

The fact that there *is* a body has blown apart all the *faking his own death* theories about Zane that Marty was coming out with earlier.

There's nothing fake about a dead body.

47

TINA

'I was talking to the taxi driver about what's happened,' Jo says.

'Surely you shouldn't be talking to *anyone* about an ongoing investigation.' Yes, I probably do watch too many crime thrillers to escape my monotonous life of term time and home time, but I'm sure I'm right.

'He said that the kill switches on jet skis aren't a hundred per cent safe, and he should know as he owns one.'

Becky looks up from staring into her glass, her red-rimmed eyes stirring something in me. Something from that day, thirty-four years ago, the only other time we've had something as momentous as this happen in our collective lives.

'What else did he say?' There can be no mistaking the pain in Becky's voice as she turns to look at Jo. I can't imagine what she's going through right now. Looking at her as she crosses and uncrosses her legs and fiddles with her hair, it looks like she doesn't know what to do with herself.

'He knew of at least two occasions over the years after an accident where the throttle had jammed itself and the jetski had carried on going without the rider on board.'

'Eh?'

'One of those times, he said, the rider was hit by his own machine.'

'You're talking absolute crap.' Cameron's risen from his place at the table and is striding to the patio doorway, looking at his wife with derision. 'Hit by his own jet ski? You're clutching at straws now, aren't you?'

'Don't speak to me, not after how *you* behaved when we were out there.'

Becky shoots Jo a look. 'I have enough to contend with right now. More trouble breaking out between us – well, I can't cope with any more. In fact, I'm going inside - I'll leave the two of you to bicker between yourselves.'

'Jo could have a point.' Marty comes up behind Cameron as Becky pushes past them. 'Freak accidents happen all the time.'

'Like they did with the two of *you*, you mean.' I scowl at him. I've had just about enough of Marty's smug niceties. Yes, perhaps he *is* a reformed character, but it's about time he knew the extent of what he put us through all those years ago. Months of stress and years of belly-dragging guilt.

'What's that supposed to mean?' Marty steps forward beyond Cameron and folds his arms.

'Tina, please.' Jo's voice is a wail. 'Just leave it alone.'

'Oh, I've kept quiet for long enough on this holiday.' I rise to my feet.

'Just shut up, Tina.' Jo's face is tight with the sudden stress I've put her under. 'You've no idea what you're talking about.'

'There's been so much shit flung around already,' I begin, 'that we might as well let our other secret out, hadn't we?'

'What secret?' Cameron looks puzzled as he leans against the patio doorway.

'I'm warning you.' Jo points at me. 'You've got it all wrong.'

'I don't owe you any loyalty.' I swat her finger away like it's an irritating fly.

As for Marty, Mr Super-nice-guy-on-the-surface, well, he's about to be ousted. 'When Siobhan returns,' I go on. 'I have a responsibility to make sure she knows that she's *also* got a partner who our friend Jo here has slept with. So that's all of the blokes here, isn't it Jo?'

'Now you listen to me—'

'Marty's made his way around three of the women in our group. But Jo can go one better than that. She's made her way around *all four* men.' I resist the urge to add the word *slut* to my revelation again.

'What the hell are you talking about?' Marty's face is filled with incredulity. Evidently, he's going to try denying it.

'I should have told Siobhan what I knew when he turned up at the airport.'

'Told Siobhan *what?*'

I'm carrying on. No one can stop me now. 'Just how well acquainted Jo and Marty are.'

Marty steps closer to me. 'Actually, I've *never* been to bed with Jo.' His arms are still folded as if he's trying to maintain a protective barrier against me.

'You're a liar. You're the boy from the youth club. I remember you.'

'Whatever theories you've cooked up, Tina, you're completely wrong.'

Marty's voice is calm – too calm – like he thinks he can charm his way out of this.

'You and Jo.' I step forward, refusing to be silenced. I'm done being brushed aside. This time, people are going to hear the truth – whether they want to or not.

'Me and *Jo?*' His brow furrows. 'Sorry, love, you've lost me.'

'Don't call me *love* again. Ever.' My voice is ice. 'You might've been all smug smiles and swagger back in the youth club days, but *you* got Jo pregnant and disappeared like it was nothing. You left the rest of us to deal with the mess.'

There's a sharp silence. Then Cameron steps in front of Marty, his face rigid and his voice tight with fury. 'Wait. Are you telling me it was *you*?'

I had no idea Jo had even told Cameron about the pregnancy. I thought that secret was locked away and buried between the four of us.

How much *has* she told him? How much *does* he know? Does he know what happened to the baby? What we had to do?

'It was *you* who raped my wife?' Cameron takes a step closer to Marty. 'You who got her pregnant when she was only *fifteen*?'

The word hangs there – *raped* – like a crack of thunder. My breath catches. This is news to me. Jo never mentioned having been *raped*. Oh my God.

Even beneath his pink sun-glow, Marty's face has turned grey. 'No,' he stammers, shaking his head as he backs away from Cameron with the pool behind him. 'You've got it all wrong. I remember Jo from when we were young, but—'

Cameron's not listening. 'You evil bastard.' Within a split second, he's grabbed Marty by the throat and has forced him into the pool. He bends him backwards against the pool's wall. 'Do you know how much *damage* you caused?' He's snarling. 'And what she's had to live with all these years?'

'It wasn't me,' Marty gasps, trying to shake himself free, but Cameron's got him too tightly in his grip. 'You've got to listen to me.'

'Let him go, Cameron!' Jo is shrieking as her husband forces Marty's head beneath the surface of the water. I've never seen a man so fuelled with anger.

'What the hell's going on?' My husband emerges from the patio door.

Cameron drags a spluttering Marty back to the surface. 'I should hold you under until—'

'No – Cameron.' Andy charges forward. 'Whatever's going on, you can't—'

'This has got *nothing* to do with you.' I grab a fistful of Andy's t-shirt as he darts past me. I can't bear to watch my husband weighing in as part of Jo's defence. But with a bit of luck, this newfound allegiance towards Jo from Cameron might alter things between her and Andy. Perhaps there's more mileage in Jo and Cameron's marriage than she's allowed herself to believe.

'Get the fuck off me.' Marty's still trying to wriggle himself free as a glass of wine gets knocked over at the pool's side as they scuffle.

'Polis,' yells a voice from the gate as two officers jump from the car.

There's no doubt now that our so-called 'holiday party' will be under even more suspicion than before over Zane. The cracks between us all are gaping fractures with truths pouring through them.

At least Marty will now be held accountable for what he did. Thirty-five years too late, maybe, but at least Jo will get justice.

I had no idea Jo was raped. None of us did. We had no idea whatsoever that her pregnancy was a result of Marty forcing himself on her. The bastard.

I hope they throw away the key.

48

JO

Siobhan stumbles from the police car, dazed and unsteady. They were only supposed to drop her off after taking her statement, instead they've walked into *this* little drama, which is bound to sharpen the spotlight on us.

'Tina's told them all it was *Marty* who raped me when I was young,' I gasp as Siobhan reaches the pool.

One officer is already speaking urgently into his radio, likely calling for backup. The other hovers nearby, eyes flicking between my husband and Marty, clearly assessing whether it's safe to step in without immediate support.

Cameron still has Marty by the scruff of the neck, his knuckles white, his jaw clenched, and even with the police now present, he shows no intention of letting him go.

'You need to arrest this *person*.' He spits the word person out like it's something foul inside his mouth.

'Please, Cameron – it *wasn't* Marty.' Siobhan rushes towards the pool's edge, but the other officer holds her back. 'Let him go.'

'But Tina just—'

'Tina's got it all wrong, Cameron. Just let Marty go – and we can tell you what this is all *really* about.'

I glance at Becky, who's emerged from the doorway of the patio to see what's going on. Who knows how she's going to take this latest revelation on top of everything else?

The officer nearest the pool is unclipping handcuffs from his belt as he steps closer to Cameron and Marty.

'It's just a stupid argument,' I begin. 'We're all incredibly stressed about Zane – there's no need to arrest Cameron.'

'There *has* been a mistake,' Marty adds. 'Really – everything's alright here.'

~

'Well, that was a complete miracle.' Siobhan reaches into the fridge for a bottle of beer. 'I don't know how we managed to talk them down.'

I glance around the kitchen, struggling to comprehend what we've become – how this group has unravelled in just forty-eight hours. Andy's slumped at the table with a beer, looking like elephant man with the injuries Cameron's inflicted to his cheek.

Marty's sitting at the side of the pool with his feet dangling into the water, looking like he has the weight of the world on his shoulders. Meanwhile, Cameron's pacing around the kitchen with clenched fists, still absolutely wired. I've never seen him like this before.

'Jo, you need to tell everyone *exactly* what you told me earlier at the cafe.' Siobhan snaps the lid off her beer bottle. 'Marty, get in here please – you need to hear this as well.'

'Do I?'

I wrap my arms around myself and lean forward on the sofa. I nod towards Siobhan. 'Can you sit with Becky?' Like Tina, I also allowed Becky to assume *Marty* was the father of my baby all those years ago, and I don't know how she's likely to react to what she's about to hear with what she's already going through.

Now, with my captive audience, it's time to relive the nightmare from my teens for the *second* time today. It was bad enough when I had to go through it with Siobhan at lunchtime.

She was supposed to be telling the others, so I wouldn't have to. I really didn't think I'd be forced to go through it all again so soon.

∽

'Never mind *Andy.*' Siobhan didn't take her eyes from me as she turned my phone face down next to my plate. 'I want to hear the truth, Jo.'

'What about?' Of course I knew *what about* – I was just playing for time.

'Tell me how you and Marty already know each other?'

I should have known Siobhan wouldn't be able to leave this alone. It was a miracle that neither Becky or Tina had blurted their misguided knowledge to Siobhan about Marty already – probably because of everything else that's been going on.

'I'm waiting.' She drummed her fingers against the edge of her plate.

'Alright.' But still, I hesitated. I'd carried this burden for years, and once I'd told another person, that would be it. The floodgates would be open. There'd be no way Siobhan wouldn't act.

'You do know you can trust me, don't you, Jo?'

I nodded, my tears welling up. Of course, I could trust them all. Even knowing that, I'd still done the worst thing I could do to Tina. But it wasn't the time to think about Tina. 'Right, I'm going to tell you everything – do you remember just after *the baby* was born?'

If I'd closed my eyes, I'd have been able to see that sparse dorm room again with its yellow walls, navy carpet and curtains. I spent a whole day staring at it all as I surfed my waves of despair.

'How could I forget?' Siobhan's eyes weren't leaving mine as our barely touched food sat in front of us.

'I'm talking about when you were all jumping to conclusions,' I continued, 'about who the father might be?'

'What do you mean?' Then a look of realisation fell over her face like a screensaver. 'Are you saying the two of them thought it was *Marty*?' Siobhan's voice was a squeak.

I nodded. 'He was the boy from the youth club.' Her face fell. 'It's true – I *did* used to know him. We flirted a bit at the youth club on the two occasions I saw him there. Well, we flirted a lot, actually.'

'I *knew* there was *something*.' Her tone was snappy, and jealous even. 'As soon as I saw your face when I introduced the two of you.'

'It's not what you're—'

'How come I never saw him?' She tilted her head to one side. 'I'd never met him before I joined the gym.'

'You were at your grandparents in Ireland when we went to the youth club. It was around the new year before we turned sixteen. A couple of weeks before Annette Speight's party.'

'I remember *that*.' Siobhan pulled a face.

'Yeah – you were definitely back at home by then. I remember it all like it was yesterday, sadly. I only wish I didn't.' When I'm lying in bed, desperately trying to escape the confines of my mind, I remember it all too clearly.

'Did the two of you sleep together? Is that what you're trying to tell me here? You and Marty?'

I could tell how important my answer was to her by how intently she was staring at me.

'He was flirting madly with me, I can't deny that – but then it turned out that he already had a girlfriend.'

'So nothing happened between you?'

I shook my head as Siobhan's shoulders sagged with what was probably relief. I relaxed slightly as well.

'Nothing other than me making a fool of myself.'

'Surely *that* isn't why you've been so off with him since I introduced the two of you the other day?'

'Seeing Marty again has flicked a switch in Becky and Tina.'

'How do you mean?'

'It's all my fault.' I fanned my fingers across my collarbone. 'It was *me* who allowed you all to assume the father was the boy from the youth club. You couldn't put a face to him, but they could.'

'Marty?'

I nodded.

'But it wasn't him?'

I shook my head.

'So why did you let it ride?' Siobhan was strangely calm considering what I'd just told her.

'I didn't – I just didn't put Becky and Tina right when they guessed wrong. It was easier that way. I had to hide who the father *really* was.'

Siobhan looked thoughtful, as if she was struggling to assemble what I was telling her. 'You need to tell me the truth about the baby's father, Jo. You've hidden it for long enough.'

'It looks like I'm going to have to.' As soon as this holiday was booked, I had a feeling my secret would emerge. I didn't want to come, but once everyone else had agreed, I'd have come across as a real killjoy if I'd backed out.

Siobhan wasn't taking her eyes off me as she waited for me to continue.

49

JO

'AFTER THE BABY, the four of us grew apart, do you remember?'

'We were doing different things, that's all,' Siobhan replied. 'Tina went into sixth form, you started college, I did my apprenticeship, and Becky revolved her life around Zane. But we still all loved the bones of each other, didn't we?'

I must have pulled a face at the mention of Zane's name. Siobhan jumped on it immediately. 'Hang on a minute, Jo – what's with the face? *Zane*?' She looked puzzled. 'You've been off with him as well since the airport, now I come to think about it.'

'You know me too well.'

'Come on, Jo – spill it.'

'I wanted to tell Becky so many times.' I wrapped my fingers around my coffee cup as though trying to draw comfort from its warmth. 'I wanted to tell *all* of you.'

'Tell all of us, *what*?'

I can hardly believe I'm going to tell her the truth, but I've got to. I haven't really got any choice.

'That he *raped* me.'

'Who? *What*?'

'Zane raped me. When I was fifteen.' There. I'd finally said the three words out loud – the first time I'd ever said them to *anyone*. I felt heavy, yet free in equal measure. Heavy that the enormous can of worms could now wriggle its way into everyone's holiday, but free in that I was becoming unburdened from a darkness that had dragged me into its centre for so many years.

'Oh my God.' Siobhan's hand fluttered to her mouth. 'Zane?'

'As he told me in no uncertain terms, Becky would *never* have believed me. *None* of you would have done.'

'Oh, Jo.' Siobhan reached for my hand across the table. I let go of the coffee cup, relief washing over me that she hadn't dismissed what I'd told her. 'I would *always* have believed you.'

'There's no way Becky would have. Or Tina.'

'I think you're wrong there.'

Both of us fighting back tears was inviting curious looks from other cafe customers. There we were, on a beautiful Caribbean island, two friends, supposedly enjoying lunch together, slumped over our uneaten meals, looking like the world was about to end.

'Who'd have ever believed a girl with an already dodgy reputation, a girl most of the others were jealous of?'

'*We* were never jealous of you.' Siobhan squeezed my hand so tightly that my wedding ring dug into my skin. 'We knew you and we loved you.'

'Becky wouldn't have loved me if I'd blown things apart for her and Zane. He was her *everything* – after all the bullying she'd been through, she'd never been happier than when he showed an interest in her. She'd have *hated* me if I'd ruined it all, just like everyone in our year already did.'

Siobhan laughed through her tears. 'The haters were only ever jealous of how pretty you were. Well - you still are, of course.'

'I hated being *pretty*.' I drew air quotes around the word. 'It always brought me the wrong kind of attention. And as for Zane...' I hated having to speak his name, 'well, he was one of the most popular boys in our year, wasn't he? Sporty, good-looking...' My voice trailed off. I didn't want to think of the boy he was. The boy who had snatched any shred of dignity I had.

'Tell me what happened?' Siobhan's earnest blue eyes didn't leave mine. I could tell she completely believed me. But how Becky was going to react after all these years was likely to be another matter.

'It was that house party we went to – the one I just mentioned,' I began.

'Annette Speight's? When her parents had gone skiing that time?'

'Yeah.' Every last detail from that night has been etched into my memory like it happened last year – not thirty-four years ago. The flash of sequins, the sting of cold air on bare legs, the way the front door still had a sagging Christmas wreath hanging on it, even though it was nearly February.

There was snow on the ground, but we didn't care — we'd squeezed into the shortest skirts and the silliest heels, wobbling down the street like we owned the night.

2 *Unlimited* was blaring through the usually quiet cul-de-sac as Annette opened the door and ushered the four of us inside. The beat thumped through my chest, full of possibility, yet full of danger I was too young to recognise.

Siobhan, Tina, and Becky had all come to mine to get ready, giggling as they stuffed coats in bags and layered on lip gloss, careful not to let their mums see what they were really wearing.

Mine wasn't home – as usual. And even if she had been, she wouldn't have cared. Not about the heels. Not about the skirts.

Not about *me*.

'Annette had been allowed to have a few *girlfriends* round, if I remember correctly?' Despite the seriousness of what we were discussing, a small smile crossed Siobhan's lips. 'But a few girlfriends turned into around fifty teenagers.'

'Yeah, but the three of *you*,' I pointed at her, 'had been collected and taken home by ten pm. There was only me who was allowed out as late as I wanted. My mother didn't give a shit.'

'I was so jealous of you being allowed out late.' Siobhan's face relaxed into a sad smile. 'It's only now that I realise I was lucky having a strict dad. It's funny how things change when you've had kids— ' She cuts herself off. 'I'm sorry. Sometimes my mouth runs away with me.'

'Don't worry. Anyway, after the three of you had been picked up, things got *badly* out of hand.'

Siobhan frowned. 'I don't remember you telling us any of how things got out of hand.'

'I probably didn't – I'll have wanted to wipe the whole thing from my mind. Anyway, there were gatecrashers, much more drink, tablets – drugs.' I swallowed and wiped at my eyes with my sleeve. People were giving us sideways glances. 'But things got especially out of hand for *me*.'

Siobhan stayed quiet this time, clearly waiting for me to elaborate.

'I don't know if you can remember, but Zane was at the party that night.'

'Vaguely.'

'He'd given Becky quite a hard time for having to leave early. He was calling her boring and all sorts. She was quite upset about it.'

Siobhan scrunched her nose as if that might help her to remember. 'It's all such a long time ago.'

'Perhaps I'd have never said a word if Zane hadn't been bad-mouthing me to Tina last night.' Anger rose in me again at the memory of Tina's words in the steam room, *once a slut – always a slut.*

Their Last Days of Summer

'She hasn't told me anything about that. She said she was trying to process it all when I tried to get it out of her.'

'When it looked like Zane was going to get Tina into bed last night, he made some drunken wisecrack about how there was only *you* to go before he'd have laid all four of us. Tina realised then that *I'd* been with him and she's put her own two and two together.'

'And concluded that you'd seduced him behind Becky's back? Is *that* the reason why Tina was so pissed off with him this morning. Why she'd slept on the sofa?'

'This is what I'm trying to tell you.'

'Sorry. I'll shut up and listen.'

'Zane told Tina that really, he'd wanted *you* in bed last night but would have to settle for *her*.'

'In his dreams. I always thought he was a decent enough guy, but I would never have touched him with a bargepole in that sense.'

'Tina understood from Zane that him having slept with me was consensual. But it wasn't. He just took what he wanted and then left me on the ground.'

Siobhan didn't say a word, she just sat there, staring at me with tears in her eyes.

'When Tina had a go at me in the steam room this morning, she called me everything from a whore to a slapper. I've never seen so much hate in someone's face.'

'I thought it was Andy who you were fighting over.' She let out a long whistle.

I closed my eyes. 'I'm not proud of myself, you know. If I could turn the clock back, I'd have steered clear of him.'

'Jo, tell me how it happened with Zane.'

'Surely, you don't want me to go over it. Please Siobhan – I don't know if I can.'

'I need to get it straight in my mind. And *then*, I'll be able to fight your corner.'

'I can't lie.' I looked Siobhan in the eye. 'After you'd all left me at the party that night, I was slightly flattered by Zane's attention to begin with, after all, he was supposed to be besotted with Becky.'

'He *was* besotted with Becky.'

'And even knowing that, I still agreed for him to walk me home. It was freezing and he'd offered to lend me his coat.'

'Go on.'

'I was telling myself he was just looking out for me. And you've no idea how much I regret it.'

The hustle and bustle from the rest of the cafe may as well have not been happening. The crunch of the coffee grinder and the echo of barked instructions from one colleague to another. All that mattered was the presence of my friend and her believing me.

Tina jumped to her own conclusions on Zane's say-so from last night – without even coming to ask for my version. But after what I've done with her husband, no one could blame her.

'We were walking through the park towards my estate.' I paused. If I were to squint, the distant lights through the snowflakes that had begun to fall would emerge in my mind.

'What time was this?'

'Well after midnight. No one else was about, and at that point, I felt grateful that I had Zane to walk me back with it being so late.'

'And?'

'He was telling me about Becky *not putting out,* as he described it.'

'He said *what*?'

'I know – anyway, he said he knew *I'd* be different.' As I noticed the disgust on Siobhan's face, I rubbed at my forehead, aching with the tension I'd put myself under. 'I thought he was joking at first. But then he grabbed me.'

'He grabbed you? What do you mean, *forcefully*?'

'Not straightaway. It was only when I said, *what the hell do you think you're doing,* and tried to back away from him that he got a tighter hold of me. I tried to fight him off, Siobhan, I really tried.' I reach for the napkin to dab at my eyes. It was the first time I'd ever talked about it.

'Oh Jo.'

'It was only when I found myself pinned down on the grass, completely overpowered by him, that I realised he wasn't joking at all. I couldn't get out from under him, Siobhan, I couldn't—'

Suddenly, right there in that cafe, I couldn't breathe. I could smell his aftershave again, the stale lager on his breath, the weight of him crushing me beneath him. I dropped my head onto my arms against the table as if trying to shield myself from the rest of the world.

'But why — why—?'

'Why didn't I say anything?' I raised my head again, my bare arm soggy with fresh tears. 'Because he warned me that if I breathed a word, he'd tell everyone *I'd* come on to *him*.' The tears were cascading down my cheeks, but I was past caring what anyone thought. 'He threatened to make my reputation worse than it was already.'

'Oh come on, Jo. You didn't have a *reputation*. You only thought you had.'

I ignored her. She was only saying that to make me feel better.

'Is everything alright?' The gap-toothed waitress who'd brought our lunch was standing over us. I didn't know whether she meant with me or with the food.

'Erm, yes, sorry. We'll eat soon.' Siobhan looked up at her. 'Just some bad news, that's all.'

'I'm sorry to hear that.' The waitress moved on to another table, but I could feel the eyes of other cafe customers on me, probably dying to know what could be wrong.

'For weeks I went over and over in my head what I might

have done to lead him on,' I continued. *Everything* was tumbling out. 'You must recall how I started dressing in trousers and jeans instead of skirts and dresses? When I could still fit into them, that is.'

'I just wish you'd told me.'

'I couldn't. I just couldn't. And from the moment I escaped from him, and ran home, I worried he might have got me pregnant – he hadn't used anything.'

'I can't imagine what you must have gone through.'

'I just felt so cheap – so dirty.' I wiped again at the tears. 'But I kept telling myself it wouldn't happen – not the very first time of going with a boy. Not that I *went* with him.' My voice tapered off.

'This is horrendous.' Siobhan wiped at her eyes with a napkin. Our chicken wraps still sat virtually untouched, going cold in front of us. I couldn't have eaten a thing.

'After the baby had gone,' – I felt sick at having to say the word, *baby*, – 'I wore my hair scraped back in a ponytail and my face bare of makeup. Do you remember?'

'It's not how things should be.' Siobhan's expression darkened some more. 'Women should be allowed to wear what they want and look however they like without fear of what a man might read from their clothes and the amount of makeup they choose to wear.'

'I just never wanted it to happen again.'

'Becky's been married for all these years to a *rapist*?' Siobhan lowered her voice with the last word. English was understood too well around here to say the word out loud.

'If I could have spoken out back then, I would have done. I was just a terrified fifteen-year-old, and the more time that passed, the harder it became to tell the truth. All I could do was avoid him and allow the rest of you to believe I'd slept with an older lad from the youth club.'

'Marty.' Siobhan shook her head. 'Well at least I know the truth now.'

'Becky thought I was jealous of her.'

'I remember. She couldn't work out why all of a sudden, you wouldn't have anything to do with Zane.'

'Why do you think I got so drunk at their wedding?'

'Now I know about *this,* I'm surprised you went at all.'

'Only because of how it would look if I didn't. When the vicar said, *Does anyone know any reason why this man and woman shouldn't be joined in matrimony,* I don't know how I kept quiet.'

'I wish you'd spoken up.' Siobhan shook her head. 'Becky's going to have to know the truth – just as soon as I can get her on her own.'

'Does she *really* need to know?'

'Of course she does. Besides, I can't have her and Tina thinking the worst of Marty.'

'They only think I slept with him, not that...' My voice trails off again.

'A leopard doesn't change its spots,' Siobhan said. 'For all we know there could have been other girls – other women. Zane got away with it once, after all.'

I hung my head. If other women had been attacked, it would be all my fault. If I'd spoken up, he would have been punished years ago.

'You'll have to tell Becky,' I say. 'I can't do it. It would have been awful enough blowing her world apart back then – but it would be even harder now.'

50

BECKY

'I'M SO SORRY, MARTY.' Jo looks from where she's been staring at the patio table straight into his face.

The early evening air is heavy with silence apart from the occasional slop of the swimming pool water against the tiles in the breeze.

'I thought we'd never see you again after those times at the youth club – and it was far easier for the others to assume it was *you* for all these years, instead of the boyfriend, then husband of one of my best friends.'

'At least I know why you've all been so off with me.' Marty's expression is a cross between anger and dislike as he moves his gaze between the four of us. 'But no, as Jo just told you, I already had a girlfriend. But girlfriend or not, I could never have treated a girl like that *animal* did.'

His words are like a knife through my heart. I've been married to that *animal* they're all talking about for nearly thirty years. The breeze blows through my hair, cooling me slightly as the sun starts to sink in the sky. I'm glad it will be getting dark soon. It'll be far more in keeping with how I'm feeling.

Now Jo's finished telling us, Cameron reaches for her hand.

Clearly, he knew about much more than she'd ever told us, but he knew the *what* rather than the *who*.

I'm wrestling with whether I'd have believed her back then if she'd told me the truth about her pregnancy and what Zane had done to her. I'd like to think I would have done, but I'm not totally sure. But at least I believe her *now*.

When Siobhan shouted the truth at me earlier — the words that shattered everything I thought I knew – I didn't question her for a second.

Because somewhere deep down, I think I'd always known something like this would be the case.

I just hadn't let myself hear it until she finally said it out loud.

'It's nearly eight,' Siobhan says. 'The police will be back to take Becky to the hospital morgue soon.'

'How are you feeling, hon?' Tina reaches across the table and rubs my shoulder. 'Are you sure you're up to it?'

'I'll have to be.' My stomach twists. I don't know how I'll be when I have to look at him laid out. Dead. It will probably be a combination of guilt, shame, misery and hatred.

'I'll come with you,' Siobhan says. ' This isn't something you should do on your own.'

'But I'm his next of kin.' My voice is flat. Identifying his body is something I've got to do, I know it is, but it's going to be horrendous. I've been told to expect bruising, swelling and lacerations, all of which might make him hard to recognise. However, there's the thirty-three-year-old ZB tattoo on his chest to recognise him by, or the scar on his left shin from an old football injury.

I've never seen a dead body before, and certainly not one believed to be my husband. But of course, I could easily confirm here and now that it's Zane on the slab *without* having to physically see him. But if I did that, the police would realise that I was there at the moment he died, the whole time...

∼

'No, no, stop – Cameron!'

It was as if Jo had been waiting for her chance. Cameron had pulled up beside us to say something to Zane. Jo took the opportunity to slide from the other side of their seat into the sea like custard skin into a pudding bowl. Then, she'd powered through the waves towards the space at the back of Andy like he was all that mattered to her.

All I could do was to hold my breath as I waited to see how Cameron would react to his wife's behaviour. And react, he certainly did. Even before Jo had time to get comfy behind Andy, Cameron jumped into the water and was already on her tail.

As he reached them, he dragged Andy from his seat even faster than Jo got on behind him and started punching him in the face before he could do anything to defend himself.

At the sound of another approaching engine, I twisted in my seat. It was Siobhan and Marty. A spray of blood rose in the air as Cameron threw another punch, slamming Andy's head against the side of the engine. And then another.

'Stop it,' I shrieked again, resisting the urge to jump into the water, to swim over and attempt to break them up myself. But if I had, I'd have only got myself caught in the crossfire. Jo was just sitting astride the seat, shrieking like a banshee. If anyone had been able to stop Cameron, it would have been her, not *me*. 'Zane, do something!'

'What the fuck would *you* care?' He twisted around on the seat and snarled the words into my face. I couldn't believe it – what was wrong with him now? He'd been acting weird ever since Siobhan said she needed to speak to me.

I shuffled as far back in the seat as I could, away from my husband. Of course I cared that Cameron was knocking ten bells out of Andy. We were what felt like miles from the shore. What the hell were we going to do?

By then, Marty was in the water and attempting to restrain Cameron. Knowing Marty as I did from the past, it didn't sit comfortably that he was the only one trying to help, whereas my husband couldn't give a toss.

It also hurt that Cameron still cared enough about his wife to attack Andy in this way. I comforted myself with the knowledge that Jo jumping ship from Cameron to Andy had to be another nail in the coffin of their marriage. I couldn't imagine how they'd come back from how she was behaving.

'You just want Cameron for yourself, don't you?' Zane turned from where they were still fighting and shoved me in the ribs. 'After last night? Go on, admit it, I can read you like a book.'

'Just stop it, will you?' I snapped, my voice brittle with panic as I scanned the sea for an escape – any escape. I searched for an empty seat, even briefly considering throwing myself behind Tina if she was to turn up here, in spite of the tensions between us. Anyone would be better than staying here with Zane.

He could be charming, disarmingly so, but when that darker side surfaced, it was like being with a stranger. And lately, that stranger had been showing up far too often.

The man gripping the handlebars wasn't the one I married. Not anymore.

51

BECKY

THERE WAS ONLY one place I could swim to get away from Zane. Cameron's now-empty seat. But Cameron was already pounding his way through the waves back over to it, so I'd have to be quick.

Jo and Marty were tending to Andy's bashed cheekbone.

'And you, you nosy bitch.'

'Who the hell are you talking to?' I twisted around in my seat, my thoughts of escape interrupted for a moment while trying to look at my husband. Surely, he wasn't saying that to *me*.

Zane swung one of his legs over the handlebars so he was facing to the side, a sneer on his face as he surveyed Siobhan ten or so metres away. What on earth had *she* said or done that could be making Zane speak to her like that? It could only be to do with her plans to talk to *me*.

'Leave me alone, Zane – I bloody mean it.' Siobhan's eyes were marble hard, and her lip curled in disgust as she looked back at him. 'You've done more than enough damage.'

What did she mean? *What* damage? It must be what she'd said she wanted to talk to me about?

Their Last Days of Summer

'Take Andy back to the shore,' Marty ordered Jo. 'Just in case there's any damage after those blows to his head. But take it steady.' Andy looked dazed, but at least he was sitting upright as he clung onto Jo, blood dripping from his face all over the back of Jo's bright orange life vest.

I was more concerned with Zane's sudden and unexplained rage. There were people around on the shore if Cameron were to follow Jo and Andy back, if things were to get out of hand again. But out here, we were on our own. And I was still none the wiser as to what was wrong with Zane.

'Be careful,' Siobhan yelled after Jo. But with the roar of their engine, they probably didn't hear her.

Zane was still perched sideways in front of me as Marty began heading back to Siobhan.

'Come on, let's go.' Really, I wanted to get away from Zane while he was in his strange mood. Cameron was still in my eyeline, but too far away to swim towards. Perhaps it would be better if I just got Zane to take me back to the shore.

'You're going to pay – for the crap you're trying to spread about me.' Ignoring me, Zane jabbed his finger in Siobhan's direction.

'Who? *What?*'

'*Crap?*' Siobhan's voice was incredulous. 'We both know that's not the case, don't we? It's time Becky knew the truth as well.'

'What are you talking about? The truth about what?' Oh God, as if there wasn't enough trouble between Andy and Cameron without Zane kicking off as well.

'Like I said, *you're* going to pay.'

Zane dropped into the water with barely a splash. His powerful arms cut through the water like a knife through butter as he swam towards Siobhan. What had she done?

'Zane, what are you playing at?' Marty paused for a moment and treaded water. 'Don't you think we've had enough aggro out here?' He'd effectively left Siobhan wide open for Zane to attack.

I could have ridden away while I was free of my husband, but I wouldn't have done that to my friend. Since we'd all returned from lunch, and Siobhan had let on that she had something to tell me, Zane's mood had turned like the tide. Whatever it was certainly needed to come out – but not in *that* way. Not two miles away from the safety of dry land. She shouldn't have said *anything* in front of him.

Marty increased his stroke to reach Siobhan before Zane did. He'd redeemed himself somewhat in the two days we'd been around him. I wondered if he even knew that his teenage fling with Jo had resulted in pregnancy. It was something that needed to come into the open. But first...

'Get him off me.' Siobhan screamed as she tried to hang onto the handlebars. But Zane was tugging her into the water. Gravity won, and before Marty reached them, Zane had forced Siobhan's head beneath the surface.

'Marty!' I shrieked. 'He's going to drown her.' Marty was swimming as hard as the current would allow and had nearly reached them, but wasn't quite close enough. For a moment, Siobhan managed to get to the surface and gasp for air, but this was followed by a lungful of water and a gurgle as Zane forced her down again.

'Marty, help her.' I was gripping the engine between my legs while looking back to see if Cameron had noticed what was happening and was coming to help. Or anyone else. But no one was coming. It was down to Marty to rescue Siobhan.

It was Zane's turn to have his face exploded in a shower of blood as Marty reached him and punched him, square on. His head flew back and he let go of Siobhan for long enough that she could get back above the surface and splutter up sea water.

After checking Siobhan was alright, Marty turned to swim after Zane, who was front-crawling at full pelt back towards me.

'Don't let him on, Becky,' Siobhan screamed. 'The man wants locking up. He *raped* Jo. I found out today. *He* was the father of her baby.'

My heart stopped for a moment. No! *Zane!* Surely not? But why would Siobhan say something of that magnitude if it wasn't true?

'You're chatting shit.' Zane snarled, blood streaking his teeth as he paused in the water, turning to bare them at Siobhan. His voice was hoarse and feral.

Was he about to circle back and go for her again? Or was he coming for me?

I didn't want to wait to find out.

There were seconds, heartbeats, where what I decided could change the course of everything. Seconds where I could choose between watching and acting. Decide between silence and justice.

If I started the engine fast enough... if I turned to my left and hit the throttle hard, I could get to him before he reached me.

I could mow him down before he ever got the chance to hurt someone else. This cowardly beast who'd tried to drown Siobhan. The same beast who raped Jo and left her, at fifteen, to carry the weight of his shame.

I didn't think. I acted. I yanked the throttle and launched the jet ski forward – straight towards my husband's head.

52

SIOBHAN

It feels like a lifetime ago since we left the UK, but in reality, it's only been seven days.

It certainly feels like a lifetime since we took off from the airport in Aruba.

Cameron took the two available business class seats for himself and Jo. It's impossible to predict what's going to happen between the two of them in their marriage, but Jo has distanced herself from Andy, and she and Cameron look to be pulling back together. Of course, that could all change when they return to the normal swing of life.

In contrast to my luxurious outbound journey, I was back in cattle class. Our plane landed in Bonaire, known as 'the B island,' for nearly two hours. In all this time, no one in our cabin was even offered a drink of water. To add insult to injury, near the end of our eleven-hour flight, we flew over the UK to begin our seven-hour layover in Amsterdam.

At least Cameron got us all booked into the airport lounge with him, so that was something. Although none of us really knew what to say to each other as we watched the endless hours tick by.

I open my mouth to ask Marty to hold up and to wait for me, but I can tell he's cooled towards me throughout our remaining days in Aruba. Whether it's because of what he's been caught up in, or whether it's because my two best friends have spent the last thirty-four years believing him to be the father of Jo's baby while she allowed them to, I don't know. He says he needs to get his head around things, and then he'll be in touch. And he's told me to get another personal trainer in the meantime.

Cameron pulls Jo's case from the carousel, setting it down with more force than necessary. Andy stands nearby, his hands buried deep in his pockets, waiting for his – and presumably Tina's luggage too. I doubt he has any real choice but to go home with her. He tried to sit beside her on the flight, but she made him move. I ended up sitting between them, stiff with the tension neither of them would acknowledge.

Becky and Marty took the three seats across the aisle, with an empty seat separating them. A seat that would've been Zane's if Becky hadn't driven at him.

I hope she knows how I feel about what she did. Something close to awe. Gratitude laced with disbelief for how she put *me* before her husband. Because when it came down to it, Becky did what none of the rest of us would have had the nerve to do.

She ended him.

As we reach the final gate, I'm so exhausted I can barely stand up straight, but there's something new to face now. Zane's parents.

They've already texted Becky to let her know they'll be waiting in the arrivals lounge and weren't listening to her protestations that she'd be alright on her own.

'How am I going to do this?' She asks me through gritted teeth. 'After all, it was all my fault.'

'It was all *his* fault.' I can't feel bad for what happened to him. After all, the bastard tried to drown me. And after how he ruined Jo's life...

'If it wasn't for me driving at his head,' she whispers, 'he'd still be alive and kicking.' Becky's staring down at the ground as we wait in the queue.

'Alive and able to have another go at me,' I reply. 'Or Jo or Tina. Or *you*. I just can't believe all these years have passed without him showing his true colours.'

'Oh, he did show them,' she replies. 'Time and time again.' She raises her vest top to reveal a yellowing bruise beneath it. 'But he was so well-liked outside the house that no one would have believed how he could be when he lost his temper at home.'

'If you'd only told me.' I rest my hand on her arm. 'I would have had you out of there like a shot.'

'But there was a nice side to Zane too.' Her eyes flood with tears. 'Probably the side that held me there.'

'It's always the case. Textbook domestic abuse.'

Becky and I have talked at length since the night she identified her husband in the Aruban Chapel of Rest. She'd been with him for so long, she accepted Zane's regular violent outbursts as the normal part of any relationship. She'd been ground down to the point where she thought she somehow deserved the treatment he gave her.

Before our 'holiday,' I assumed the two of them were happily married. It goes to show that no one can ever really know what happens behind closed doors.

It was only in the moment when Becky discovered Zane had raped Jo, and she witnessed him forcing my head beneath the water that she made the split-second decision that he wasn't going to hurt anyone else.

Their Last Days of Summer

With their tear-streaked and gaunt faces, the much older versions of the people I recall from the top table at Zane and Becky's wedding need no introduction. They're perched on high stools at the coffee bar in the arrivals lounge, waiting for their daughter-in-law. If Becky can just get through this, it's another hurdle she'll have cleared. She's cleared the worst one – she's out of Aruba and back on Yorkshire soil.

'You can do this, hon.' I drape my arm around my friend's shaking shoulders. It's twenty degrees cooler here at Leeds Bradford Airport than it was in Aruba, which will take some getting used to after that warm breeze.

But I'm glad to be back in the UK, even if Marty has already taken himself off to the taxi rank without even saying goodbye to any of us. I doubt if I'll ever see him again after today, and I can't say I blame him. I turn back to Becky. 'Just let them drop you back at home and then tell them you need time on your own.'

'At least we haven't had to accompany Zane's body back,' Becky sniffs. 'His parents are flying out to do that.'

'But you've still got the funeral to get through,' I remind her. 'And a very important part to play there. After that, you're free.'

The look on her face is difficult to read. Clearly, she doesn't know yet what a good thing being free will be.

Now that the holiday is over, all four of our relationship statuses may be shifting to *single*. Andy and Tina haven't exchanged a single word since the flight from Aruba, Becky is now a widow, and Jo and Cameron – well, that's anyone's guess. Whatever was simmering between Jo and Andy appears to have cooled – unsurprisingly, really. Five days of relentless police questioning and the looming threat of criminal charges tends to snuff out even the most reckless kind of chemistry.

That, and the spiralling legal fees, have dragged us all firmly back down to earth.

Despite our differences, we agreed early on to stick to one version of events. Becky was riding with Cameron while Zane had veered off alone, far beyond the designated zone.

He was always good at pushing boundaries. That was something we could all agree on. With the four of us reinforcing one another's accounts, the authorities had little choice but to accept Zane's death as unexplained. Possibly even accidental.

Our lawyer says the police are tentatively entertaining a theory Jo once was scoffed at for – that a rider could be hit by their own jet ski. That possibility may have been helped along by Cameron and Becky ensuring Zane's machine was found at just enough of a distance from his body.

Whatever the investigators believe but are unable to prove, we've been allowed to fly home. That's all that matters now. Zane's parents have been informed they can begin the process of bringing their son home too. And from what we're hearing, the Aruban Public Prosecutor is preparing to close the file.

As Cameron put it, Aruba is a small island, one built on tourism. They can't afford the kind of headlines that Zane's death might generate if anyone were to look too closely.

If someone had told me, before this holiday began, that one of us wouldn't make it home and another would be their killer, I'd have called them unhinged. And yet here we are.

53

SIOBHAN

I LET myself in through the weird-feeling familiarity of my front door, stepping over the pile of post before heading to the kitchen to put the kettle on. I'm knackered but need a brew before I pull the blind down in my room and crawl beneath my duvet.

Goodness knows what it will be like for Becky entering her house. A place where Zane will be nowhere, yet still *everywhere*. We've all been trying to convince her that her actions were justified, but I have little doubt that the guilt will continue to eat her up. Speaking of eating, none of us has done much of that in the remaining days until the police let us go. Most people pile on weight during a holiday, but I think we've all lost a load with the stress.

As I pour my tea, my eyes rest on the photo of my beautiful daughter, Indy, which is pinned to the fridge door.

I don't deserve Indy, who is now at university, I know I don't, and I read the same thing in Jo's eyes when she visited me in hospital, not long after Indy's birth.

Until that moment, she hadn't been sure which of the three

of us had left her newborn baby inside the porch of St Mary's that September day.

'Now that I've got Indy and I'm a few years older, I don't know how I could have left the baby like I did,' I told Jo as I lay, pink and blooming with maternity, while my baby slept in the cot at the end of my bed.

'It was *you*?' She stared at me, her eyes full of tears.

'I'd do anything to turn back the clock.'

'Well, you can't change a thing.' Jo's voice was strangled as she looked away and studied the shiny white floor. 'And neither can I.'

She left immediately after that, without looking at Indy, without looking at me, without even saying goodbye.

Over the years, I've longed to ask Jo whether she's ever considered making contact with her daughter. I've also wanted to broach the topic of what might have happened if we'd taken another decision between us. To have sought help instead of acting as novice midwives before covering it all up. The outcome of Jo's sorry situation was as much our responsibility as it was hers, yet she was the only person vilified in the media.

The baby girl we safely delivered will be in her mid-thirties now – I've never felt relief like it when I found out she had survived. By now, Jo's probably a grandmother. She's never known motherhood, apart from playing stepmum to Cameron's two daughters, and that hasn't been a happy role. She never had any more children, saying she couldn't bear to be pregnant again. It's like she's spent the whole of her adult life punishing herself for what happened to her as a teenager.

I too, will never stop punishing myself for the catastrophic role I had in the baby's fate. I walked away from the poor mite at the start of her life, leaving her as vulnerable and alone as any human could ever be.

And now, the bitter irony exists that I was also there after her biological father was left in the water for dead.

My attention turns to another photo, one of me, Jo, Becky and Tina, taken on a nineties weekend when we were thirty. On the surface of it, we were great friends, bound together by shared experiences and happy memories.

But really, what was binding us together was guilt and fear. Guilt at the decision we'd made.

Fear that one day, what we did to that defenceless baby would tunnel its way back out. Fear also that, along with Jo, the rest of us might get the judgment we deserved.

54

THIRTY THREE YEARS AGO

THIS IS A BIG YEAR, our head of year just said in assembly. Our G.C.S.E. year. *How we spend it has the power to either set up our futures or tear them down.*

But I've already torn down *my* future.

Every minute of every day, I ache for that baby girl I gave birth to. I always knew it was going to be a girl – I could just tell.

If we'd stayed together, I'd have been the mum my own mother has *never* been. She thinks being a parent is about leaving me plenty of money for a takeaway or paying me a generous clothing allowance. She thinks it's providing a home my friends are jealous of, and paying for every trip and away-from-home excursion she can find – when really, she only wants to get me out of her hair.

I've always been jealous of my friends' mums. Yeah, Tina might be overweight and bulimic, but at least her mother worries about her. Becky's family might be short of money, but what they lack in money, they make up for in love. Siobhan and her mother are like best friends, and people often think they're sisters.

There can be no denying that the friendship between the

four of us hasn't been the same since what happened. It's a miracle none of my friends' mothers have found out the truth about the baby. Not yet, anyway.

The *baby in the bag* story didn't just make the Whitby news, it was in the news all over the country. Mum called 'the mother' evil, saying things like *she deserves to have her fanny sewn up* – her words, not mine, and that she was an irresponsible coward who needed locking up. What would she have been saying if she knew she was the baby's grandmother?

Nobody, not even my friends, knew what it was like for me that morning. My insides felt like they were being ripped out. I lay there afterwards, unable to stop being sick into the bin while bleeding all over the place. Luckily, the girls had plenty of sanitary pads between them. If the word *lucky* can be used to describe anything that day.

My baby girl *was* lucky, however. The news reporter said the rucksack's zip had been left open enough to let plenty of air in. Plus, the baby had been wrapped in a towel and left in a sheltered and safe place. When the church warden found her there, she was sleeping soundly. She had no idea she'd been abandoned and that she was all alone in the world. But she wasn't alone for long.

People took to the letters page in the newspaper, all desperate to adopt the *baby in the bag*. I desperately watched each scrap of news, weeping when they flashed photos of my daughter onto the screen. She was so tiny, so helpless, and I'd allowed my friends to take charge and for them to take her away from me.

I don't know her name, only that to start with, she was called *Mary* after the church she'd been found at. She'll be nearly a year old now and has barely been talked about in the news since she was sent to foster parents until her *forever family* could be found.

Becky and Zane are still together, and she has no idea that he raped me and that 'Mary' is *his* daughter too. I'm too ashamed to tell *anybody*, besides, just as Zane warned, nobody would ever believe me.

Somehow, I just need to put it all behind me and try to get on with the rest of my life. But I'll *never* stop thinking about my baby girl.

Maybe, just maybe, one day I'll get to see her again.

EPILOGUE
MARY

I KNOW it's Jo as soon as the bell on the cafe door tinkles. Her hair's blonde, probably highlighted, but we stand at the same height and looking into her eyes as she approaches is like looking into a mirror. She's even got a similar way of dressing. We're both dressed in skirts just above the knee, ankle boots and woolly tights. We could have almost compared notes about what to wear as we got ready to meet.

I go to shake her hand, but at the last moment, I relent and allow her to hug me. If anyone else in this bustling space is paying any attention to us, they'll probably be able to tell that we're mother and daughter.

What they won't know is that this is only the second time we've ever met in our lives.

'Mary.' She says the name that stuck with me like it means everything to her, and judging by the tears shining in her eyes, it probably does.

'Hi Jo.' I can't call her *Mum*. How can I? I've had wonderful parents who've been right behind me since I was eighteen months old. They've loved me, protected me and ensured I've wanted for nothing after my sorry beginnings. If either of them have felt wounded at my decision to meet Jo after all these years, they've kept it very well hidden.

'Thanks for agreeing to see me.' As she sits, I can see she's shaking nearly as much as I am. 'It's far more than I deserve.'

'You explained everything when we Facetimed,' I reply. 'I really *can* understand. I guess being the mum of a fifteen-year-old myself helps.'

There's a hunger in Jo's eyes I can't fulfil just yet. I haven't even told Ame that she's got a second grandmother, nor does she know anything about me being *abandoned* before being adopted. There's never been the right time to tell her, and besides, after my high-profile start in life, my parents did everything they could to make sure my years after they adopted me were normal and that I was kept out of the media.

'Would you like to see a photo of Ame?'

My friends have all warned me to go easy with this meeting, and not to expect too much from it, but the woman's my *mother*. My actual flesh and blood.

Yes, I love *Mum*, but it's impossible not to feel bonded to Jo now we're sitting across a table from each other. I've tried to hate her over the years, but I haven't got it in me. If I were the product of some woman having a fling in her twenties or thirties who'd *then* decided to dump me, I might have felt differently, but Jo was the same age as Ame is now. Fifteen years old and still a child.

'I'd love to.' She dabs at her eyes with a tissue and tucks it up the sleeve of her jumper. This is crazy, even our jumpers are a similar shade of blue.

I fumble around on my phone for a few minutes. My fingers are shaking too. 'This is one of her with her dad, my husband Ben.'

She takes my phone from me, drinking in the image of her granddaughter. 'She looks just like you.'

'And *you*.' I laugh. 'Obviously, I don't take after my father.'

The waitress arrives to take our order, leaving my comment about my *father* hanging in the air.

'A tea for me,' Jo says. 'What are you having?'

'Tea for me too. If it's in a cup, can you leave the tea bag in?'

'You clearly take after me in the tea department as well.' Jo smiles for the first time since she arrived. 'But we have very different jobs, don't we?'

'Mum said it was inevitable I'd end up being a midwife.'

I'm pretty sure Jo flinches when I refer to Mum as *Mum*. But she's got to expect that nothing's going to change my relationship with the woman who brought me up. The woman who put a roof over my head and loved me as if I was her own.

'It's to be commended that you've found a career bringing babies *safely* into the world.' Jo reaches into her sleeve for her tissue again. 'I'm so proud of you.'

The pride she speaks of isn't hers to own, but I'll let it slide. 'When we Facetimed, you mentioned your friends who were at my birth.'

Jo's eyes cloud over. 'I don't see so much of them these days. We went on holiday together earlier this year to celebrate turning fifty, but it was a disaster.'

'Oh? Why's that?' I can't believe Jo's fifty. I hope our genetics extend to me looking as young as she does fifteen years from now.

'We're all very different people from who we were thirty-five years ago,' she replies. 'And perhaps we weren't holding our friendship group together for all the right reasons.'

'You're still friends though, right?' Ben thinks it's weird that I've a yearning to meet these women Jo's told me about. But they're the only connection I have with my life before my adoptive parents. The foster parents I had before them are dead now.

'Yes, our friendship's just not what it used to be.'

'Everything changes, doesn't it?' I glance up to see where

the waitress is with the tea. I've got so much to say to Jo, we have so many years to make up for and yet, none of the right words are finding me. We don't know each other well enough for the silence which now hangs between us to be comfortable.

'Have you got a picture of them?'

'Who?'

'Your friends.' I've thought a lot since Jo told me about them, especially about the one who was on her own with me. The one who placed me in a bag on the ground and then walked away. I have to wonder how much they talked Jo into leaving me like she did.

She tugs her phone from her bag and, with still-shaking fingers, pulls up a picture which she holds in front of me. I stare at the screen for a few minutes. From their sun-flushed skin and the palm trees in the background, the four women, only one-and-a-half decades older than me, are obviously abroad. This must be the recent holiday Jo's referred to. But their smiles, the way their arms are easily slung around one another, and their matching cocktails suggest a far stronger friendship than the one she's described.

Something's gone *badly* wrong on that holiday.

'You said one of them left me at St Mary's?' I raise my eyes from the screen to Jo's. Hers are still watery. Really, I can hardly believe that I'm sitting here with my mother, my *real* mother, after all this time. It's surreal.

Jo points at a pretty, bohemian-styled woman with wavy, auburn hair. 'Siobhan has a daughter of her own now – Indy. But she's spent her whole life fearing she's going to lose her, as she's been in and out of hospital with kidney troubles.' She dabs at her eyes again. 'And she still spends every day of her life beating herself up over what she did to you.'

'Can I meet her sometime? Can I meet them all?' I want to ask Siobhan what was going through her head as she walked with me to the church porch. I want to know what I looked and felt like to her. And I also want to tell her she *can* enjoy her daughter. I forgive her. I'd be only hurting myself more if I didn't.

'I guess so. If you really want to?'

'I really do.'

'I expect you'll want to know about your father since you mentioned him before.' Jo's avoiding my eyes now. I wonder why.

The waitress arrives back with our tea. 'Can I get you anything to eat with this?'

'Not for me, thanks,' I reply.

'Nor for me.' As the waitress walks away, Jo pats her middle. 'I couldn't eat a thing. I can't tell you how nervous I've been about meeting you.'

'So what do you want to tell me about my father?' I'll wait to see what she's got to say before I divulge anything.

'He's dead.' Two flat words, devoid of any emotion. But she must have felt something about him *once* for me to exist in the first place.

I stare at her. *Dead?* I wasn't expecting that. 'Bu-but I only met him earlier this year.'

'You did? How? I mean—' Her words are filled with shock.

Gosh, she has no idea about what I'm going to tell her. With the close proximity of time in between my deciding to meet Zane – and then Jo leaving her name at the General Register Office, I assumed they must have conferred to at least some extent about finding me.

'Zane's wife — Becky is it?'

'Yes.'

'Well, she told him around ten years ago that you'd got pregnant at fifteen, and how it had resulted in *the baby in the bag* on the news.'

I hate referring to myself in this way, but it *is* what they all called me.

'According to Zane, the two of you had a secret fling when you were fifteen, and Becky wouldn't have had any idea *he* was my father when she was telling him about me.'

'But—'

'The dates had all tallied when he thought about it,' I continue. 'So Zane registered himself with the Adopted Contact Register around ten years ago.'

'Ten years ago?' Jo echoes. She looks pale. 'He never said a word to me.'

'But he's dead?' I can feel something unexpected bubbling up inside. 'I mean, how?' I might not have liked the man, but it still feels like part of me has died, too. After all, he gave me life. That's all he ever did for me, granted, but without him, I wouldn't be here.

'He was on the holiday I've talked about.' Jo's face darkens. 'He had an accident.'

'So was he your friend's boyfriend when you and he...' My voice trails off. Judging by Jo's expression, there's a lot more to this story than meets the eye.

'Yes.' She reaches for the teapot. 'But honestly, it's all ancient history.'

'But I want to know about it. It's *my* history.'

'How often have the two of you met?' She's dodging my question. But I have a right to know things, and I won't stop until I get to the full story. If not today, then I'll be pushing for information when I meet Jo's friends.

'It was only the once,' I reply. 'He said his wife, Becky never wanted children, which was why he wanted to meet me. I told him that wasn't a good enough reason.'

I'd wanted Zane to hold his arms out and tell me he'd have been there my whole life if he'd only known about me. I hoped he would care enough to want to make up for lost time. But there was none of that. However, it doesn't feel right to discuss this with Jo. Not yet.

'I'm honestly gobsmacked that he left his details on the contact register.'

'Well, *you* left *yours* a few months ago, didn't you?'

Jo shuffles in her seat, clearly unsure how to respond.

'He also didn't seem happy about me looking so much like you and finished the conversation saying he was glad he'd met me, and that I'd satisfied his curiosity.'

'And that was it? He didn't say anything about seeing you again?'

I shake my head. I won't tell her that I went home and bawled my eyes out. That I didn't have anyone I felt like I could talk to about it. I'd had far higher hopes when we met, and had been left with my innate sense of rejection snaking through me.

We have a second cup of tea, and Jo tells me about her friends. Siobhan's had a wobble within her marriage this year but has realised that the grass isn't greener on the other side and gone back to her husband, Caleb.

Becky, the woman who's technically my stepmother, is now a widow. She had no idea that her husband was also my father, but she knows now, so it will be extra strange meeting her.

Jo's other friend Tina has two sons and is getting divorced, but gets on better with her husband now than they ever did when they were together.

As for Jo, she's also on her own, but says her fifties will be about getting to know herself and working out what's important.

'Which is you, Mary,' she says.

I don't know how to respond to that, but I am beyond thankful that her reaction to me is poles apart from what my *father's* was.

'Listen, you don't owe me a thing, but I hope you'll see me again. And again and again. I've got a lot of making up to do.'

'So long as eventually, you tell me the full story,' I reply. 'I think I have the right to know.'

'When the time's right.' She nods her head. 'As I've discovered, the truth always comes out sooner or later.'

The End

Thank you for reading *Their Last Days of Summer* – I hope you enjoyed it and would be hugely grateful if you would consider leaving a review on Amazon, which will help other readers to find it too!

If you want to read more of my work, check out *The Wife I Was on Amazon*, my next psychological thriller, where you'll meet Georgia, who's trapped between this world and the next. She has unfinished business – and others to protect from the same fate she's suffered.

It's a story especially written for the spooky season, but can be enjoyed at any time of the year.

And for a FREE novella, please Join my 'keep in touch' list where I can also keep you posted of special offers and new releases. You can join by visiting my website www.mariafrankland.co.uk.

BOOK CLUB GROUP DISCUSSION QUESTIONS

1. Discuss how thirty-five years changed each of the four women.
2. Which of the female characters did you feel the most sympathy for? And the least? Did this change as the story progressed?
3. What about the male characters?
4. How did the outcomes align with your expectations? For example, which woman did you suspect had given birth? Were you right about who'd left the baby at the church? What about who died? And the person who killed them?
5. Going on holiday with people means you get to know each other well and can bring things bubbling to the surface. Do you have your own experiences of this?
6. How well did the Aruban backdrop tie in with the darkness between the characters in the story? Did you envy their location or feel relieved you weren't there?
7. Another contrast in the story is that between wealth and poverty. What instances did you notice?
8. Discuss what fuelled the partner-swapping game. Could different pairings have changed the direction of the story?

9. Talk about how the romantic relationships between the four women with their partners have evolved during the story. What realisations might they have come to about themselves?

10. Some difficult themes are dealt with in this book. What retribution has been achieved by the end of it?

11. What might Mary's life have been like if Jo had fought to keep her?

12. Discuss how all four women have been affected over the years by their part in Mary's abandonment.

13. Discuss the factors that might have led Zane to turn out the way he did.

14. What are your thoughts on Jo telling Mary the 'whole' story?

15. What would you like to see happen next?

PROLOGUE - THE WIFE I WAS

I'M SO TIRED. I've never been this exhausted in my life, not even when I was suffering from the crushing new mum weariness. I felt like it would never end, but one morning, as if by magic, Etta had slept through the night.

Divorce, however, is a new kind of hell. They say it's one of life's top three stressors. And we all know stress causes insomnia.

Night after night, I lie in the spare room, staring into the shadows, willing daybreak to arrive and yet dreading it in the same breath. It's impossible to hold down a demanding job working shifts and to have the energy for the needs of my ten-year-old daughter.

But tonight, I'm being looked after. I was astonished by the bubble bath already run for me when I walked in through the door. A cup of cocoa was thrust into my hands along with a barked command to soak, relax and sleep.

I sip at the hot drink as I peel off my uniform, a cursory glance in the mirror telling me that, yes, I look like crap. My skin is pale and crepey, my eyes are dark in my face, and my hair, when I release it from the bun that's contained it all day, does not tumble around my shoulders like it did in my youth. Instead, it sticks out in all directions. I miss the woman I used to be.

I open the mirrored cabinet, relieved not to have to look at my reflection anymore and reach for the tablets prescribed last week by my doctor. I never wanted to take sleeping pills, but needs must. They knock me out in less than an hour, so taking one now means I'll be ready for oblivion by the time I get out of the bath. I swallow one with a sip of cocoa. It sticks in my throat, and I gag. I take a huge swig from my mug to force it down.

As I slide into the fragrant bubbles, I let out a long sigh and close my eyes. Within minutes, my current predicament melts away as my limbs feel at one with the heat of the water. For now, nothing matters. Not my failed marriage. Not the impossible pressures at work. Not even the hours I miss with Etta.

For now, here in this bath, my worries are lulled into oblivion by the sound of bubbles popping around my ears and the scent of whatever they're emitting. I force my eyes open and squint at the bottle on the shower rack. I think it says lavender and chamomile, but I'm struggling to focus. I raise my shoulders out of the water and lean forward, needing to centre myself and not fall asleep. Not in the bath. I take another drink of the velvety chocolate from my mug before falling back again. I won't be staying in here for long – I can barely keep my eyes open. I'll just have a moment, and then I'll wash my hair.

Etta's smiling face enters my thoughts as the sound of my breath lulls me some more, and then Dexter's face, filled with contempt as it has been so often in recent months. That we're still together in the same house through all this is becoming unbearable. Especially since I never wanted this separation.

Memories of happier times begin floating through my

Their Last Days of Summer

mind. His smiling eyes, when he went down on one knee. Him brushing away his tears as the midwife handed him our newborn Etta. The day he carried me over the threshold into this, our dream home.

But all dreams come to an end.

I'm warm, too warm. And all of a sudden. I can't get my breath. I really *can't* get my breath.

With all my might, I attempt to sit up, but I haven't got the strength. Something's pressing on my chest, firm and determined, crushing me, holding me against the flat of the bath. I can't move, I can't fight. I need to breathe or I'm going to die

Through the film of water, I see the shadow of a figure looming above me. Is it Dexter?

The cocoa and the pill swirl inside me like a sickness. My strength has dissolved as much as the pill I recently swallowed. I can't even scream.

My panic sharpens, then softens. The edges of my world blur. The weight on my chest continues, the unyielding hands continuing to hold me under the water.

Eventually, I have little choice but to surrender my life. There's nothing else I can do. At the age of thirty-seven, I've been murdered.

Find out more on Amazon

ACKNOWLEDGMENTS

Thank you, as always, to my amazing husband, Michael. He's my first reader, and is vital with my editing process for each of my novels. His belief in me means more than I can say.

A special acknowledgement goes to my wonderful advance reader team, who took the time and trouble to read an advance copy of Their Last Days of Summer and offer feedback. They are a vital part of my author business and I don't know what I would do without them. This is my twenty-fourth full-length novel and it becomes harder and harder to think of first names for my characters. Therefore, I'm really grateful to members of the group who offered their own names up for me to use! They are:

Tina (Tina Abril)
    Andy (Put forward by Sarah Tomey)
    Jo (Jo Woodcock)
    Cameron (Put forward by Jess Hess Elliott)
    Becky (Rebecca Charlesworth)
    Zane (Put forward by Rachel John Fournier)
    Siobhan (Put forward by Kelly Shelton)
    Marty (Put forward by Gemma Rachel Marie)

I will always be grateful to Leeds Trinity University and my MA in Creative Writing Tutors there, Martyn, Amina and Oz. My

Masters degree in 2015 was the springboard into being able to write as a profession.

And thanks especially, to you, the reader. Thank you for taking the time to read this story. I really hope you enjoyed it.

INTERVIEW WITH THE AUTHOR

Q: Where do your ideas come from?

A: I'm no stranger to turbulent times, and these provide lots of raw material. People, places, situations, experiences – they're all great novel fodder!

Q: Why do you write psychological thrillers?

A: I'm intrigued why people can be most at risk from someone who should love them. Novels are a safe place to explore the worst of toxic relationships.

Q: Does that mean you're a dark person?

A: We thriller writers pour our darkness into stories, so we're the nicest people you could meet – it's those romance writers you should watch...

Q: What do readers say?

A: That I write gripping stories with unexpected twists, about people you could know and situations that could happen to anyone. So beware...

Q: What's the best thing about being a writer?

A: You lovely readers. I read all my reviews, and answer all emails and social media comments. Hearing from readers absolutely makes my day, whether it's via email or through social media.

Q: Who are you and where are you from?

A: A born 'n' bred Yorkshire lass, now officially in my early fifties. I have two grown up sons and a Sproodle called Molly. (Springer/Poodle!) The last decade has been the best: I've done an MA in Creative Writing, made writing my full time job, and found the happy-ever-after that doesn't exist in my writing - after marrying for the second time just before the pandemic.

Q: Do you have a newsletter I could join?

A: I certainly do. Go to www.mariafrankland.co.uk or click here through your eBook to join my awesome community of readers. When you do, I'll send you a free novella – 'The Brother in Law.'

Printed in Dunstable, United Kingdom